Prai

"A cathartic tangle of love, rage, and religious trauma. . . . King-Miller explores the fraught dynamics of mothers and daughters, bodily autonomy, and generational curses in an inventive possession tale unlike any you've read."

—Hailey Piper, Bram Stoker Award–winning
author of *Queen of Teeth*

"*This Is My Body* blends faith and body horror into a queer cosmic romp that would make any exorcist blush. In this fresh possession epic, a marriage made in hell between David Cronenberg and William Peter Blatty, Lindsay King-Miller discovers there are entire chasms left to be purified within the human soul."

—Clay McLeod Chapman, author of
Wake Up and Open Your Eyes

"A necessary and unique possession tale, *This Is My Body* looks religious trauma and queerness straight in the eye. Intense and gory! A great exploration of the spectrum of belief, both worldly and otherworldly."

—Jenny Kiefer, author of *This Wretched Valley*
and *Crafting for Sinners*

"When I pick up a Lindsay King-Miller book, I know to clear my schedule for the night, because I won't want to stop turning the pages, nor stop underlining its sharp, musical prose. *This Is My Body* is a gripping ride through claustrophobic, gnarly body horror; creeping generational trauma; and, ultimately, the hope of reckoning and retribution."

—Cynthia Gómez, author of "The Shivering World"

"Heart-wrenching, propulsive, and always scare-the-fuck-out-of-you terrifying, *This Is My Body* expertly charts the endless interiors of pain and trauma to uncover the raw, screaming humanity waiting deep within. Lindsay King-Miller's latest is a vicious, unrelenting tour de force that will rip your guts clean out and show them to you. An absolute triumph."

—Matthew Lyons, author of *A Mask of Flies*
and *A Black and Endless Sky*

"Gay, gory, and genuine—King-Miller uses her gift for lived-in characters and settings to effortlessly drag the reader through hell and out the other side."

—Mattie Lubchansky, author of *Boys Weekend*

"A queer, thorny, deeply satisfying novel about religious trauma, the horrors of parenting a middle schooler, the forked tongue of memory, and the dangers of trying to go home again. *This Is My Body* flips the conventional possession narrative on its head. You think you know what kind of story this is? Oh, sweet child—you have no idea."

—Emily C. Hughes, author of *Horror for Weenies*

THIS IS MY BODY

Lindsay King-Miller

QUIRK BOOKS
PHILADELPHIA

Library of Congress Cataloging-in-Publication Data
Names: King-Miller, Lindsay, author.
Title: This is my body / Lindsay King-Miller.
Description: Philadelphia : Quirk Books, 2025. | Summary: "Brigid becomes afraid that her teen daughter, Dylan, might be possessed, so she reaches out to her estranged uncle and uncovers both family secrets and immediate danger to herself and her daughter"—Provided by publisher.
Identifiers: LCCN 2024053382 (print) | LCCN 2024053383 (ebook) | ISBN 9781683694649 (paperback) | ISBN 9781683694656 (ebook)
Subjects: LCGFT: Paranormal fiction. | Queer fiction. | Horror fiction. | Novels.
Classification: LCC PS3611.I5897 T48 2025 (print) | LCC PS3611.I5897 (ebook) | DDC 813/.6--dc23/eng/20241122
LC record available at https://lccn.loc.gov/2024053382
LC ebook record available at https://lccn.loc.gov/2024053383

ISBN: 978-1-68369-464-9

Printed in China

Typeset in Bembo, Pliego, and Gandur New

Designed by Elissa Flanigan
Cover photos by Tetyana Afanasyeva/Shutterstock.com, Chui Wui Jing/Shutterstock.com, Cosmin Manci/Shutterstock.com, Possent phsycography/Shutterstock.com

Quirk Books
215 Church Street
Philadelphia, PA 19106
quirkbooks.com

10 9 8 7 6 5 4 3 2 1

For everyone who gave up waiting on
Saint Anthony and went out to find
what they needed for themselves

CONTENTS

Prologue

The girl was handcuffed to the bed. For hours she had been screaming, but now her voice was gone and she merely panted, exhausted but not resigned. Her eyes were huge and sunken in her pale, strained face. Her white nightgown was soaking wet, and so was the bare mattress underneath her; she shivered in the breeze from the open window. Lit by candles arrayed on the dresser, her skin seemed to writhe from underneath, like something was crawling inside her.

The small bedroom felt crowded with five people in it. The girl's parents sat near the head of the bed, clutching each other's hands, not touching their daughter. In the far corner, a woman recited the rosary in a low, droning voice. Beneath the monotonous Hail Marys, the girl's parents whispered to each other.

The immobilized girl breathed loudly, but said nothing. Neither did the man at the foot of her bed, wearing the black vestments of a priest. His hands were clasped before him and his eyes fixed, blue and ferocious, on the girl.

Brigid watched from the hallway, her eye pressed to the gap in the doorframe where the wind whistled through. It was the dead of night and she should have been long asleep, but when she closed her eyes, all she could see was the demon, waiting to be cast out. She didn't want to miss the miracle.

The girl on the bed squirmed in her bonds. Her wrists and ankles were horribly bruised and abraded, blood seeping onto the dingy gray-white of the mattress in a sickening stigmata. Brigid remembered the soft curves of her body when her parents first brought her to this house. Now, only a few days later, skin hung from her bones like a secondhand jacket, too tight in some places, too loose in others. Her cheekbones and brow loomed, shadows swirling beneath. Her lips were chapped dull white, except in the corners of her mouth, dark red with more old blood.

Brigid thought she was the most beautiful girl in the world.

Father Angus, Brigid's uncle, raised his hands and the parents fell silent. Out in the hall, Brigid held her breath. Only Brigid's mother, Adelaide, continued speaking, endless streams of prayer without pause or inflection.

"Demon," Father Angus commanded over his sister's recitation. "Leave this child's body. Release her soul."

The girl spat at him, or tried, but her mouth was too dry. "Fuck you, old man," she rasped. Her mother, an arthritic knuckle of a woman, sobbed and buried her head in her husband's neck.

Unmoved, implacable, the priest circled the bed until he stood near its head, his shadow falling over the wretched figure of the girl. From somewhere in the folds of his robe, he produced a flask of holy water. With one hand, he forced the girl's jaw open, his hard fingers digging into the papery skin of her cheeks, and with the other poured the water in.

The girl struggled, but Father Angus clapped his palm over her mouth and held fast. Her whole body spasmed, choking and coughing, arching off the bed with the strength of her resistance.

Brigid watched and knew her soul was bound for hell, because in that moment she wanted the girl to win. In her nine years of life she had never seen anyone defy Father Angus. It was wrong: her uncle was a man of God, speaking in God's stead on earth, and to disobey him was to hate the true and the good. But the girl was so beautiful, and she fought so hard. Brigid wanted her to break the chains that held her, rise into the sky, and strike them all down in hellfire.

The girl on the bed finally went limp, and the priest took his hand away.

"You can't have her, you son of a whore," said the demon inside the girl's body. "She's mine."

PART 1

Chapter 1

B rigid shifted uncomfortably in her seat. These hard plastic chairs with no arms and too-straight backs were meant to make you feel small and abject, to remind you of your powerlessness, and it was working.

The principal shook his head sorrowfully. "Well, here we are again, Mrs. Byrne."

"It's Ms.," she said to him, as she did every time they met. She couldn't prove it, but she was certain he remembered—that his insistence on getting it wrong was another version of the terrible chair, a subtle reminder that he considered her inferior. Which was all the more infuriating because he was at least five years younger than her and wearing sneakers with a suit.

"Of course," he said unapologetically. "Mizz Byrne, I'll be honest with you, we're struggling with Dylan's behavior."

That was always his opening line. *We're struggling*, as if he expected her to sympathize, to soothe his feelings where her daughter had apparently injured them.

"What happened?" Brigid asked instead.

He sighed. "Well, as you know, Dylan has been having some interpersonal difficulties this year." Brigid tried to keep her frustration off her face. Telling him to cut to the chase wasn't going to help Dylan. Principal Halyard explained in great detail things Brigid already knew, such as that Dylan didn't have many friends and that she'd been wearing a lot of black lately.

"As educators, we strive to meet each child where they are, taking into account any challenges they may be facing in their home life . . ." Brigid wasn't imagining it; the principal gave her a pointed look as he said those words. *Challenges* like having a lesbian for a single mom, she supposed he meant, though he'd deny it if she asked. "But when those challenges become a disruption or even a danger to the other students, of course it becomes necessary to intervene."

"A danger to other students?" Dylan? What did he think— that her withdrawn, daydreamy daughter was at risk of snapping and becoming a school shooter? "Mr. Halyard, can you tell me what this is about?"

"Certainly, I'm getting to that, Mrs. Byrne." He stopped to see if she would correct him again, but this time she couldn't be bothered, so he went on. "At lunchtime today, Dylan snuck into an empty classroom—"

"Well, that hardly seems—"

"And when two other students suggested she come back to the courtyard, she instigated a physical altercation and punched one of them in the face."

Brigid was not expecting that. She'd been prepared to hear that Dylan had taken a marijuana edible or carved band names into a desk or some other quiet act of rebellion, but violence was nowhere on her list of imagined possibilities. She must have been staring; the principal was smiling back at her, smug now that he'd managed to break her stride.

"Where is Dylan now?" she managed.

"In the art room with the school resource officer," he said. "The injured student is at the nurse's office, putting ice on his eye." There was a subtle rebuke in his voice: she should have asked about the kid who was hurt first. She was selfish, the kind of parent whose child ran roughshod over the world because she'd never been taught that other people's feelings mattered. Shame surfaced like mushrooms after a hard rain, spores awakened from long dormancy. *Your sins, Brigid—*

"Who were the other kids involved?"

"Jordan Vance and Kai Shriver. Kai is the one Dylan hit."

Once more, Brigid was unprepared, and she watched the principal's satisfied expression as she flailed. "Kai? But he's Dylan's best friend." They'd been hanging out less since the school year began, but Kai had been a fixture of Dylan's small social circle since third grade, one of the few classmates Dylan ever invited to their house.

"Friendship can be complicated at this age," Principal Halyard smarmed.

"What *happened*?" Brigid was certain now that he wasn't giving her the full story. Dylan didn't just decide out of nowhere to assault her closest friend. Something else was going on.

"Mrs. Byrne, I've told you what happened." This time he leaned hard on the *Mrs.*, making sure she couldn't miss him getting it wrong.

"I'm a dyke and I've never been married, you pompous fuck," Brigid said, and the way his eyes widened was almost worth the shame that pulsed through her body like adrenaline.

She could see in his eyes that he wanted to say something horrible back, and she wished with a sudden violence that he would—just do it, just say it, just open his mouth and let her know what he really thought of her, and of Dylan. But instead he ground his teeth together and took a long, deep breath. "Ms. Byrne," he said, dripping with false obsequiousness, "I've given you all the details I have about today's incident. If there was a previous conflict between your daughter and Kai Shriver that contributed to the altercation, I don't know what it is. Perhaps you could ask Dylan, if she wishes to confide in you."

"Of course I'll ask Dylan," she said. Her flare of rage had died as quickly as it came, and now she felt defeated, exposed, outmaneuvered. Whatever point Principal Halyard was trying to make about her family, she had the sinking feeling he'd succeeded. "May I see her, please?" Forcing herself to add the *please* at the end of the question caused her physical discomfort, a sensation like nausea but higher in her chest.

He nodded curtly and pushed a button on his desk phone. "Please have Officer Ray bring Dylan to my office," he said, and disconnected without waiting for a response.

Brigid stared at him in silence, her thoughts and guts roiling. Dylan and Kai must have fallen out before today; there was no way they had gone from close confidence to physical attacks in the span of the last few hours. And she'd had no idea. What else was her daughter keeping from her? How angry would she have to be to punch someone? And why hadn't she said anything to Brigid?

Dylan had been moody lately, irritable, spending more time in her room, but that was normal for a girl who had just started eighth grade, wasn't it? Brigid didn't want to push; she knew Dylan would come to her when she was ready.

But Dylan hadn't come to her. Brigid tried so hard to be someone her daughter could talk to, never to shame or silence her. She did everything she could to make their house a place of openness and honesty, the furthest thing imaginable from her own childhood home; to light every shadowy corner, to chase away fear with love. But it wasn't enough. Dylan was keeping secrets, and if they were big enough to make her hurt Kai, they must be hurting Dylan even more.

And Brigid, blithely waiting for Dylan to confide in her, had allowed it to happen.

Principal Halyard looked at her without speaking, and she glared back at him, refusing to flinch. It gave her a twisted feeling of triumph, knowing that he couldn't possibly have as much disdain for her as she had for herself.

The principal cracked first. "Should we discuss—"

At that moment the door creaked open. "Here she is," said the receptionist, a thin, middle-aged woman with hair bleached to straw. There was a long pause before Dylan walked into the office.

She looked awful, Brigid realized with a sinking heart. Had she looked like this when she left for school this morning? The previous night? The week before? Had Brigid simply let it slide?

Dylan's ponytail didn't conceal the fact that her normally lustrous red hair was greasy and unwashed. Her posture was always as terrible as any teenager's, but today she looked *hunched*, curled in on herself as though she wished she could retreat from the world entirely. Her hands were shoved deep in her pockets. A scabby crack in the center of her lower lip showed that she'd been chewing on it, and her eyes spoke eloquently of pure exhaustion.

"Sweetheart . . ." Brigid got to her feet, opening her arms for her daughter to fall into them, as she clearly needed to do. Instead, Dylan moved past her, barely glancing at her mother as she sank into the adjacent horrible chair.

"Thank you for joining us," the principal said. Brigid wished Dylan would look her way so they could share a knowing eye roll—*this fucking guy, right?*—but Dylan kept her head down, staring at her hands in her lap. Brigid could see that the fingernails were bitten painfully short. "Now, I've had phone calls with Kai's and Jordan's parents—"

"Before you contacted me?" The question burst out, indignant, before Brigid could stifle it.

Principal Halyard flattened his lips in a way that might pass for a smile, in dim light. "Our responsibility is to notify the families of the children who were harmed before taking any other action. You'll be relieved to know they don't currently wish to file charges against Dylan for assault." He watched Dylan for a hint of response. She picked a fleck of dark green polish from her thumbnail.

"Since this is Dylan's first seriously disruptive behavior, we're assigning one week of in-school suspension. She'll be meeting with the guidance counselor and working on her schoolwork independently. Next week, on Friday afternoon, she'll have a mediated discussion with Kai, along with Kai's parents—and you, *Mizzzz* Byrne, if you care to join us. Once that's complete, she'll be cleared to return to her normal class schedule." Brigid looked at Dylan, but her daughter gave no sign she was even listening. "Given the circumstances, we think that's more than fair," Principal Halyard concluded. Brigid wondered who he was including in the word *we*.

"All right," said Brigid. "We can . . ."

"There's one other thing," Principal Halyard said, and Brigid bit her tongue, swallowing her irritation that he had waited for her to speak only to cut her off. "Kai Shriver feels, and I can hardly blame him for this, that he is no longer comfortable sharing a class with Dylan." This, finally, got Dylan to raise her head, staring at the principal in horror. "They currently have an art elective together, second period. From now on, Dylan will take choir instead."

"No," Dylan said. Her voice was raspy, like she'd been crying, although her eyes were dry.

"You won't have too much work to do to get caught up," Principal Halyard said. "I have a folder of sheet music here that you can work on during your suspension. Something to keep you busy, eh?"

"No," Dylan said again. "I love art class. That's not fair."

"Kai feels unsafe with you in the class, and we have to respect that," the principal said.

"So let him switch if he wants to." Dylan balled up her hands into fists, pressed them on her thighs as if trying to hold herself in place.

Principal Halyard smiled sadly and shook his head. "It certainly doesn't seem fair to make an assault victim switch classes just to avoid his assailant."

The word *assailant* hit Brigid's system like she'd tasted something bitter; her whole body shuddered, trying to reject it. "Don't you think that's excessive? We don't know if there were circumstances that—"

The principal looked hard at Dylan. "Is there anything else you want to say about this incident, Miss Byrne? Do you want to tell us about the circumstances?"

Dylan shot Brigid a panicky look, clearly hoping her mother would say something else in her defense, but Brigid didn't know what to say.

There must be something else going on, she thought desperately. *Please, Dylan, tell us what it is.*

But Dylan said nothing.

Chapter 2

B rigid drove Dylan to school the next day. Normally, unless the weather was bad, Dylan walked; the little mountain town of Bristlecone was small, and the middle school was only a mile from their apartment building. But Dylan was so withdrawn that morning, picking at her breakfast cereal and shrugging in response to attempts at conversation, that Brigid worried she wouldn't be able to summon the momentum to leave the house on her own.

Neither spoke on the way to school. Brigid's mind spun over the things she should say, the questions she should ask, to draw Dylan out of the silence that seemed to swathe her. She couldn't find the words. They were drowned out by the accusations echoing in her mind, the deep, resonant voice saying she had failed as a mother. Then she pulled up in front of the school and the chance was gone.

"Don't forget this," Brigid said apologetically, handing Dylan her folder of choir music through the window. Dylan's responding scowl almost made Brigid flinch.

It was only another five minutes to Brigid's work, another trip she usually made on foot, but driving home to park seemed like an unnecessary detour. She tried to use the silence in the car to calm herself, breathing in deeply through her nose, then out through her mouth, like her therapist, Marco, had taught her. Still, she was nervy and tense when she arrived at the Tenth Muse.

The shop was already unlocked, and Nadine, a white-haired woman in her early seventies, was inside, checking the shelves for low stock. Brigid didn't greet her. She had learned in the years since hiring Nadine that the older woman required silence to "ground herself" in the morning. When Nadine was ready to converse, she would let Brigid know.

In the meantime, Brigid opened the register and settled in. Standing behind the counter, looking out at her shop, she finally felt a hint of the calm she'd been grasping for all morning. This was her space—much more hers than the apartment where she lived. Every inch of this small building was crowded with things she loved. The floor-to-ceiling bookshelves that lined the walls were crammed with her carefully curated stock, Dion Fortune and Starhawk squeezed in beside Audre Lorde and Leslie Feinberg. Smaller freestanding shelves held crystals, candles, tarot cards, and locally made jewelry and art. Some of it was tourist kitsch, the kind that drove the economy of so many small towns in the Rocky Mountains, but most of it was here simply because Brigid found it beautiful.

She took another slow breath in through her nose, this time inhaling the mingled scents of incense, herbs, and new books that permeated the store. Holding this perfume deep in her lungs, she felt her pulse begin to slow, the tension in her neck ease. She was okay. Dylan was okay. Whatever had happened with Kai, they would talk about it when Dylan was ready, and they'd find a way to work through it.

Brigid met the eyes of a painting across the shop, one she'd hung in that exact spot for this exact purpose. The painting depicted the Celtic goddess Brigid, naked in an apple tree, her modesty protected by curtains of dark red hair that fell to her knees. Her head was ringed in a gold halo that Brigid knew, if she stood closer, would reveal itself to be made of bees.

Brigid the goddess was a mother, healer, and poet. She wasn't Brigid's namesake—that was Saint Brigid of Kildare, a much later addition to the iconography of Ireland—but Brigid loved the idea that her devout Catholic mother had inadvertently named her after a pagan deity. The painting exemplified the satisfaction she felt every time she stepped into the Tenth Muse and looked around the space she'd built: a celebration of spirituality in all its forms, diametrically opposed to the authoritarian, hierarchical religion she'd been raised in. No, Brigid didn't believe in any of the deities that lined her walls, but she loved knowing that *someone* did. That there was a whole world beyond what she'd been taught as a child.

Brigid the goddess looked back at Brigid the woman with glossy, inscrutable blue-black eyes. Brigid the woman breathed slowly and tried to imagine the wisdom and calm of the goddess radiating through her body. A pre-Christian matriarch would never have to worry about her daughter lashing out at a friend in school. The goddess Brigid would simply listen to her sacred intuition, which would guide her to a deep understanding of why Dylan was struggling and how to restore her joy.

Brigid closed her eyes and felt around for her sacred intuition. It reported that she hadn't eaten enough breakfast that morning, because her stomach had been in knots of anxiety about Dylan, and she should probably dash up the street and buy a donut.

"You could use a reading," said Nadine, close to Brigid's ear. Brigid's deep, calming breath exploded from her lungs in a yelp that became a giggle.

Nadine didn't laugh. She rarely did, at least not at work. Nadine was a retired kindergarten teacher, although Brigid always had difficulty picturing her surrounded by children. She had applied to work at the Tenth Muse the week it opened and believed in basically everything they stocked with an intensity that balanced out Brigid's blanket skepticism.

"You're stressed," Nadine said. "There's a question hanging over your aura. Let's see what the cards have to say."

Brigid had known Nadine long enough to understand that "let's see what the cards have to say" was her way of inviting a personal conversation. Nadine had little tolerance for small talk, but she was always happy to offer a reading. Usually Brigid took her up on it, even though she didn't believe in divination. The cards Nadine used were beautiful, and it was an overture of friendship that Brigid didn't feel she had the luxury to refuse.

But she couldn't share what was on her mind today. It wasn't just her problem, it was Dylan's too, and she had to protect her daughter's privacy. She smiled at Nadine and said, "Just a little tired today. I forgot to make coffee this morning."

"I've known five-year-olds who were better liars than you," said Nadine, but she didn't sound irritated—at least, no more than usual. When Brigid didn't respond, Nadine shrugged and began shelving a box of newly delivered books.

Brigid turned on the computer, but instead of updating her web store, she searched for therapists in Bristlecone. There were only a few who worked with children, and none of them took her insurance. After several minutes of looking through the options, she made Dylan a telehealth appointment with a psychologist in Boulder. The first new client appointment available was seven weeks away. *Maybe this thing with Kai will have already blown over by then*, Brigid thought with no real optimism. She added Dylan to a wait list, in case there were unexpected openings.

The morning brought in enough customers to keep her busy, and by the time Nadine went home in the early afternoon, Brigid's worries about Dylan had mostly slipped her mind. She was arranging a display of candles and incense when she heard a voice that tripped a long-forgotten wire in her brain.

"Oh, my goodness, is that you, Brigid Byrne?"

For a throat-tightening moment, Brigid could only think: *They found me.* Her heart galloped and her legs tensed to run.

Then rational thought intervened. She looked in the direction of the strangely familiar voice and saw not the looming shadow that haunted her childhood nightmares but a short, stocky middle-aged woman with graying curls framing her round, pleasant face. The sight of her reminded Brigid of a certain blend of fondness and anxiety, an urgent desire to be liked, and the smell of PTA bake sale muffins.

"Eileen Mulligan," said the woman before Brigid could come up with her name. "Alexandra's mom."

"Oh, wow." Brigid caught herself just in time to avoid saying "holy shit." "Mrs. Mulligan!"

Mrs. Mulligan chuckled. "You're not in middle school anymore, dear," she said. "I think it's fine to call me by my first name."

"What brings you to Bristlecone? It's so good to see you!"
Brigid finally remembered to add.

"I went for a hike up here this morning, and now I'm just
exploring the town," said Mrs. Mulligan, whom Brigid would
never be able to think of as Eileen. "I'm retired now, you know,
so I'm finally getting around to all the hiking I always meant to
do." She laughed, and Brigid did too. Her own laughter sounded
forced to her, but maybe Mrs. Mulligan didn't notice.

"That sounds nice," Brigid said.

"And you work here, do you? How long have you lived up
here in the mountains?"

"Yes, this is my store," said Brigid. "I've been here for a while.
I went to college in Vermont, but then I moved back to Colorado."

Mrs. Mulligan nodded. "I was so sorry to hear about your
mother," she said. "It must have been a shock to you. She was
so young."

Brigid hid her wince. "Thank you. It was hard, but that was
a long time ago."

"Of course." At least Mrs. Mulligan took the cue to drop the
subject. But that didn't stop her from following up with "And
do you make it down to Denver much to visit your uncle? You
know, I still live in the same house as when you and Alexandra
were little. I see him around the neighborhood sometimes."

"Not really," said Brigid, and this time she must not have
done a very good job hiding her discomfort.

Instead of being put off, though, Mrs. Mulligan gave her a
small, conspiratorial smile. "Well, I can hardly blame you for
that," she said quietly. "Especially if he's still as much of a shit-

head as he used to be."

Brigid, shocked, burst out laughing. "Mrs. Mulligan!" she exclaimed.

"Please, dear, it's Eileen." Mrs. Mulligan shook her head as if embarrassed, but she looked satisfied with the effect of her comment. "He *never* says hello to me, and I know he recognizes me, that self-righteous old fart. Oh, I know we're around the same age, but I believe that man was an old fart before he hit puberty." Brigid snorted. "Do you remember that when you were kids, he wouldn't let you come over to our house because I was divorced?"

"Among other reasons," Brigid said before she could stop herself.

Mrs. Mulligan raised her eyebrows. "Yes, well, there was that too," she said. "Is that why you stopped seeing him? Or did he stop seeing you? I'm sorry, that's personal. I probably shouldn't be asking you that." But she was still looking at Brigid with open expectation, and for once, Brigid found she didn't mind talking about it. There was something comforting about knowing that Mrs. Mulligan already knew her Uncle Angus—knew him well enough, anyway, that Brigid wouldn't have to explain.

"No, I haven't spoken to him since I left for college," she said. "My choice, not his, although I doubt he minds much."

"Well, I wouldn't feel sorry for him if he did," said Mrs. Mulligan. "Goodness. Pulling you out of school like that, over nothing but a little puppy love."

Brigid felt her cheeks get warm. It wasn't entirely true, she thought, that it had been just puppy love. Certainly the way she had felt about Zandy had been more intense than that, if not more sophisticated. But she wasn't going to correct Zandy's mother, of all people, on that point.

"Am I right in guessing that you still . . ." Mrs. Mulligan raised her eyebrows significantly. "Not that I suppose you'd want to talk to your uncle much, either way."

Brigid couldn't help but laugh. It was such an inappropriate question, but the delivery was so well-meaning that she couldn't fault it. "I do still kiss girls, yes," she said. "I mean, women." It had been quite some time since any kissing had taken place, she thought ruefully, but that was another detail Mrs. Mulligan didn't need.

"Are you married, then? Now that it's legal?"

Brigid thought of Gwen, then pushed the thought away. That had been a long time ago, and anyway, Gwen hadn't wanted to get married, even if they could have. "No, never married," she said lightly.

"Well," said Mrs. Mulligan with a look of satisfaction, and Brigid realized too late what kind of conversation she'd inadvertently stumbled into. "You know, I'm sure Alexandra would be so interested to know that I ran into you. She still lives in Denver, too. Housing has gotten so expensive there, but of course she doesn't need much space, since it's just her."

"Very subtle, Eileen," said Brigid, forcing herself to use the older woman's first name. It felt profoundly strange in her mouth.

Mrs. Mulligan waved her off with a laugh. "Now, why don't you just write down your number for me, so I can pass it along to my daughter? I'm sure you girls have lots to talk about."

Brigid handed over her number without further protest, then rang up a random assortment of purchases she was sure Mrs. Mulligan was just buying to be polite.

"I hope we see each other again soon," Mrs. Mulligan said

pointedly as she left the store.

Alexandra Mulligan. It was silly; they hadn't seen each other in thirty years. Who knew what sort of person she had become, or whether they'd even like each other anymore? Maybe Mrs. Mulligan would lose Brigid's number, or, more likely, Zandy would spot the attempted setup from a mile away and resist her mother's interference by never calling. Besides, Brigid realized, she hadn't mentioned Dylan. Even if Zandy was interested in reconnecting with her middle school crush, the discovery that Brigid was now a single mother, with all the baggage that entailed, would probably douse that old flame in an instant.

Still, she spent the rest of the afternoon staring off into space, a little flush on her cheeks, a smile on her lips.

Chapter 3

Brigid was twelve years old when she met Alexandra Mulligan. Technically they'd known each other since the previous year, when the students from three different Catholic elementary schools on the north side of Denver all came together to start sixth grade at Twelve Apostles. But Brigid hadn't made friends that year, or any year previously. The kids from her home parish knew all about her feverishly devout uncle; they had learned long ago that Brigid wasn't allowed to go to other kids' houses until Father Angus questioned their parents to make sure she wouldn't be exposed to anything ungodly. They knew trying to be friends with Brigid was more trouble than it was worth, and they made sure the rest of the school knew it too.

Sometimes Brigid imagined how her life would be different if she had a father. He'd be nice, she thought; he'd play outside with her and take her to the movies and read to her from books that weren't the Bible.

But if Brigid's father did those things, it wasn't with her. He'd left Adelaide when Brigid was only four years old—or more precisely, he'd made *them* leave, so his new girlfriend could move in. He and Adelaide had never been married, and her parents had cut her off because of it. But they were dead, and Adelaide's brother, Angus, owned their house now, and he allowed his sister and niece to move in with him, even though Adelaide's sin in conceiving Brigid had been grievous.

Angus never let the two of them forget that they lived on his charity. He was a big man, tall and wide-shouldered, with red hair and pale blue eyes, and he cast an enormous shadow that encompassed the house and everyone in it. Adelaide enrolled Brigid in Catholic school at his insistence. Father Angus didn't preach in, or even attend, a church, but he spent most of his days reading the Bible in his study and his evenings delivering sermons over the dinner table, explaining to his sister and his niece how the modern world was tempting them toward eternal damnation.

Brigid floated through her days alone, hating Father Angus, and knowing that hatred was a sin for which she was doomed to burn. With the prospect of hell awaiting her, a friendless middle school existence was downright tolerable.

But one day toward the end of seventh grade, Alexandra Mulligan leaned over to Brigid and whispered, "I love that book." It was reading period, and Brigid was staring at a Nancy Drew mystery without really absorbing the words. She had grabbed it from the shelf at the front of the room where Sister Rosa kept books for students who forgot to bring one from home. Brigid never brought books from home, because she had no interest in reading any of the books that were allowed in her house.

She blinked at Alexandra, not knowing how to respond.

"Oh?" Alexandra was a tall, lanky girl who played softball. She wasn't especially popular or pretty; she was too gangly and boyish, and her hair was always a mess. Still, she laughed a lot, and playing a sport meant she automatically had friends. Brigid was on guard against the possibility that she was being teased.

But Alexandra's smile was earnest. "My mom has a whole box set of Nancy Drew from when she was a kid," she said. "I've read them all. Which one's your favorite?"

"I don't know," Brigid said. "This is the first one I've read."

"Oh, cool," Alexandra said, undeterred. "I can lend you the others if you want."

"Maybe when I'm done with this one," Brigid said. She didn't particularly want to borrow an entire Nancy Drew box set, but she also didn't want Alexandra Mulligan to stop talking to her. The longer she looked at Alexandra's smiling face, the prettier the other girl seemed to become. It didn't matter that her bangs had gone too long without trimming, or that her lips were dry and chapped. Alexandra had a slightly lopsided smile and a gap between her bottom front teeth, and Brigid never wanted to stop looking at her.

After class, Alexandra waited for Brigid, and they walked down the hall together until they had to split off to go to separate classes. "Call me Zandy. I hate being called Alex," she said. "Do you want to sit with me at lunch?" Brigid, who usually sat at the end of a table with no one talking to her, nodded gratefully. She snuck the Nancy Drew book home and read it under her covers after bedtime just so she'd have something to talk to Alexandra—Zandy—about the next day.

Brigid had known all her life that she was unforgivable and riddled with sin, but when she started spending time with Zandy, the precise shape of that sin became clearer. From the first time they sat together at lunch, Brigid knew she wanted to kiss Zandy, that she felt about her the way other girls in their class felt about boys like Toby Cruz or Mark Romano. Sometimes, when she snuck looks at Zandy during reading period and saw her looking back, Brigid even imagined that Zandy felt the same way.

When she finally worked up the nerve to invite Zandy to her house, she was apologizing almost before the words were out of her mouth. "They're really weird and strict, I'm sorry. We don't have video games or movies or anything. And I'll have to help my mom with dinner, so that might be boring for you. I totally understand if you don't . . ."

"Of course I'll come over," Zandy said, smiling like sunshine.

After school, they walked close together, shoulders bumping occasionally. It was springtime, and garden beds bloomed all down the street. Zandy stopped to bury her face in a profusion of early lilac blossoms with a sigh that made Brigid tremble. "Doesn't this time of year feel magical?" Zandy asked.

Brigid didn't know what to say to that. What did magical feel like? Maybe it felt like standing next to Zandy.

Brigid's mother greeted them at the door, and Zandy gave her a big, bright smile, but it was different from her usual smile. This one was stretched out, shined up. It covered the gap in her bottom teeth. Adelaide returned it with a strained smile of her own. Zandy introduced herself as "Alexandra," and Adelaide offered the girls apple slices. While they were eating, Father Angus came into the kitchen and stared at them. Brigid looked at the table, closing herself around her feelings like a clenched fist.

"Don't be rude, Brigid," Adelaide said. "Introduce your

friend."

Brigid stood up. "I'm sorry," she said. "This is Alexandra Mulligan. Alexandra, this is my uncle, Father Angus."

"Uncle Father?" Zandy looked like she might giggle at that, but she saw Brigid's face and didn't. She stood up too. "It's nice to meet you, Father," she said. Angus looked at her, nodded, and left the room.

"We're going to go work on our homework," Brigid told her mother, and they finally escaped from the kitchen and up the stairs to the second floor. Brigid pulled her bedroom door shut behind them as quietly as possible, just in case her mother or uncle heard and demanded she open it again.

"Wow," said Zandy when they were alone. "You weren't joking. They're intense."

"Yeah," Brigid said. She fought the urge to apologize again.

Zandy opened her mouth like she wanted to say something else, then changed her mind. "Do you really want to do our homework?" she asked. "Because I brought a deck of cards."

Brigid didn't know how to play Spit, but Zandy was happy to teach her. They sat on the bed, playing one card after another as fast as possible, trying not to giggle too loudly. Brigid's favorite part of the game was every time she and Zandy went to play on the same card at the same time and their hands brushed over each other. After a few rounds, Brigid found herself watching Zandy's hands more closely than she was watching the cards, reaching out whenever she saw her beginning to move.

As Brigid played a king on top of a queen, Zandy's empty hand darted out and caught Brigid's wrist. Brigid looked up and saw Zandy grinning at her, the real, asymmetrical smile that revealed her teeth. Zandy turned Brigid's hand over and cupped it in her own, stroking the tip of her thumb over the mound of Brigid's palm. Warmth crept up Brigid's neck.

"I'm glad you invited me over," Zandy said. Her voice was very low, and she stared into Brigid's eyes as she said it. Brigid swallowed hard.

"I'm glad you came," she said, trying to match Zandy's tone. Zandy licked her lips, and Brigid followed the path of her pink tongue, entranced.

The door opened with a creak. "Brigid, I need you to come help with dinner," her mother said. Zandy let go of Brigid's hand and played another card. She looked entirely unfazed, but Brigid noticed she'd played a six on top of Brigid's king.

Adelaide looked at the cards spread across Brigid's quilt. "You said you were doing homework."

"We finished it all," said Brigid quickly.

Adelaide pursed her lips. "No cards in the house, girls," she said. "Your uncle wouldn't like it." Brigid thought about asking what God could possibly have against cards, but as usual, she didn't have the nerve.

"Sure thing, Mrs. Byrne," Zandy said, sweeping up the pile of cards, then smoothing them into a tidy rectangle with just a few quick gestures. Brigid realized she was staring at Zandy's hands again and made herself look away.

"Alexandra, I'm sure your mother will be expecting you home for dinner," Adelaide said before she left the room.

Although Angus was quick to veto Brigid spending time at the Mulligans' house, Zandy came to the Byrnes' house more and more frequently. Sometimes they played cards, despite Adelaide's warnings; sometimes, especially as the end of the school year loomed and final projects came due, they actually did their homework.

The first day of summer break was an annual tradition of misery for Brigid. No club or camp was acceptable to Father Angus—even Twelve Apostles' summer Bible study was "too modern"—so vacation meant a ten-week slog of household chores and dinner-table sermons, unbroken by the slightest novelty or fun. Brigid hadn't even bothered to ask Zandy what she was doing over the summer, dreading a litany of adventures she would never be able to share.

But the day after seventh grade ended, Zandy knocked on the Byrnes' door. Adelaide looked almost as surprised to see her as Brigid felt. "Alexandra, how nice to see you," she said in a voice that communicated the clear opposite.

"Hi," said Zandy very politely. "I'm going to the park, does Brigid want to come with me?"

"Yes," Brigid said before Adelaide could respond. Thinking fast, she turned to her mother and said, "It would be good to get some exercise, since I don't have gym class over the summer. And we could stop at the library to pick up our summer reading books."

Adelaide looked at Brigid skeptically, and Brigid willed herself to return the gaze, not to glance at Zandy. Finally, her mother said, "You'll still need to do your chores when you get back. And I want to look at your library books before you start reading them."

"Of course," Brigid said, stifling her smile.

"Thank you so much, Mrs. Byrne!" Zandy chirped. She was halfway down the block before the door closed behind Brigid.

Brigid stood shocked for a moment before running after her. Zandy crossed streets without looking, her long, loose hair a flag in the wind behind her, laughing in the sticky sunshine. Her legs were longer and stronger than Brigid's. They turned a corner and poured into Rocky Mountain Lake Park, cutting through grass still wet from the early-morning sprinklers.

Zandy passed the playground and collapsed under a huge blue spruce tree, where Brigid finally caught up with her. The shade felt sweet and holy after only a few minutes running in the sun. Brigid lay down beside Zandy, spreading her arms out in the cool grass.

Above her, the shadows of tree branches shifted and danced. Then another shadow crossed her field of vision. Zandy was sitting up, leaning over Brigid.

Brigid caught her breath. In the dark beneath the tree, she could barely make out Zandy's face; her expression was inscrutable. Still, Brigid felt understanding pass between them. Grass prickled the back of Brigid's neck, an ant crawled over her wrist, and Zandy swooped in to kiss her.

Zandy's lips were dry and warm, her breath hot in Brigid's mouth. It was almost unbearable in combination with the summer heat, but Brigid didn't want it to stop. Zandy's hair fell loose around their faces like a curtain, a secret room within the sheltered cavern of the tree, protecting them from the world.

Brigid didn't know what she was supposed to do. She'd barely even seen kissing in movies. But the feeling of Zandy's lips brushing over hers was amazing, as though her lips were suddenly the most sensitive skin on her whole body, tingling and alive to the slightest pressure. Brigid lifted her head to press her mouth more firmly to Zandy's. *I love her*, she thought, amazed.

They broke apart, and Zandy giggled self-consciously. "Was that okay?" she asked.

Brigid didn't think about Adelaide. She didn't think about Father Angus. She resolutely did not think about the fires of hell, which would one day consume her soul. "That was perfect," she said.

Chapter 4

The sun was almost down outside the Tenth Muse's huge front windows. Brigid knew the sidewalk was still busy, full of locals and visitors enjoying the cool mountain air of early October, but she couldn't see anything beyond the reflection of the store's brightly lit interior.

It had been a busy afternoon, but now, less than an hour before closing, no one was left but Dylan, Brigid, and her newest employee, Cypress. Brigid had picked Dylan up from school and brought her back to the store, much to Dylan's dismay.

"I don't want you home alone right now," Brigid had said.

"What do you think I'm going to do?" Dylan fumed. "Ride my bike to Kai's house and throw a brick through his window?"

"I don't know *what* you might do, and that's what worries me," Brigid had responded.

Now, Dylan drifted moodily from one shelf to another, picking up books and rifling through their pages before putting them back out of order. She stuck her finger into an amethyst geode and wound a gauzy scarf around her wrist. Brigid fought the urge to snap at Dylan, tell her to stop messing with things. She tried to focus on alphabetizing tiny vials of essential oils, but she was too distracted, tracking Dylan's chaotic path around the Tenth Muse, keeping mental notes on everything she'd need to set right later.

Dylan took a necklace from a jewelry rack, a rose quartz heart on a black velvet cord, and swung it in circles. The whirring sound it made cutting through the air seemed to vibrate inside Brigid's head. She opened her mouth to tell Dylan to stop, but her daughter was already moving on.

"What's this?" Dylan picked up a smooth disc of gleaming black stone from its wrought-iron stand.

Before Brigid could answer, Cypress, behind the counter, jumped in. "Obsidian mirror. Obsidian is protective, but the mirror is especially good for scrying and communicating with the dead." Cypress was a student at Grand County Community College, but they barely looked older than Dylan. Today their long, skinny braids were gathered in luxuriant pigtails, amplifying their aura of baby-faced innocence.

Dylan turned the mirror over in her hands, leaving, Brigid was sure, fingerprints that would need to be wiped away. "Scrying?"

"Divination. Seeing the future, or things that are hidden."

"Like secrets?"

Cypress nodded, came out from behind the counter and went over to Dylan. They pulled a pendant out of the jangle of necklaces they wore and held it away from their chest so Dylan could see it: a smaller version of the obsidian disc on a string of black beads. "It lets you see beyond the surface of things, to understand the truth."

"Cool!" Dylan reached out to touch it, then glanced at Cypress and pulled her hand back. "Sorry, I should have asked." Brigid gritted her teeth. Why was this the first time in three hours Dylan had expressed a hint of respect for someone else's property?

"No worries, but yeah, I prefer that mine is the only energy it absorbs," said Cypress. "Obsidian mirrors have been in use since the ancient Aztecs. They're really powerful. If you have a question, the mirror can show you what you need to know."

"How? Like, what would you do?" The frown that had creased Dylan's forehead since Brigid picked her up from school was gone now. She looked fascinated, listening to Cypress with an attention she hadn't shown Brigid in weeks, maybe months.

"Just looking into it and clearing your mind might be enough," said Cypress. "But you could do a more involved ritual, too. A lot of magic is just symbolism. If I wanted to clear away the barriers to understanding something, I might spill some water on the surface of the mirror and then wipe it off." Then they grinned conspiratorially at Dylan. "Be careful, though. It might show you the truth about yourself, too, and not everyone's ready for that. Don't start digging up secrets unless you want your own to come to light."

Dylan nodded, turning the larger obsidian mirror around in her hands again. Brigid couldn't stand it anymore.

"It's not magic, Dylan," she said, trying to keep the irritation out of her voice. "It's just a different way of thinking about the world. Some people might look at a black mirror while they meditate, and it helps clear their mind, but that doesn't mean the mirror itself has powers."

If Nadine had been there, she would have launched into a lecture about respect for forces beyond one's own comprehension, but Cypress merely shot Brigid an offended look and went back to the counter.

Dylan crossed her arms. The frown was back. "So you don't believe in any of this? Even though you charge people money for it?"

Brigid took a deep breath and tried to untangle her reflexive defensiveness from her genuine opinions. "It's not that I don't believe in it. I would say that if people find meaning in it, that meaning exists. People find meaning in all sorts of things."

"Why did you open this store in the first place if you don't believe in magic?"

The simple answer to that question was: Gwen. Gwen thought it would be hilarious. "You could devote your life to doing all the stuff your uncle and your mom thought was Satanic," she'd said one night over wine. "Spend your days selling pentagram necklaces, and your nights . . ." Then she'd run her hand up Brigid's thigh, and for quite some time they hadn't talked about it.

But Brigid had liked the idea, enough to stick with it even after Gwen was gone. It wasn't really about defiance; the little rebellious thrill of *my mother would hate this* faded after a few months. Running the Tenth Muse had become an affirmation of Brigid's choices in life, of having escaped the punishingly rigid Catholicism of Adelaide and Angus Byrne. There were so many ways to interpret the mysteries of the universe, and none of them were more wrong or right than any other.

"I guess I believe that people make the magic they need," she said now. "Everything I sell here is symbolic, like Cypress said. It's the intention people bring to things that makes them powerful."

Cypress opened their mouth, possibly to interject that they hadn't said that, exactly, but they closed it again.

"That's a cop-out," said Dylan. "You're saying you think everyone is right? Every religion is true? That doesn't even make sense. They all contradict each other."

"I don't think I know enough to rule anything out." Brigid could hear the strain in her own voice now, and she was certain Dylan could, too.

"But do you actually *believe* in anything? Like, do you believe in God?"

"That's personal," Brigid snapped.

Something happened to Dylan's face, and watching it made Brigid's heart ache. It was like watching Dylan fold in on herself, an origami box closing around something too precious to share. "Sorry," she said quietly.

Shit. Dylan had been *talking* to her, for the first time all day, and Brigid shut her down. Guilt and regret bloomed in an instant. "No, honey, I'm sorry," Brigid said, but Dylan wasn't looking at her anymore.

The bell above the door rang then, and a group of college students came in. Brigid hated herself for feeling relieved by the interruption. She helped them find the tarot deck they were looking for, and by the time they were gone, Dylan had disappeared into the store's back room. Brigid hoped she was doing homework, but knew it was more likely she was messing around on her phone.

As Brigid counted out the cash register, her own cell phone rang. She didn't recognize the number, but it had a Colorado area code, and she hoped fleetingly that it might be the therapist with an earlier appointment.

"This is Brigid," she said.

"Wow," said a low, feminine voice. "Brigid Byrne. You sound very businesslike."

Brigid's breath caught, because she knew that voice, even if it had sounded very different the last time she'd heard it. "Holy shit, Zandy?"

"Yeah," said Alexandra Mulligan. "You gave my mom your number. I hope you're not disappointed that I'm calling you instead."

Brigid laughed. It was too loud and high-pitched, and the sound of it made her cringe. "Yeah. I mean, no. I'm sorry. I—yes, I gave her my number to give to you."

"Good, because you made her week. 'That Brigid is such a nice girl!'" Zandy said, doing a solid impression of her mother's distinctive voice. "'Wouldn't it be lovely if you two reconnected? I wonder what she's been up to all these years! She happened to mention that she's not married, isn't that interesting?' I assume you happened to mention it because she asked point-blank," Zandy added in her normal voice. "She's hoping you reappeared from the past to wife me."

"No!" Brigid blurted. She was glad Zandy couldn't see her face.

"Yeah, I'm not the marrying kind," Zandy said. "My mom is having a much harder time accepting that than she did with the gay thing." Doing Mrs. Mulligan's voice again, she said, "'Alexandra, people spent their whole lives fighting for your right to get married. After all that, are you really telling me you can't be bothered?'"

Brigid laughed. "Okay, I won't propose to you. You talked me out of it."

"So, wow. Brigid Byrne. What a blast from the past," Zandy said.

"I missed you," Brigid said before giving herself a chance to overthink it.

"Shit, I missed you too," Zandy said. "So when are we going to get together? I'm still in the old neighborhood, although it doesn't look much like the old neighborhood anymore. What about you?"

"I'm in Bristlecone," Brigid said. "Up in the mountains, near Winter Park."

"Do you ever come down to Denver? To visit your folks or anything?"

Brigid tensed. "I don't have anyone to visit."

"Shit, I'm sorry," Zandy said quickly. "I forgot about your mom, I'm—I shouldn't have brought up your family. I was just thinking if you were ever in town, maybe we could get together."

"I'd love that," Brigid said.

"Yeah? Do you have any plans to be in Denver?" Zandy's voice was warm and hopeful, and Brigid felt it like a physical heat, radiating through her core.

Impulsively, Brigid said, "I can come down tomorrow." Her face flushed as soon as she said it. Not only was it impractical, it was embarrassing. She'd come on too strong.

But Zandy only said, "Are you sure?" in a tone that sounded like she actually hoped Brigid would say yes.

"Yes," Brigid decided. "It's been a stressful week. Getting out of town for a few hours would be good for me. I should be home before my daughter gets out of school, though. Can you do lunch?"

"Absolutely," Zandy said. "Do you remember Lorenzo's? It's still there. It's practically a historic landmark."

Brigid was startled to feel a pang of nostalgia at the thought of Lorenzo's, with its big neon sign shaped like a chef's hat. She'd walked past it on the way home from school every day for two years. During that one short summer of freedom, before Father Angus discovered them and her world came crashing down, she and Zandy had gone there in the middle of the day for gelato. It was rare for her to miss anything about Denver, but in that moment she missed Lorenzo's.

"That's perfect," she said. "Can you meet me there at noon?"

"It's a date," said Zandy, and obviously Brigid knew that was a standard phrase to confirm plans, knew it couldn't be considered suggestive, but she still had a fluttery feeling in her chest as she hung up the phone.

From among the shelves, Cypress said, "We need to order more of those little ceramic incense burners."

"I think we have more in the back. Can you go look?" Brigid asked. She'd completely lost count of the register while talking to Zandy. Five, ten, fifteen—

Cypress screamed.

Brigid's brain filled with white noise as she turned and ran toward the back room, her limbs feeling unbearably heavy, unforgivably slow. *What if I'm too late*, she thought, rounding the counter too sharply and slamming her hip into its edge. Pain lanced down her leg, but she didn't stop.

In the back room, Cypress was on their knees beside a huddled shape on the floor. *Dylan.* The floorboards beneath Dylan's body were stained with something dark, and for a long moment

Brigid saw blood. That was her daughter, lying there in a pool of blood; that was her daughter lying there dead.

"No," she said.

Dylan lifted her head and stared at Brigid. "It's coming," she said.

"Oh, my baby," Brigid said wildly. She pushed past Cypress and threw herself over Dylan, half embrace and half collapse, sobbing into her daughter's hair. "Dylan, sweetheart, you're okay."

Over the earthy, alive smell of Dylan's body, Brigid breathed in the tang of something sharp and chemical. Spray paint, she realized. That was the dark spot on the floor she'd mistaken for blood. Dylan had found the supplies left over from repainting some old bookshelves and had sprayed a shape on the floor in thick layers of black.

She sat up and pulled Dylan to sitting. Dylan stared past her, not meeting her eyes, but she was unmistakably alive, and anything beyond that was negotiable. "Holy shit, you scared me," Brigid said over her shoulder to Cypress. "Why did you scream like that?"

"I thought," Cypress said, and never finished the sentence. Instead, they got up and left the room.

Brigid clutched Dylan to her chest. Limp in her arms, Dylan let herself be rocked back and forth. Eventually Brigid's pulse slowed to somewhere in the vicinity of normal. She brushed Dylan's hair away from her face, leaving a few black streaks where the ends of her hair had fallen into the wet paint, and looked at her unfocused eyes. "Are you okay, Dylan? What happened?"

"It's on the way," Dylan said. Then, in a sudden burst of energy, she pulled herself out of Brigid's grasp and crawled a few feet away. She drew her knees up to her chest, covering her face with her paint-spattered hands.

Brigid looked down at the floor. Dylan had used the black paint to inscribe a circle wide enough that her body, curled in the fetal position, had fit entirely within it. But with Dylan out of the way, Brigid could see that she'd also drawn some kind of symbol or rune in the middle of the circle, each line at least as thick as Brigid's forearm.

Looking at that symbol made Brigid's head hurt. It was too dark, too dense. The paint smelled fresh, but didn't look wet; there was no gloss to it, no reflection. It seemed to absorb all light. Brigid swayed with vertigo as an optical illusion overtook her. For a moment, the rune looked like an absence, a shape carved out of the floorboards, opening into an endless, lightless void. The longer she stared at it, the stranger she felt. Its layers of black played tricks on her, making her imagine shifting, unstable shapes, something moving in that abyssal darkness. Something coming *up*, toward her.

Brigid dragged her gaze back to Dylan. "Did you draw this?" It must be the paint fumes going to her head; that was why she felt so dizzy and strange.

Dylan hunched forward and dropped to her hands and knees. Her head hung before her, hair brushing the floor. She was close to the edge of the painted circle, and Brigid had a brief, absurd impulse to pull her hair back, keep it from falling down the hole.

It's not a hole. Nothing was waiting down there to grab Dylan's hair and drag her into the black.

Dylan gasped. She coughed. She rocked back and forth. After a moment, Brigid realized Dylan was heaving, as if trying to expel something from her throat. Was she choking? "Dylan!" She tried to think of the first-aid class she'd taken. How did you do the Heimlich maneuver? But if someone was coughing, it meant their airway wasn't blocked, right?

The coughing became awful, wet retching sounds. Tears ran down Brigid's face, and she clung to Dylan like the mast of a storm-tossed ship. She shouted for Cypress, or maybe she didn't—she felt her lips moving but heard nothing except Dylan's agonized breathing. They struggled together until Dylan was half in Brigid's lap. Dylan flailed, elbowing Brigid hard in the neck, but Brigid didn't let go.

Gradually, the coughing subsided. Dylan stared up at Brigid, her face slick with tears. "I can't get it out," she said.

"What?" Brigid asked.

"I don't know," Dylan said. Her voice was raw from coughing and despair.

Chapter 5

Dylan refused to eat dinner—her throat hurt too much—and went to bed immediately. Alone in their small kitchen, Brigid stood at the open window and let the cold air rush into her nose, her throat. Below her, the pines for which the town of Bristlecone was named sloped down the mountain, then up again into the distance. Usually she loved this view, but tonight she barely saw it.

She was fucking this up. Her child was in pain, and Brigid didn't know how to help.

A bird landed on the windowsill, startling her. It was a tiny thing, small enough to fit in the cup of her hand, pale gray except for a stripe of velvet black on the top of its head. It stared back at her, cocked its head, fixing her with bright black eyes.

"Hey, little one," Brigid said softly. The bird kept staring, and Brigid had the silly thought that she wanted to pet it. When she reached out her hand, the bird vanished into the deep blue night.

"I don't want to do this by myself," Brigid whispered.

It had never been her plan. She'd wanted to raise a child with Gwen. She'd dreamed of their happy little family of three at the park, cooking family meals, curled up on the couch together for movie nights. Gwen was sturdy and even-keeled, smoothing out Brigid's sharp edges. She'd be the safe and stable foundation on which their baby's joyful life could be built.

But Gwen hadn't wanted children, no matter how Brigid tried to convince her. She usually changed the subject instead of arguing outright, but Brigid could feel the tension growing. Despite Gwen's reassurances, Brigid feared she wasn't in this for the long haul.

Brigid redoubled her efforts to prove she was worth it, tightening her grip as she felt Gwen slipping through her fingers. She put in long hours renovating the Tenth Muse, then came home and cooked elaborate meals. They fucked frantically. Brigid knelt for hours at the altar of Gwen's body. *Please*, she begged without saying the words, *let me take care of you forever. Please stay.*

Then Brigid's uncle called. Only later did it occur to her to wonder how he'd gotten her number. "Your mother has passed away," he said. His voice sounded ragged from crying, and that shocked Brigid almost as much as his words. "She committed the sin of despair." Brigid waited for him to go on, but he didn't. He just sat there on the open line, and she did too, neither of them speaking a word. It was a solid five minutes of silence before she finally hung up.

That night she curled into Gwen's arms, her eyes dry, her whole body feeling hollow. "It's over," she said. "It's finally over." She had told Gwen very little about her childhood, about her family, and she could see that it frightened Gwen, her obvious relief at her mother's death.

"When is the funeral?" Gwen asked.

Brigid had no intention of going to any funeral, especially not a service presided over by Father Angus. "I think you should talk to someone," Gwen said, but Brigid ignored that, too.

There was a little money, after the will was settled. Adelaide had a small life insurance policy in addition to what she'd squirreled away from the part-time bookkeeping job she'd held all those years. Brigid was surprised her mother hadn't left everything to Father Angus, but she wasn't too proud to take what was offered. It couldn't confer any obligation, now.

With her mother gone, Brigid felt even more acutely the desire to settle things between herself and Gwen, to have a family of her own. "It's time," she told Gwen, flushed with excitement. Surely Gwen would feel it too, now; surely Gwen would understand. They couldn't get married, not in Colorado, but a child would be even better, would tie them to each other, blood-deep and lifelong.

Gwen's face crumpled. "I don't think it's the right time," she said. "I don't think we're ready. I don't think you're ready. This isn't a decision to make in a hurry, especially while you're mourning."

"I'm not mourning," Brigid said, and Gwen threw up her hands and left the room.

The next few months were as hazy in her memory as a dream. Looking back, Brigid could see that she'd been nearly out of her mind with grief while completely unwilling to admit it. Somehow, she had become convinced that a baby was the answer. If she had a family of her own—the very thing Adelaide had warned would be forever lost to her if she pursued her *sin-*

ful, unnatural tendencies—that would prove that her mother was wrong, that Brigid wasn't broken, that she needn't regret how things had ended between them.

So Brigid made an appointment with her gynecologist.

She was sure it was the right thing to do, sure that Gwen's protestations would disappear when she saw Brigid's dedication to their shared future. She looked through pages of sperm donor profiles and chose one with Russian heritage to match Gwen's. She scheduled her appointments during work hours and never mentioned them. Three months in a row, after a urine test to confirm she was about to ovulate, Brigid lay on her back while an apple-cheeked nurse threaded a tube into her cervix and poured reheated sperm into her uterus, and Gwen didn't know anything about it. She might have protested if she'd seen Brigid's inheritance disappearing in thousand-dollar chunks, but they still had separate bank accounts.

The first two months, the negative pregnancy tests caught Brigid in the chest, a crushing blow that knocked the wind out of her. She cried in the bathroom at the store, scrubbed her face, came home, and had dinner with Gwen like nothing was wrong.

When she took the third test, she closed her eyes and steeled herself for disappointment, but it didn't come. The strip showed two pink lines, the second one pale but unmistakable. It had worked. She was pregnant.

Brigid left work early to buy a bottle of champagne and make grilled salmon, Gwen's favorite. When Gwen arrived home she found Brigid beaming, spilling over like the champagne bottle, foaming and fizzing with the good news. Brigid still remembered the smell of fish and garlic in the air when Gwen's mouth fell open in horror and she knew she had made a mistake.

"We talked about this," Gwen pleaded. "I said we need to wait."

"I don't need to wait," Brigid said. "I know what I want, and I want it to be with you. I love you." She pressed a hand to her belly, slightly soft, no different than the day or the week or the month before, but she could swear she felt a tiny answering pang from deep within.

Gwen shook her head. There were tears in her eyes. "I don't see how you can say you love me and then try to . . . to hijack my life like this."

Brigid took a step backward. "That's not fair."

"This isn't fair!" Gwen gestured to the dinner, the champagne, the pretty blue dress Brigid had changed into. "You did something I told you I wasn't ready for, and you act like you're giving me a present! Were you ever even listening to me? Do you even *know* me?"

Panic flared in Brigid, hot and bright and much too late. "Gwen, I'm sorry. I love you. I didn't mean to upset you."

"Jesus, I'd feel better if you did! If you were trying to piss me off, at least this would make sense!" She pressed the back of her hand to her forehead, as if checking for a fever. "Look, I need . . . I need some time. I need to think."

Desperate to make her stay, Brigid blurted the only thing she could think of. "Please don't go. I'll get rid of it if you want me to."

"Do you mean that?" Gwen looked at her hard.

And Brigid lied, "Yes, I mean it." Surely Gwen would flinch, now. Surely she wouldn't actually make such a demand. She would say it had to be Brigid's decision, and they would talk about it more, and she'd have another chance to argue her case, and in the end Gwen would stay.

But instead Gwen said, "Okay. Yes. Please do," and Brigid couldn't control the expression that bloomed on her face. Gwen saw it and knew what it meant. "God dammit, Bridge," she said, not angry, just terribly sad.

They said more things after that, but Brigid couldn't remember them anymore, which was probably a blessing. Gwen didn't leave that night, but she packed her things and was gone by the end of the week—not just gone from Brigid's apartment but gone from Bristlecone, gone from Colorado. She went back to Philadelphia and lived with her sister for a while, and Brigid stayed where she was, alone and pregnant and an orphan.

After Dylan came, Brigid was so tired and working so hard she didn't have the energy to be lonely. Every second she was awake she was either at the store or taking care of the baby. Though she was exhausted, there was satisfaction in it, too. The love she felt for her daughter was thin and gritty, like the dregs in a cup of coffee; it was all Brigid had to offer, but it was enough. Dylan thrived. Brigid wished Gwen could see her, but Dylan didn't need Gwen. She had one mother who adored her, and if they didn't live luxuriously, they never went hungry either.

Now thirteen years had passed, and Brigid had nothing in the world except Dylan. And Dylan was faltering.

"What do I do?" Brigid asked aloud in the dark, quiet kitchen, but no one answered, because no one was there.

Chapter 6

T he first thing Zandy said to Brigid's face was "You look like hell."

It had been a cold, strained morning in the apartment. Brigid made oatmeal for breakfast, topped with apples and toasted walnuts the way Dylan liked, but Dylan wouldn't touch it. "My throat is still sore," she'd mumbled.

Brigid looked closely at her daughter, trying to decide whether she looked thinner than usual under her oversized sweater and baggy jeans. Did she need to look for a therapist who specialized in eating disorders? "What about some yogurt? That won't hurt your throat."

"No, thanks. I need to get going."

Brigid checked the clock. "I was planning to drive you. We don't need to leave for a few more minutes."

"No," repeated Dylan, the loudest she'd spoken all morning. "I can walk to school. You don't have to watch me every second. I'm tired of you treating me like a toddler."

Brigid dug her fingernails into her palms and tried to keep her voice level. "Dylan, I know you're having a hard time right now, and I'm trying to do what I can to support you—"

Dylan had rolled her eyes. "Bye, Mom. Have a good day," she said pointedly, and turned toward the door. Brigid had battled the impulse to shout at her, to run after her and grab her shoulder, but then what? Wrestle her into the car? She'd never dealt with defiance like this before, and she was suddenly, bleakly aware that she had no idea what might happen if she put her foot down. She was, she realized, afraid to see how far her daughter might go.

"I'm going to call the school to make sure you get there on time," Brigid said. Dylan let the door slam shut behind her.

Having already scheduled Cypress to open the store, Brigid had fought the impulse to cancel on Zandy and go back to bed. The brief argument had left her exhausted, scraped down to her bones.

But Brigid thought of how genuinely happy Zandy had sounded at the prospect of seeing her, and she made herself shower, brush her hair, and get dressed. Driving away from Bristlecone, she felt the pressure in her chest slowly ease. The slopes on either side of the road, thick with spruces and pines and the occasional bright yellow aspen grove, cradled her protectively. Morning sunlight gleamed off early snow on the higher peaks. It felt good to be in the car alone, listening to Brandi Carlile and watching the Rocky Mountains roll past.

Eventually, the mountains fell away to hills, and the hills gave way to malls and gas stations, and then she was in the city. The dilapidated roller coaster of Lakeside Amusement Park, closed for the season, stood sentry by the side of the road and welcomed her home.

The bright bubble of calm that had carried her down from the mountains trembled and dissolved as she exited the highway. What would Zandy think of the person Brigid had become? Forty-one and single, with a struggling store, a troubled child she didn't know how to help, and no significant relationships to speak of. Would Zandy be disappointed? Would she regret getting back in touch with Brigid?

Though she'd lived here most of her childhood, the Northside that Brigid drove through now was a strange patchwork of nostalgic and unfamiliar. The Victorian painted ladies and 1950s ranch houses Brigid remembered were now interspersed with larger, more angular constructions, and recently scraped-clean lots suggested more were coming. Local restaurants, secondhand stores, and video rentals had been replaced by craft breweries and a store that appeared to sell CBD products for pets.

The neon sign outside Lorenzo's, at least, was exactly as she remembered. It was cozily dim inside the restaurant, and Brigid's vision swam for a moment as her eyes adjusted from the golden autumn sunlight. Half blind, she turned toward the voice, low and rich and affectionate, saying "You look like hell."

"I feel like hell," Brigid said reflexively, and then she said, "Oh, Zandy."

Alexandra Mulligan had grown into a tall, fat, handsome woman, standing before Brigid in jeans and a short-sleeved button-down shirt with a floral pattern. Her once wild hair was cropped close, buzzed on the sides and rakishly tousled on top. She wore glasses with thick black plastic frames, and her forearms were tattooed. But her eyes were the same eyes, her smile the same smile.

"Jesus," Zandy said. "Brigid Byrne." Eye contact went on and on, and Brigid smelled spruce and sweat. Then, as if remembering herself, Zandy said, "Have a seat," and gestured toward the table she'd just risen from.

"Thank you," Brigid said, and sank into a chair as though her legs were about to collapse under her, as though she'd just run miles instead of walking across a breezy parking lot. Her pulse was a frantic drumbeat.

Zandy passed her a laminated menu that looked like it hadn't changed since they were thirteen, but Brigid barely glanced at it. She couldn't stop staring at Zandy, at the girl she'd loved looking out from this stranger's face.

They exchanged a few pleasantries until the server came to take their orders. As soon as he was gone, Zandy leaned closer and said abruptly, "So why do you feel like hell?"

Brigid laughed. "Right into the deep end, huh?"

"Hey, if you want to fuck around with where'd you go to college and what's your favorite Marvel movie, we can do that," Zandy said. She shrugged. "But you drove all this way at the drop of a hat. I figure maybe you did that because you have some real shit to talk about."

Brigid's throat felt dry. "You're right," she said. "It's been a hard couple of weeks, and I haven't had anyone to talk to."

"You've got me, babe," Zandy said. "Lay it on me."

So Brigid did. She started with Dylan's suspension, doubled back to explain about Gwen and why it was only the two of them now, then described Dylan's bizarre behavior the night before. Zandy listened thoughtfully, nodding and humming but otherwise reserving any response. Their food was delivered while Brigid talked, but neither of them paused to take a bite.

"I'm such a shitty parent," Brigid concluded miserably. "All she has is me, and I'm not enough. I'm letting her down."

"Look," Zandy said, "I don't know a lot about your situation growing up. I remember you lived with your mom and your uncle, and he was seriously scary, and she was . . . I never really got to know her."

"I didn't either," Brigid admitted. "Sometimes it felt like she was shutting me out, and sometimes I thought there was nothing there to know. Like she was just an extension of him."

"Yeah," Zandy said. "And I know it was bad for you. I think it was probably worse than you ever told me, and I thought that back then too, but I didn't know how to ask."

Brigid's face felt hot, and a phantom pain flared in her knees.

"I'm not asking now, either, unless you want to talk about it," Zandy said quickly.

"Maybe another time," Brigid managed to say.

"I just think, you know, you had a family and it wasn't all that fucking great," Zandy said. "I know you feel bad that you haven't given your daughter more, but you're doing better by her than anyone ever did by you. You know how hard it is to break an abusive cycle? And you're doing it on your own, with no partner, no backup?" She shook her head. "I always knew you were so damn amazing, Brigid Byrne."

Tears welled up in Brigid's eyes, and she tried to blink them away without Zandy noticing. She didn't deserve Zandy's praise, she knew, and just hearing it made her feel guilty, but if she tried to say anything right now she'd weep all over the table.

Zandy took pity on her. "Eat your pasta, it's getting cold." Gratefully, Brigid twirled up a forkful of fettuccine alfredo, and for a few minutes they were occupied with chewing.

"Anyway," Brigid said when she was sure she had control over her voice, "I've talked enough. Tell me what you've been doing for the last three decades."

While Zandy talked about her cats and her nonprofit job teaching music to kids, Brigid struggled to focus on her words. It wasn't that she wasn't interested. Zandy's life sounded wonderful, warm and full in a way Brigid envied. It was just—she kept getting distracted by a quirk at the corner of Zandy's mouth, or the way her fingers moved when she gestured.

"Not that I'm not flattered, but you're staring," Zandy said with a grin.

Brigid flushed. "It's just so good to see you again," she said. "I never thought I would, after . . ." She didn't need to finish that sentence; Zandy knew what she meant.

Zandy's grin faded. "I came by your house, you know," she said. "After they pulled you out of school. I came by so many times, and I stood there on the sidewalk, but I never got up the courage to knock on the door." She grimaced. "I'm sorry. I was terrified of him. I don't know what I thought, that he'd tell my mom I was a deviant or something. Which of course she already knew, we just weren't ready to admit it to each other."

"I didn't blame you," Brigid said wholeheartedly. "I never would have even walked down that street again if I were you."

"And now I see him around the neighborhood, and he's just . . . this old man," Zandy said. "It's weird how time changes things."

Brigid had no response to that. Time hadn't changed anything for her, except putting distance between herself and her uncle's house. She was as afraid of him as she ever had been.

Zandy noticed her silence. "You don't see him these days,

huh?"

"Not since I left for college," Brigid said.

"I wonder if he's still preaching," Zandy mused. "Actually, that reminds me, I've wondered this for years. What church was he with? It wasn't Apostles, and no one at Saint Agnes remembers him."

"He didn't . . . Wait," said Brigid. "You go to Saint Agnes?"

"I'm in the choir," Zandy said.

Brigid stared at her. "You're still Catholic? But you're so . . ."

Zandy laughed. "Dykey? There are plenty of gay Catholics."

"Don't they say it's a sin?"

"The Pope does, but it's not like I see him around," Zandy said. "Saint Ag's is great. They can't officially say they're affirming, but there are lots of us there and no one gives me a hard time."

Brigid couldn't imagine. "But why?" She knew it was an inappropriate question, but she was so curious. "I mean, you're an adult. You could just . . . not."

"It sounds like you're not going to relate to this, but I believe in God," Zandy said.

"The Catholic God? Wine into blood and unbaptized babies go to limbo for eternity?"

"They don't have limbo anymore," Zandy said. "The Pope made an announcement. Shut the whole place down. I think it's a Spirit Halloween now."

Brigid laughed at that. "The rest of it, though?"

Zandy shrugged. "I was raised Catholic, so that's how I relate to God. It's the framework that makes sense to me, even if I disagree with some of the dogma."

Brigid thought about her store, all the books and crystals and accoutrements people used to connect to whatever idea they had about the divine. Tin cans on strings, carrying vibrations back and forth. Speaking in the hope that something was listening, listening in the hope that something was speaking. Everyone was just trying to feel less alone.

"You're right, I don't relate," she admitted. "But that doesn't make it a bad thing. I'm glad you have something to believe in."

Zandy looked at her without blinking. Her eyes were big and light brown, flecks of gold shimmering like mica in granite. "What do you believe in, Brigid Byrne?"

Brigid thought of paint fumes and black runes. She thought of rosary beads and a thick red rug. "I'm still trying to figure that out," she said.

Chapter 7

On Friday morning, Brigid woke before her alarm. For a moment she couldn't remember the source of the tension that buzzed inside her, chasing away sleep, but then it dawned on her. This afternoon was Dylan's mediation with Kai Shriver. Brigid would have to go to the school and face not only Principal Halyard, but also Kai's mother.

Dylan was already in the kitchen, smiling nervously alongside the full coffeepot.

"Aw, sweetheart, thank you," Brigid said. She poured herself a mug, added milk, and took a deep drink. The taste made her shudder. Dylan, not yet a coffee drinker herself, had brewed a pot that tasted like being buried alive.

Brigid made eggs, and they sat down together. In the buttery light of the autumn morning, Brigid tried to convince herself to be optimistic. "How are you feeling about today?"

Dylan looked down. "Do you think they'll let me back in art class?"

"I don't know," Brigid said slowly. "Maybe if you can work things out with Kai so he feels safe." She couldn't quite bring herself to use the word *apologize*.

"He's not scared of me," Dylan said, still looking at her un-eaten eggs instead of meeting Brigid's eyes. "He's just being an asshole because he can."

"You did hit him," Brigid ventured, hoping this was it, hoping Dylan was about to open up, explain why she'd been fighting with Kai in the first place. But Dylan just sighed and stood.

"I'm not really hungry," she said.

"You didn't eat dinner last night either," Brigid protested. Dylan shrugged. Brigid had given up arguing about driving her to school, so she just watched in silence as Dylan shouldered her backpack and slumped out the door.

In the early-morning quiet at the Tenth Muse, Brigid went to the back room and looked at the stained floor. The morning after Dylan painted it, she'd scrubbed until the floorboards' finish was ruined, but the ghost of the rune lingered.

Chairs and boxes were still piled against the wall, where Dylan had moved them to clear the floor for her painting. Brigid began returning them to their original spots, arranging them to partially cover the remaining stain. As she shifted a stack of boxes, something that had been balanced atop one of them fell to the floor.

It was a book called *Spiritual Defense*. Brigid vaguely remembered ordering it from her supplier's catalogue, but it must have been three years ago or more. The edges of the pages were dust-grimed and shelf-worn, but inside, the book was nearly pristine. Its spine was cracked in one place, falling open to a page with a large black-and-white illustration. A man in a long ceremonial robe stood with his arms spread, palms out. His forearms were cut open and bleeding, two slashes that crossed rather than traced the radial arteries. The blood from both arms spilled down in broad streams that joined beneath him to form the symbol Dylan had drawn on the floor.

Sigil 5, said the caption below the picture. *For protection, or to banish unwanted spirits.*

Brigid flipped through the book. The text seemed to be a strange mix of esoteric Christianity and the kind of neo-pagan mysticism Brigid's customers favored. Apparently, all bad luck was caused by malevolent spirits—the author never used the word *demons*—who gravitated toward negativity. The reader could ward off their attacks through a combination of occult practices, prayer, and positive thinking.

Brigid rolled her eyes at the terrible writing and the non-sensical mash-up of belief systems. Some of it sounded like a watered-down version of Father Angus, while some of it was just repackaged self-help. No wonder *Spiritual Defense* looked like it had been sitting on the shelf for years.

But why would Dylan seek help from such a source? Brigid couldn't help remembering the terror on her face that night in the back room, the way she'd shaken and convulsed. What had frightened her daughter so badly?

She went back to the counter and searched for children's therapists again—an action that was beginning to feel like a compulsive gesture, like nail-biting. The options were all the same: no new clients, long wait list, didn't take her insurance. What were you supposed to do if your child was truly in crisis? Brigid wondered.

Nadine arrived just before noon, and Brigid left for Dylan's mediation. It was a beautiful October day, bright blue sky and pine-scented breeze, the green mountainside sloping above the town punctuated with bursts of golden aspen leaves. Brigid tried to walk slowly, to drink in the peace, but she still arrived at the middle school before she was ready.

Melinda Shriver was waiting in the conference room, wearing a pristine white blazer and looking irritated. Brigid had known the woman for years but never felt totally comfortable around her, always slightly anxious that Melinda secretly disliked her. Now, as she saw Melinda's scowl deepen the moment she laid eyes on Brigid, she was relieved that she didn't have to wonder anymore. Melinda definitely disliked her.

As Brigid sat down across the round table from Melinda, Dylan was escorted into the room by a young, round-faced woman who must have been the guidance counselor. Dylan glanced at Brigid but didn't return her greeting, and slipped into a chair halfway between Brigid and Melinda, facing the door. The guidance counselor sat beside her.

Brigid saw how Dylan's shoulders, already drawn up tight, rose further when Kai Shriver sauntered into the room. He dropped his backpack into one chair and sat in another, leaning back with his arms folded across his chest. It was clear which of them was afraid of the other, Brigid thought. She looked to the counselor to see whether she noticed the disparity in body language, but the woman was looking down, writing on a notepad.

Principal Halyard was the last to arrive. He broke the tense silence in the room with a "Hey there, folks" that made Brigid clench her teeth. "Great to see you all today." He looked expectantly at Brigid, then at Melinda, but neither of them could bring themselves to agree that it was great to see him. At least they had that in common, Brigid thought.

"Well, let's chat, shall we?" he finally said. "I know these kids have been friends for a long time, and it would be a shame to lose that special connection. Today we're here to create a space where we can all share our feelings and hopefully come to a better understanding of how we can move forward together."

Dylan twisted a lock of hair around her finger. Kai chewed on the inside of his cheek. No one was in a hurry to share their feelings.

Brigid took a deep breath. "I think we need to talk about what happened before the fight last Tuesday," she said. "I don't know what's going on, but it's clear that Dylan was already feeling uncomfortable around Kai, and—"

Melinda cut her off. "I will not allow you to victim-blame my son when your child is the one who assaulted him."

"No one's blaming anyone," Principal Halyard said. "I think it's good to get everything out in the open. Dylan, Kai, would either of you like to share? Did you have conflict prior to last Tuesday?"

Brigid reached across the table, past the counselor, to touch Dylan's hand, but Dylan pulled it away. "It's okay, sweetheart," Brigid said as quietly as she could. "You're safe. You can tell us." Dylan scowled down at the table, refusing to meet anyone's eyes.

"She just stopped hanging out with me," Kai said to the principal. "We used to be friends. All I did on Tuesday was ask if she'd come eat lunch with Jordan and me."

"Imagine a world where you could take no for an answer," Dylan said, barely loud enough for Brigid to make out the words, but still dripping with venom.

"So that's it?" Kai said. He sounded indignant, but the look on his face was more like amusement. "You're never going to talk to me again? Just because I didn't want to be your boyfriend?"

Dylan's head snapped up. Her face was horribly pale. "Shut up," she said.

"Just because we made out one time? Look, I'm *sorry*," Kai said, and now the amusement was unmistakable. "I didn't mean to lead you on. I just think—"

Dylan launched herself across the table at Kai. He yelped and shoved himself back, tilting his chair on two legs and almost falling. The rest of the adults leapt to their feet, but Brigid sat staring, unable to move. Kai's hands flew up in front of his face to fend Dylan off. Both children were shouting, wordless and full of rage and fear.

Finally, Principal Halyard got his arms around Dylan's waist and dragged her away from Kai. For a moment, Brigid's heart leapt in horror, thinking Kai must have hit Dylan in the mouth, because her lower face was smeared with blood. Then she realized Kai was still shouting—screaming, now—with his right hand clasped to his chest. The blood was his. Dylan had bitten deep into the meat of his palm.

"Jesus Christ!" Melinda yelled. "What the hell is wrong with you? Why would you do that?"

It was obviously a rhetorical question; Melinda didn't wait for Dylan to respond before she shouted at Principal Halyard to get the nurse, call an ambulance, *do something, goddammit*. Only Brigid was silent and still, and so only Brigid heard Dylan's reply, barely louder than a whisper:

"I was hungry."

Chapter 8

The school nurse washed and bandaged Kai's hand and said she didn't think it needed stitches. Principal Halyard managed to convince Melinda Shriver not to file a police report. Brigid should have helped, but she couldn't think of anything useful to say. Her tongue—her whole body—felt heavy, full of sand.

"We'll have a disciplinary meeting regarding Dylan next week," the principal said to her. "Right now, I think the best thing would be to take her home. And of course you understand she's not allowed on campus until further notice."

Brigid just nodded. Dylan shot her a look of anger and betrayal, but what else was she supposed to do? How could she defend her daughter when they'd all watched her attack Kai with no apparent provocation? When his blood was still drying on her lips and chin?

They walked home in tense silence. Dylan fell behind Brigid, and every time Brigid tried to match her pace, Dylan only slowed more.

"Will you please wash your face?" Brigid said once they were inside the apartment. Dylan disappeared into the bathroom without a word.

Brigid sat at the kitchen table and opened her email, found the message from Dylan's potential future therapist. *I'll make sure to let you know if an appointment opens up sooner . . .* The phone screen blurred, then disappeared as Brigid squeezed her eyes shut against tears.

She heard the bathroom door opening and forced herself not to look up, not to make Dylan feel scrutinized. There was no sound of footsteps; Dylan was standing in the bathroom doorway, not retreating to her room, but not joining Brigid in the kitchen either.

After a few seconds that felt interminable, Brigid stood up. She knew that pressing Dylan for an explanation would only lead to a fight, but she couldn't sit still any longer. Though it was still early afternoon, hours from dinnertime, she went to the refrigerator and pulled out eggs, bagels, a block of cheddar. Breakfast for dinner, Dylan's childhood favorite.

Without a word, Dylan joined her at the counter, got out a bowl, and began cracking eggs into it. Brigid closed her eyes and breathed deeply, enjoying the shared silence.

As Brigid grated the cheese, Dylan spoke. "We kissed," she said, staring down at the egg yolks she was methodically breaking with a fork.

"Oh," said Brigid, carefully neutral. "You and Kai?"

"Yeah."

Brigid said nothing else as she put a pan on the stove and dropped in a pat of butter to melt. After a minute, Dylan added,

"We weren't dating or anything. It wasn't like that."

"Okay," Brigid said. "What was it like?"

Dylan poured the eggs into the pan. "We just wanted to . . . you know, try it. We're friends, or we were friends, and it seemed like it would be simpler. And safe. Instead of, like, trying to find a boyfriend, or a girlfriend for Kai."

After a long moment of Dylan staring motionless at the pan, Brigid nudged her gently out of the way, so she could stir the eggs before they scorched. "Then what happened?"

"He started telling people."

"Telling people?"

"About what we did. About me." Dylan's voice had dropped to a near whisper. "He made it sound different than it was. He made me sound . . ." She trailed off. Brigid imagined all the ways that sentence could end. "Different," Dylan concluded.

Brigid transferred the spatula to her left hand so she could wrap her right arm around Dylan's shoulders, the two of them still not looking at each other. Dylan, who had been tensely upright, slumped against her with palpable relief. "That asshole," Brigid said. Dylan sniffled a laugh.

"I thought we were really friends," she said. "I didn't think he saw me that way. Like, you know, a *girl*." She sneered the last word. "Then his friends started talking about me too. Some of them would come up to me and say stuff, you know, ask me if I would make out with them. And other things."

"So that was why you stopped hanging out," Brigid said, seething as she sprinkled cheese over the eggs. She was going to have words with Principal Halyard, the sanctimonious fuck. He'd punished Dylan for defending herself while never noticing that Kai and his friends were tormenting her. "And then what happened on Tuesday?"

"Mrs. Meehan said I could eat lunch in her classroom," Dylan said, her voice shaky. "Kai and Jordan, they followed me in. They were saying . . . gross things. I told them to leave me alone, but they wouldn't. So . . ."

"I understand," said Brigid. "And I see why you lashed out today." Kai and his friends had spent so much time worrying her, like foxes with a rabbit. Brigid could hardly blame Dylan for wanting to get a bite in.

Something shuttered in Dylan's eyes. "I didn't mean to do that," she said quietly. "It felt like . . . I was watching from the backseat, or something. Like I wasn't the one in charge."

Brigid chewed her bottom lip as she piled eggs and cheese onto the bagels. Dissociation, she thought. She really needed to get her daughter to a therapist. Setting the plates on the table, she said, "Sweetheart, I'm so sorry you went through all that. What Kai and Jordan did to you is sexual harassment, and I'm going to talk to your school about it. There's absolutely no reason you should be punished and they shouldn't."

Dylan stared at her in horror. "Please don't, Mom," she said. "I don't want anyone to know. Don't tell them."

"You don't need to be embarrassed," Brigid insisted. "You didn't do anything wrong. They're the ones who should be ashamed of themselves. If I just . . ."

"I said no!" Dylan shoved Brigid with both hands.

It felt like being hit by a truck. Incredible pressure exploded from two hot points of impact, one on her chest and one on her shoulder. Brigid flew more than fell backward and slammed into the refrigerator. The handle bit into her side, just above her right hip. She landed on the floor in a heap, stunned, her vision kaleidoscopic.

Brigid heard a horrible wheezing. After a moment, she realized it was the sound of air croaking from her aching lungs. She struggled to get back to her feet. Finally, her diaphragm relaxed and she inhaled with a desperate whoop.

Dylan stood at the table, head cocked to one side as she watched Brigid with interest, but no concern or regret. Brigid felt a rush of revulsion alongside the pain and shock. How could her daughter have *thrown* her like that?

I didn't mean to, Dylan had said just a moment ago, but this hadn't been an accident or a moment of panic. Dylan had hurt Brigid on purpose.

Brigid backed toward the doorway and down the hall, leaving the bagels on the kitchen table. Dylan watched her go without a word.

Chapter 9

Father Angus Byrne's house wasn't dark all the time. It couldn't have been. Surely there had been spring days with the windows thrown open, or winter evenings lit by twinkling Christmas lights. Surely someone hummed a song as they folded laundry, or sitcom laughter crackled from another room.

But that wasn't what Brigid remembered. She remembered shadows and silence.

When Brigid's father threw them out, Father Angus took them in, but he always made it clear that it was out of duty more than love. For her part of the bargain, Adelaide handled the mundane tasks of keeping the house while her brother attended to his study of God's word.

Angus lived ascetically, so Adelaide and Brigid did too: plain food, simple clothes, little entertainment outside of the Bible. A part-time bookkeeping job at a florist shop, combined with a pittance of child support from Brigid's erstwhile father, provided for their groceries and utilities. Brigid didn't wonder until years later how Angus had kept the lights on before Adelaide moved in.

It was also some years before Brigid discovered that priests were traditionally associated with churches. Father Angus's job, as far as she could tell, was to read the Bible in his study, and sometimes aloud to his sister and niece. He delivered sermons, but mostly over the dinner table, full of hellfire and the devil, the wickedness of the modern world and their duty to fight against it.

Sometimes, too, he left the house for hours or days, with little explanation. Brigid didn't usually ask where he was; she was just glad he was gone.

One evening, when Brigid was nine, a man and a woman came to the house. Father Angus must have been expecting them; he opened the door before they could knock on it. They looked like they were around her mother's age, the woman nervous and stringy, the man all bluster, sticking out his elbows like he was trying to take up extra space.

As Angus welcomed them inside, he caught sight of Brigid watching. "Go help your mother with dinner," he said, and Brigid hurried down the hall. When she reached the kitchen doorway, though, she turned and looked back. Angus and the guests had disappeared into the big, seldom-used living room. If she lurked in the doorway, they'd see her. But the living room shared a wall with Angus's study.

Eavesdropping was a sin, Brigid knew, and so was going in her uncle's study without an express invitation. It didn't make her hesitate. Neither did the enormous cross on the far wall, Christ's wooden face staring down in exquisitely carved anguish. Brigid tiptoed across the plush red rug, so much softer and nicer than anything else in the house, and pressed herself against the wall opposite the crucifix, listening with her whole body.

". . . to meet you, Mr. and Mrs. Santoro," she heard Father Angus say in his voice like faraway thunder. The vibrations of it carried through the floor and the walls, but she couldn't hear any of what the Santoros said in response. After a pause, Father Angus said, "I see. And how old is your daughter?"

More silence in which the Santoros were presumably speaking. Brigid imagined their voices like tiny insects, fluttering into walls, never making it out of the room. "Oh, yes, Father Vincent," said Angus. "A good man, I'm glad he . . ." His voice dropped, as though he was trying to match the quiet of the Santoros. Brigid scowled, pressing her ear to the wall so hard it hurt. She couldn't hear a thing.

A hand on her shoulder made her jump, but it wasn't until she looked around that Brigid wanted to scream.

There was Adelaide, her face too close, huge and pale. Sometime in the last five years, she had become painfully thin. Her cheekbones jutted like rocks from a frozen river; her skin was old tissue paper, limp and wrinkled, reused too many times to wrap presents no one wanted. Even Adelaide's hair looked like it was starving.

"Just what do you think you're up to?" Despite the obvious anger in her face, Adelaide's voice was barely a whisper. She was trying not to draw Angus's attention, and Brigid couldn't be sure whether Adelaide meant to protect her daughter or herself.

Brigid scrambled to come up with an excuse, but Adelaide held up a bony hand to silence her.

"Please don't lie to me, Brigid. It's tedious."

"Are you going to tell him?" Brigid asked, feeling sick and

helpless.

Adelaide looked at her for a moment, then sighed. "Kitchen. Now."

It wasn't an answer, and Brigid's stomach squirmed with dread as she followed her mother back to the kitchen. Adelaide handed her a head of lettuce, then returned to her lasagna in progress.

Brigid washed and ripped the lettuce under cold water Her mother stirred meat into sauce, then layered it over noodles in the casserole dish. Adelaide never once brought the spoon to her lips, never checked the sauce for taste.

After a few minutes, Adelaide said, "People who eavesdrop sometimes learn things they wish they didn't know."

Brigid wanted to ask what that meant, but she was interrupted by the sound of the front door opening, then closing again. A moment later, Father Angus entered the kitchen, looking thoughtful.

"We are called upon to help a troubled soul," he announced, using the deepest resonance of his preaching voice. Adelaide set her spoon down and turned to face him, clasping her hands in rapt attention. Brigid, now slicing tomatoes for the salad, didn't look up. "The next few days will test our faith," Angus said. "I need you both to summon all your strength and be on guard against the devil's lies. Do you understand?"

Brigid watched her knife go up and down. Tomato skins split. Watery red juice spilled and spread over the cracks in the wood. She heard Angus's footsteps heavy on the floor.

Then his hands were hot and terribly soft, cupped around her cheeks. He turned her face toward his, and she gasped when she saw the ice blue of his enormous eyes, inches from her own.

"Listen to me, damn it," he said. His breath was warm on her face. Father Angus never swore, never said *damn* or *hell* unless he meant it literally. "What I have to do will harrow all our souls. I need you to be the strongest you've ever been, or you'll regret it for eternity. Do you understand, Brigid?"

She could hardly move, he was gripping her face so tightly, but she managed to twitch a nod. With a great sigh of relief, Angus let her go. Brigid looked back down at the cutting board, at the tomato juice oozing onto the counter, and fought the burn of oncoming tears. Adelaide was still standing perfectly still, hands folded before her like a schoolgirl reciting her lesson. Without another word, Angus left the kitchen.

He didn't come back for dinner. Adelaide waited and waited, but wouldn't dare go and summon him, nor would she begin eating without him. Brigid sat and fidgeted, too queasy and confused for hunger.

Finally, she got up the nerve to ask her mother, "What's he talking about? What's going to happen?"

It was rare for Adelaide Byrne to laugh, but she laughed then, sounding dry and more pained than amused. "How am I supposed to know?" she asked. "Go ahead and eat your dinner."

Under her mother's stern eyes, Brigid forced down a few bites of lasagna. She picked some lettuce leaves out of her salad and crunched them without dressing, avoiding the tomatoes. The thought of their cool slimy flesh on her tongue made her want to gag.

The next morning was gray and bitter cold. Angus, who usually slept in, was in the kitchen with Adelaide when Brigid got up for school, dressed in the priest's robe he seldom wore. A full pot of coffee was brewing, instead of the half pot Adelaide usually made for herself and her brother. Brigid resolutely did not ask what was going on; if they didn't want to tell her, she didn't want to know.

"Sit down, sweetheart," said her mother. "I'll make you some toast."

Adelaide never made Brigid breakfast. "I'll just eat on my way to school," Brigid said, reaching for an orange on the counter.

"You're not going to school today," said Angus, his voice too immense for the small kitchen. "Your mother has already called to excuse you for the rest of the week."

"Why?" Brigid finally asked, shocked and indignant. She didn't love school, but it was her only escape from this dismal house. He couldn't take that away from her, she thought desperately, knowing that of course he could.

"We need you here" was all he said, and then he looked away from her, as decisive an end to the conversation as hanging up a phone.

Brigid fumed in silence while her mother made toast with too much jam and set it in front of her. She'd just put the first bite in her mouth when the doorbell rang.

"Brigid, answer the door," said her uncle.

The cold that hit her when she opened the front door was like a physical force. The air stank, too, the frigid wind blowing from the east, carrying the stench of barnyards from the plains beyond the city. Adelaide always said that smell portended snow.

The Santoros stood on the doorstep. The woman looked even more nervous than she had before, the man even angrier. In between them stood a teenage girl. She was probably five or six years older than Brigid, a head taller and beginning to soften into curves, looking around her in confusion and dismay.

"Well, go inside," said Mrs. Santoro to what must have been her daughter. She didn't greet Brigid or acknowledge her at all. Brigid stood back to let them enter.

"Welcome," said Father Angus from behind her. Brigid saw the teenage girl's eyes widen at the sight of him: tall, broad, gowned in black, filling most of the space in the narrow hallway.

"What is this?" the girl asked her parents, taking a nervous step backward. But her parents stood firm behind her, preventing her retreat.

"Serafina, isn't it?" Angus asked. He didn't wait for the girl to respond. "My name is Father Angus Byrne. Your parents have explained to me that you're struggling, so I suggested they bring you by to talk with me. Perhaps I can offer you some spiritual guidance."

"What did you tell him?" Serafina asked over her shoulder, not taking her eyes off Father Angus.

"That we're worried about you, darling," her mother said. Brigid heard spider silk in her voice, sticky and gleaming.

"Let's go in the kitchen and have a cup of coffee," Father Angus suggested. "Or tea, if you prefer that, Serafina. We can talk about what's troubling you. I think you'll find there's very little that can't be solved if you put your faith in Jesus."

Serafina shook her head, but her parents were moving forward, bearing her along like a current. They swept past Brigid and into the kitchen.

Moving slowly, feeling as though she was wading through deep water, Brigid followed. Serafina sat at the table opposite Father Angus, her body curled forward over a steaming mug of tea; Brigid couldn't tell if she was trying to get warm or just making herself as small as possible. Her parents stood on either side of her, like sentries at a gate.

From the doorway, Brigid could barely hear Serafina say, "There's nothing wrong with me."

"Your parents say you've been acting strange," Father Angus said gently. "Not like yourself."

Brigid expected the older girl to deny this allegation, but instead Serafina's mouth twisted into a strange chuckle. "Oh, is that what they told you? I'm not myself?" She looked over her shoulder at her father, then twisted around to look at her mother. "You're both such fucking liars," she said loudly.

Brigid clasped a hand over her mouth. She was terrified of being found out and punished if she even thought that word, but Serafina had said it out loud. To her parents. In front of a *priest*. Brigid was half horrified, half in awe.

"Young lady," said Mrs. Santoro, voice trembling.

"Don't talk to me like I'm your daughter," said Serafina. "I don't even know you."

"Please, let's all calm down and drink our tea," Father Angus said.

"If you're not our daughter, who are you?" Mr. Santoro said. It was the first time Brigid had heard him speak, and his voice was higher than she would have expected, out of sync with his rough, burly frame. "What are you? Where's our little girl?"

"Your little girl is fucking dead," Serafina snarled at him, and then she bent over the table and threw up.

Brigid still had her hand pressed tight over her mouth, and now she screamed into it.

Everyone else was too distracted to notice. Adelaide came running with a roll of paper towels. Mrs. Santoro leapt back from the pool of vomit spreading across the table like a vile, many-fingered hand. Mr. Santoro was roaring with anger, shaking his fist at his sweating, heaving daughter. Only Father Angus was still. Brigid watched him, transfixed.

"Saint Michael the Archangel, protect us in battle," intoned Angus.

Serafina stood, shoving her chair back in one sharp motion. Her parents each grabbed one of her arms and held on desperately as she fought and squirmed. Brigid could see the strain and fear on their faces; the sapling of a girl between them was on the brink of shaking them both off. *She's so strong*, Brigid thought with that same mix of dread and admiration. Surely no human girl was that strong.

"Let go of me!" Serafina screamed, arching against her parents' grip on her arms. She bent backward from the waist, until her dark hair brushed the floor and her upside-down face snarled at Brigid in the doorway. Brigid thought she saw green and gold sparks in the older girl's eyes. She thought she felt infernal heat rising from her skin, even across the distance between them.

"Demon, go forth from this child!" Angus bellowed. "I consign you back to hell!"

Serafina stood upright and spat in his face.

"You want to talk about hell?" She said it in a whisper, but it carried like a shout to Brigid's ears. "You can't send me to hell. I brought it with me."

Angus didn't flinch from her saliva, which Brigid could see shining on the rough gray stubble of his soft jawline. "My child," he said with a tenderness Brigid had never heard from him. He reached out one hand to stroke her face. Serafina shivered, and a tear ran down her cheek. Through the window, Brigid noticed snowflakes beginning to fall.

The girl and the priest stood there, eyes fixed on each other like blades locked in battle, for what seemed like hours but could only have been a few seconds. In the long quiet, Brigid watched as Serafina's mother drew a syringe from her purse. She thought about yelling a warning, but she couldn't make herself break the silence, too afraid of what would emerge from its shattering. Very slowly, Mrs. Santoro slid the needle into her daughter's neck.

Serafina's body jolted so hard it appeared, for a moment, that her feet rose off the floor. Then she went limp, slumping into her father's arms.

"Thank you, Giulia," said Father Angus. To Serafina, who stared hazily up at him with loathing in her heavy-lidded eyes, he said, "This would have been easier if you'd simply drunk your tea."

"You," Serafina breathed, but then her head lolled back and her eyes fluttered closed. It was as though something switched off in the room, an electronic device that had been humming at a nearly inaudible frequency. In its wake came stillness and relief.

"Don, let's get her upstairs," said Father Angus. "Adelaide, clean this up and then help Giulia get settled." He came around the table to lift Serafina's dragging body out of her father's arms, her long hair draping over his arm like wet seaweed. The Santoros surrendered their burden with relief. Giulia rubbed her hands on her skirt, as though wiping away grime.

As Angus carried Serafina out of the kitchen, Mr. Santoro trailing behind, Brigid stepped back against the wall. She pressed herself flat, trying to fade into the wallpaper. But as they passed her, Serafina rolled her head to the side—a strange, stiff movement, as though the motion were unfamiliar. Her eyelids *clicked* open like a doll's, and she stared straight at Brigid.

"They'll get you too," she said.

Chapter 10

Three days passed in a sleepless, snow-drifted blur while Serafina Santoro lay handcuffed to Father Angus's bed.

Angus slept—in short stretches and at odd hours—in Adelaide's bed. Adelaide slept in Brigid's room, the two of them squeezed back-to-back in the twin bed. Adelaide was a light sleeper, tossing and turning and muttering under her breath from bad dreams, and her feet were cold. Angus could have taken the twin and let the two of them share the queen in Adelaide's room, but Brigid didn't dare say that to her uncle. He moved from room to room like a storm cloud, black robes and dark circles under his eyes, the air around him crackling like lightning.

Giulia and Don Santoro slept on the couches downstairs. At least, they did in theory; like Angus, they slept sporadically and without regard for the clock, sprawling fully clothed across the furniture only when their bodies threatened to give out. Otherwise, they were in the master bedroom with Serafina, talking to her and praying over her as she wept or screamed or cursed.

"Let me go," she wailed, and it seemed Brigid could hear two voices layered over each other: the plaintive cry of a terrified girl and the snarl of a rabid dog. Brigid, in the kitchen making lunch as the sun went down, tried to tune out the screams. She focused on the snow falling outside the window, trying to trace an individual flake's trajectory from sky to grass.

On the first day, after carrying Serafina's unconscious body up the stairs, Father Angus had come back down to the kitchen and finally explained to Brigid what was going on. "Serafina is possessed," he said.

Brigid stared, waiting for more. She'd heard the word before—Angus talked about possession a lot—but she wasn't clear on the exact meaning.

"That girl is sharing her body with a demon," her uncle said. Snow-gray light through the windows made his face shadowy. "She has left her soul unguarded, and Satan's emissary has built itself a home inside her. It wrestles her for control of her body, and it will drag her soul to hell if it can."

A tide of horror washed through Brigid, so intense she was briefly unable to speak. To have something evil inside you, to be invaded, taken over—the idea made her feel sick. She wondered if that was why Serafina had thrown up. Pity and disgust made her throat tight.

"You stay away from the girl," Father Angus said. "I don't want the demon in her to set its sights on you next. You're not strong enough in your commitment to the Lord to withstand that kind of spiritual assault."

Brigid looked down in shame. He was right. She remembered how thrilled she was when Serafina had said that terrible thing to Father Angus. The evil in Serafina had spoken, and the evil in Brigid had delighted to hear it.

"I want to help her," she whispered.

"You can do that by praying, and by keeping the household running smoothly," Angus said. "My job is on the battlefield of the soul. Yours is here in the kitchen with your mother. We each have a part to play. Promise me you won't go in that room or speak to Serafina."

"I promise," Brigid said with all her heart.

It took about six hours to break her promise. The snow was already a foot deep outside. Angus and Adelaide were talking in the kitchen, and the Santoros were whispering in the living room, and no one saw Brigid walk through the doorway of the master bedroom where Serafina—and the demon—lay bound.

The older girl's eyes were open, the sheen of sedation gone. With her arms spread wide and cuffed to the bedposts, she was a living echo of the silver crucifix she wore around her neck. The blankets and sheets beneath her were in chaos from her struggles.

Brigid stopped in the doorway and stared. Serafina's cheeks were red with exertion, her eyes glittering with rage. She was beautiful. Half-remembered stories of female saints danced out of Brigid's reach, stories of girls captured and tortured, broken for the sake of their faith, exalted by suffering.

But this wasn't that, she reminded herself. The power that animated Serafina wasn't sanctity but sacrilege.

"Hey, kid," Serafina said. To Brigid's profound gratitude she spoke quietly, not trying to attract attention from elsewhere in the house. "You know where they keep the key?" She rattled her cuffed wrists as though Brigid might not understand what key she wanted.

Brigid shook her head, bereft of language. A demon was speaking to her. She was terrified for her life, but at the same time, she also felt more important than she ever had. If she'd known where the key was, she might have run to fetch it.

"God damn it," Serafina said to herself, and Brigid stifled a gasp at the blasphemy. "I can't get it—" She tried to push herself up to a sitting position with her feet, flailing and grunting as the sheets slipped underneath her. Brigid felt vaguely embarrassed and wondered if she should look away. With her arms spread and bound, Serafina couldn't get enough purchase to drag herself upright. She bared her teeth in a snarl of frustration.

"I'm sorry," Brigid whispered.

"If you're sorry, then get me out of here," Serafina spat. Brigid jumped back as though she might be singed by the heat of Serafina's anger.

"I'm sorry," she repeated. "I can't."

"Who the hell are you, anyway?" Serafina asked. Her voice was like glass splintering. "What are you doing here? Are you that creepy priest's kid or his child bride?"

"What?" Brigid said thinly. Suddenly the wildness in Serafina's eyes didn't seem magical. It seemed dangerous. Those glittering eyes scraped over her body, making her feel exposed and dirty.

"Does he fuck you?" Serafina demanded in a hiss. "Are these cuffs supposed to be for you? Are you just standing there waiting for me to clear out of your spot?" Brigid shook her head frantically. She didn't know what Serafina was suggesting, exactly, what that nasty word meant or why Serafina said it like she was throwing fistfuls of sand at Brigid's face, but she had a horrible feeling that if the girl—the demon—kept talking, she was going to scream, or cry.

Whatever was looking at her through Serafina's narrowed eyes, she did not want it to see her cry.

"Bet he fucks you," it sneered, and its voice did not sound at all like a teenage girl's anymore. "Bet you like it. You want me to fuck you, little girl? You'd like that, too. Want me to stick my tongue up inside you? I'll split your fucking worthless flesh in half with it. I'll cut you to pieces and lick up the blood."

Brigid felt frozen. Her feet wouldn't move to run. She wanted to scream, but if she screamed, her uncle would hear. He'd know she disobeyed him, that he was right not to trust her, that she was weak and heavy with sin. And worse than that, he'd hear what the monster in Serafina's skin was saying about Brigid. Even imagining the shame of it was more than she could stand.

"I know what you are," she said, hearing her own voice like it was coming from the bottom of a very deep hole. "You came from the devil. You're trying to get me and take me to hell."

The demon laughed, and the worst part of all was that the laugh *did* sound like a teenage girl's, high and bright as a bell. "Oh, I can tell you what hell is like, kid. They're all lining up down there to get a taste of you." Serafina lurched against her cuffs, thrusting her hips grotesquely into the air.

Flinching back from the sudden movement broke through Brigid's stunned stillness. She turned and ran, as quietly as possible, down the hall, and made it to her own room before she started crying. That sweet, musical laughter followed her all the way.

After that, Brigid stayed away from Father Angus's bedroom. When she had to go up or down the stairs, she circled as far as possible around the door and dashed past it without looking inside. It stood open all the time, and if she didn't look away she caught glimpses of Serafina within, still stretched out in a horrible echo of the sacred symbol. Sometimes Serafina called after her, but Brigid never responded.

Father Angus and the Santoros spent most of their time huddled around the girl in the master bedroom. Adelaide was in and out, bringing them food that Brigid made and taking away their dishes for Brigid to wash. Occasionally she joined in their vigil for a while. Sometimes they prayed over Serafina; other times they just talked to her, cajoling and threatening by turns, pleading with her to find the strength to cast out her intruder. When they crowded around her bed in their folding chairs, Brigid couldn't see Serafina from the hallway; when they recited rosaries over her, Brigid couldn't hear her voice.

It was deep in the night when Father Angus finally drove the demon out of Serafina. Brigid woke with a jerk to discover that she was alone in her bed. Adelaide, who had fallen asleep beside her sometime in the yawning gray hours after dinner, had slipped away. Perhaps it was the click of the door closing behind her that had broken Brigid's fragile sleep.

Brigid sat up in bed. Outside her window, snow blanketed the ground and clouds blanketed the sky, diffusing the moonlight into a strange violet glow that hinted at morning, though sunrise was hours away. Father Angus's voice rumbled from the other end of the hall.

Shivering in her flannel nightgown, Brigid pushed back the covers and slipped out of bed. The floor in the hallway was cold under her feet. Father Angus's bedroom door stood half-open as usual, and Brigid sidled up behind it, peering through the crack at the doorframe into the room. For the first time in two days, she looked in at the girl with the demon inside her.

Serafina looked ruined. Her hair was lank and greasy, sticking to her face with sweat in some places and ratted up in tangles in others. Her face looked thinner than when she arrived, her cheeks hollow and jaw sharp. It occurred to Brigid for the first time to wonder whether they'd been feeding her while she was tied up in here. Adelaide had been in and out of the kitchen to request a sandwich for Angus or a cup of tea for Giulia, but she'd never asked Brigid to make any food for Serafina.

The sheets and blankets had been removed at some point, and Serafina lay on the bare mattress, sweat stains spreading around her. Brown, sludgy blood oozed down her forearms from the cuffs that had rubbed her wrists raw. Her eyes were surrounded by bruise-like circles. Brigid had never seen a person look so utterly exhausted.

But the eyes staring out of those dark rings were still bright and alert, glittering with a fire that made Brigid tremble, even hidden behind the door. Those eyes intrigued her and terrified her, made her want to move closer and run away. Those eyes said that whatever was inside Serafina, hungry and weakened though it might be, was still fighting for its life. Fighting for the girl's soul.

The room was freezing cold, icy air whispering out into the hall. Someone—probably Adelaide—had opened the window, trying to air out the stale, hot smell of Serafina's body and not entirely succeeding. Brigid shivered, and saw Serafina shiver too.

No one else seemed bothered by the cold. The Santoros huddled by the head of the bed. In the corner armchair, Adelaide sat reciting a rosary. Her voice was monotonous and tired; Brigid wondered how long she had been praying. Father Angus paced by the foot of the bed, looking deep in thought.

Suddenly, he rounded on the shackled girl. "Demon," he shouted with the full force of his preacher's bass, "leave this child's body! Release her soul!"

"Fuck you, old man," said Serafina through cracked and bloodless lips. The words surged through Brigid on a tide of joy mixed with shame. It was wrong to say such a thing, it was terrible, and yet Brigid's heart danced when she heard it.

Father Angus pulled out his bottle of holy water and forced its contents down Serafina's throat while the girl flailed and struggled. When he took his hand away, Brigid saw steam rise from Serafina's mouth. Was it from the holy water scalding the demon, or just hot breath in the cold air?

"By the power of God," Angus recited, "cast into hell Satan and all the evil spirits."

"You can't have her," the thing inside Serafina panted. "She's mine." Brigid wondered whether anyone would do battle like this for her own soul, whether anyone, even the forces of hell, would ever want her so badly.

Through the open window, the cold night gusted, sounding like the howl of some far-off but ravenous beast. The house groaned in reply. "You shall not prevail," Father Angus said, louder than both. Below it all, Adelaide kept praying, as though she didn't even notice what was happening in the room around her.

"Why won't you just let me go?" Brigid couldn't tell whether Serafina was asking the question of Father Angus, or the demon, or possibly both. The girl's tired face twisted as though fighting back tears, but from where she stood Brigid could see that her eyes were dry.

Instead of replying, Angus bent over the bed and laid his

hands on the girl: one on her forehead, one on her belly.

Serafina screamed with all the strength her wrecked voice could muster. The sound was small and desperate, swallowed up by the wind. She fought, her whole body jerking from side to side like lightning crackling between clouds, but the cuffs and Father Angus were stronger by far. The priest pushed down, as though trying to shove her straight through the mattress, pinning her in place.

The Santoros, whom Brigid had almost forgotten were there, leapt to their feet. "Don't hurt her," cried Giulia.

Serafina's eyes rolled wildly before focusing on her mother. "Don't hurt me?" she said, an improbable edge of laughter in her voice. "Don't hurt me?" She snapped her jaws, biting the air like an animal. "You fucking bitch, I'll—"

"It's not your daughter speaking," Father Angus reminded the Santoros. "We cannot hesitate to cut out the tumor for fear of shedding blood. The healing will be worth the pain."

Serafina screamed again, but it sounded even weaker. "No," she sobbed, voice broken with crying but still no sign of tears on her face. Even the tongue in her wailing mouth looked dry as a desert streambed.

"Let go of the child," Father Angus said. His voice was almost soothing, almost kind. "This can all be over."

Serafina wailed, contorting helplessly. Brigid could almost see the infernal hands on her, claws sunk deep in her weary flesh, trying to pull her from Father Angus's grasp in a hellish game of tug-of-war.

The lights in the room flickered. In the instant they went dark, Serafina arched up off the bed, *hard*, with an echo of the same strength Brigid had seen the day the Santoros arrived. She screamed once more, and this time it sounded like pure despair.

Then Serafina's eyes closed. The lights came back on, steady yellow, pushing back the encroaching night. The girl's body went slack beneath Father Angus's hands, and Brigid's chest folded inward like a crushed soda can. *No*, she thought. Was this the end? Was the evil defeated? The thought should fill Brigid with hope, with the glory of God triumphant, but instead it made her feel hollow. Even the wind was gone, and without it the bedroom smelled like sickness and blood.

She looked away from the girl on the bed, the priest bent over her saying "Thanks be to God," and out the window, searching for the moon. But all she could see was thick gray clouds, glowing with their own sorrowful light.

Chapter 11

"Who are you texting?" Dylan asked.

It was late Monday morning and the kitchen was full of sunshine, a breeze blowing through the open window above the sink. Dylan was grousing her way through the stack of schoolwork she was supposed to complete during her suspension, and Brigid had stayed home—ostensibly to catch up on paperwork, but really to keep an eye on Dylan—while Nadine covered the store.

Reflexively, Brigid turned the phone face down on the table. Then she flushed. "A friend."

Dylan's eyebrows crept upward. "What friend?"

"Cypress." That was an obvious lie. If it had been Cypress, she would have said so to begin with. Dylan folded her arms and glared, and Brigid felt so awkward and teenaged it almost made her laugh.

In fact, she was texting Zandy. They'd been keeping up a running conversation since their lunch—which hadn't been a date,

Brigid kept reminding herself—the week before. Zandy texted funny things her students said, or pictures of dogs in her neighborhood. Brigid struggled to think of anything interesting to reply, but Zandy didn't seem to mind; if Brigid didn't respond within a few hours, Zandy would just text her something else. They hadn't made any plans to get together again, but that was okay, Brigid thought. She wasn't trying to rush things.

"Why won't you tell me?" Dylan said now. "Are you talking about me?" Her glare deepened, distrust etched in her face. "Is that a therapist?"

"No, honey, sometimes I have conversations that aren't about you," Brigid said, trying to keep her tone light. As a matter of long, almost superstitious practice, Brigid did not discuss women she dated with Dylan. She wasn't dating Zandy, of course, but mentioning her to Dylan still seemed dangerous, as if that would undermine any possibility of a future relationship.

Dylan stood up from the table abruptly. She'd been working on her homework; now she scooped up her books and papers in one dramatic gesture. "You can't keep secrets from me forever," she hissed, and stomped off to her room.

"Okay, then," Brigid said aloud to the empty kitchen. She was annoyed, but at the same time, it was almost a relief to have such a prosaic argument with her daughter.

The breeze turned cold as a cloud crossed the sun. Brigid stood up to close the window. She leaned over to breathe in the smell of pines, then jolted backward.

Outside on the windowsill was a smear of gray feathers, sticky with gore and punctuated by a scatter of broken bones. Brigid gagged as the smell hit her—metal tinged with rot. At one end was a cluster of deep black feathers, and Brigid's stomach lurched as she realized there was an eye staring out of it, like a shiny black bead.

She thought of the little bird she'd tried to pet the other day, and her eyes stung with sudden tears. What had done this? she wondered. Could a coyote or a feral cat get up to the second floor? Maybe it had been a larger bird, a hawk or an eagle.

Swallowing hard, Brigid used a thick sheaf of paper towels to wipe the bird's remains from her sill. Then, although the sun had emerged again and the air outside was warm, she closed the window and locked it. Her reflection looked back at her from the glass, eyes lost in deep shadow.

After three days at home with Dylan, Brigid reluctantly returned to work. Leaving Dylan home alone worried her, and she called several times a day to check in, but she couldn't foist responsibility for the store onto Nadine and Cypress forever. As autumn unfurled over the Front Range and hikers, hunters, and sightseers poured into the mountains, the Tenth Muse was busier every day. October was Brigid's Christmas season. Some of the demand was festive—witchy jewelry for costumes, Ouija boards for parties—but many of Brigid's customers were searching for deeper mysteries.

Nadine complained about the Halloween crowds every year, and Brigid commiserated with her, but the truth was she enjoyed spooky season. She liked the hope on her customers' faces as she rang up black candles and books about astral projection. She liked moving the displays around, arranging ritual knives and dark-colored gemstones to look like props from a gothic movie. She liked the endless restocking, even, because of what it represented: all those people looking for some evidence of life after death, for some truth that would outlast their own fragile bodies. It was a little bit sad and a little bit beautiful.

This is the time of year when people believe they have souls, she texted Zandy. It was a weird thing to say, but she was pretty sure Zandy wouldn't judge her.

I believe that all the time, Zandy texted back almost immediately.

The Tenth Muse had closed half an hour ago, and Brigid was alone. She should be rushing through her tasks and getting back to the apartment as soon as possible, eager to check on Dylan, but there was something so peaceful about the dark, empty store. And she had Zandy on the other end of the phone—words on a screen, not even as tangible as a voice in the dark, but not nothing, either.

What else do you believe in? she texted.

Zandy's answer appeared a minute later. *Like in a flirty way or are you actually asking for a rundown of my personal relationship with Jesus?*

Brigid laughed. The silence of the store seemed to absorb her laughter, swallow it up. *Like what about Halloween, do you like it or think it's evil? Do you believe in the devil?*

Almost as soon as she hit send, the phone rang. There was no picture of Zandy saved in Brigid's phone, but her name was evocative enough. Brigid thought of her hands—strong and wide, short nails, no rings—and felt shivery. She took a breath and let it out slowly before she picked up.

"That's some deep shit to ask over text," Zandy said.

Brigid laughed. "Sorry. It's just been on my mind lately."

"I like Halloween," Zandy said. "I don't think Catholics in general have an issue with Halloween. Saint Ag's has a carnival with a costume parade every year."

Brigid rearranged a stack of SALE stickers, just to be doing something with her hands. "What about the other thing?"

Zandy was quiet for a moment, and Brigid wondered where she was, what she was doing with her own hands. "The devil?"

"Yeah. All that stuff. Demons. Evil."

"In the literal red-guy-with-horns sense, no," Zandy said. "It seems silly to me. But I guess I have to admit that there's evil in the world, and I don't know where it came from."

"The Catholic Church says demons are real," Brigid pointed out.

Zandy gave a little sigh. It sounded both exasperated and fond, and it made Brigid feel strangely warm. "I already told you, I don't agree with everything—"

"I saw my uncle exorcise a girl," Brigid said. The words hung in the air, surprising her, as though they hadn't just come from her mouth.

Zandy was quiet for a string of seconds. "That's wild," she said finally. "Do you want to tell me more about that?"

"I was nine," Brigid said. "I think she was fifteen or so. Her parents brought her to our house. She scared me, but I was drawn to her, too. At the time I thought it was the power of the devil. Like, I thought I was really evil back then, that there was something wrong with me deep down. Wrong with my soul. And so this girl . . . this attraction to her that I felt . . . Her name was Serafina Santoro." She was telling this out of order, she knew, but she couldn't take the time to arrange it into a coherent shape.

"Okay," said Zandy. "Sounds Italian. She was from the neighborhood?"

"I think so. I remember when she came over, she was wearing a Catholic school uniform." That detail bloomed in Brigid's mind like ink on paper: the cardigan and plaid skirt Serafina had worn on their doorstep. She must have thought she was on her way to school when her parents took an unexpected detour to Father Angus's house. Hadn't it been a school day? Brigid was pretty sure she'd been in her own uniform when the Santoros arrived. She thought of them both with a kind of horrified wistfulness, two girls who'd gotten up that morning with no idea what the day would bring.

"And you liked her?" Zandy prompted gently.

"I was fascinated by her. She was so angry, and she cursed at my uncle and spat at him. I didn't have the courage to do that back then. I never did, actually. I got out of his house, but I never told him to his face to go fuck himself. Serafina did. So I thought that was amazing, and then I felt guilty for thinking that."

"What happened to her?"

"He tied her up," Brigid said, and heard Zandy draw in breath, slow and deep. "She was in our house for three days. And he prayed over her, until . . . until the demon left."

"So you believe in demons, then?" Zandy asked.

"No," Brigid said. Zandy didn't respond, as though she knew to wait for the real answer behind the reflexive one, so Brigid tried to find it. "I don't exactly know what I believe about that," she admitted. "When it was happening, I believed there was a demon and that my uncle cast it out. That was all real to me. So I remember it as something that really happened, even though . . . it didn't. It can't have." She could picture Serafina's eyes, that green-gold shine in the ceaseless dark of Brigid's childhood home. No human eyes glowed like that. But was that light real, or just a trick of her memory?

"Right," Zandy said slowly.

"You don't believe it," Brigid said. It stung, Zandy doubt-ing her, even though that didn't make sense—she'd just said she knew it wasn't real. But didn't she want Zandy to believe it *for* her, just a little bit? To argue against her skepticism, to convince Brigid to trust her senses, her memory, over her rational mind?

"I'm open to the possibility, but not convinced," Zandy said. "And I'm having trouble getting past the part where your uncle tied a girl up. That's . . ." She seemed to be choosing her words carefully, and that hurt too, the idea that Zandy couldn't speak her mind plainly, that her unvarnished thoughts might not be safe with Brigid. "That scares me. It makes me worry for that girl, because it doesn't sound like the adults in her life were using good judgment. And I think it makes me worry for you, retroactively, for the same reason. I still don't know very much about what happened to you when we were kids."

Flooded with an energy she couldn't name and didn't know what to do with, Brigid shoved her chair back and stood up. Her phone still lay on the counter, and she paced back and forth as though invisibly tethered to it. "Her parents were terrified, Zandy. I remember. They had no idea what to do with her." She could barely picture the Santoros' faces, but she remembered Serafina's, all eyes and bared teeth. She could still hear her voice, aching with rage and disgust, the awful accusations she'd spat at Brigid. If Brigid told herself now that a troubled teenage girl had said all those things, would she be able to make herself be-lieve it? "She was so . . . I don't know. She wasn't normal."

"Lots of people aren't normal," Zandy said, her disembod-ied voice rising from the phone speaker, thin and distorted, like a twist of smoke from a candle going out. "I wasn't a normal kid. Neither were you. We still deserved to be treated well." She spoke without heat, carefully calm. Brigid hated it.

"This was different," she said. "This wasn't like . . . what my uncle did to me."

"Why are you defending them?" Zandy said, and now there was heat in her voice, just a little. For some reason that brought Brigid a flush of satisfaction. She imagined Zandy on her feet, pacing, just as Brigid was now, her round Irish cheeks going deep pink. "Their teenage daughter acts out and they get a priest to . . . what, abduct her? This sounds like the Catholic version of those creepy camps that steal kids from their houses in the middle of the night."

Brigid stopped pacing and slammed her hands on the counter, to either side of her phone. "You don't understand," she said loudly, too loudly. "You don't know what it's like to be scared for your child."

There was a long quiet after that, so long she almost checked whether Zandy had ended the call, except somehow she knew better. This was an open silence, a silence with someone on the other side. Zandy was still there, with her, listening to the nothing they were both saying.

"Are you scared for your child?" Zandy asked finally.

Brigid opened her mouth, but nothing came out. There were only two possible answers to Zandy's question, but neither one of them felt like the truth.

Chapter 12

Every summer of Brigid's childhood blurred together in her memory, a long sweaty stretch of boredom and chores, killing time at the florist's shop while her mother was working and reading in the basement, next to the rattling washing machine, to escape the heat upstairs. Every summer except one: the summer she was in love with Zandy Mulligan.

After they kissed in the park, Zandy came over almost every day. "Why is she here all the time?" Adelaide wondered more than once, not always waiting until Zandy was out of earshot. "Doesn't she have anything better to do?" Brigid tried to keep her face blank and not let on that the question stung.

Despite her visible distaste for their friendship, Adelaide begrudgingly allowed Brigid to spend more and more time out of the house with Zandy, as long as she promised they wouldn't be at Zandy's house, and as long as she always came home on time.

Finally, Brigid had a chance to explore the neighborhood she'd lived in since kindergarten. Zandy took her to parks, libraries, empty elementary school playgrounds, all of them as revelatory to Brigid as stepping through a portal to Narnia. Brigid didn't get an allowance, but Zandy did, and sometimes made extra money babysitting kids on her block. She was always happy to cover Brigid for a scoop of pistachio gelato at Lorenzo's or a slushie from the gas station, something so cold and sweet it made her teeth hurt.

Once, Zandy even took her to Lakeside Amusement Park. Brigid had never felt so terrified and delighted as she did on the Cyclone: first the hot, rattling darkness of the tunnel, then the swoop in her stomach as they began to climb the towering hill. They looked down on Sheridan Boulevard, where cars hummed past, shrinking away smaller and smaller as the roller coaster's tracks stretched ever upward. When they finally crested the hill and began picking up speed, plummeting downward, Brigid screamed so loud and so long it made her ears hurt. Then she made Zandy wait in line to ride the Cyclone three more times. On their fourth and final ride, Brigid gathered all her courage and leaned over to kiss Zandy in the darkness of the tunnel. She got a mouthful of hair and the side of Zandy's ear.

On the way home, Zandy pulled Brigid into an alley and kissed her against a stranger's garage door, in the shadow of a Dumpster. They stole kisses all summer, whenever they could find a spare few minutes and a sliver of privacy: between the shelves at the library, the bathroom at Lorenzo's, the dressing room of a vintage store on 32nd Avenue. And over and over, under the spruce tree at Rocky Mountain Lake Park, the drooping branches creating a cool blue space outside of time.

Kissing Zandy felt so good, Brigid lost herself in it entirely. Later, at home, she squirmed under her mother's and uncle's questions about what she'd done all day. Guilt and shame crept in, and she hated herself and dug her fingernails into her palms and prayed rosaries in her room at night, begging God for forgiveness. She didn't let herself think about Serafina—that memory was too raw, too horrible to contemplate—but she felt the edges of the evil inside her, the place where she had let the devil in. She felt herself on a hill, like the one at the beginning of the Cyclone, but this track plunged down and down forever into an eternity of fire.

In bed, covers pulled over her head even though she was sweating and miserable, Brigid cried as quietly as she could, repenting. She promised God she would be good. She would never touch Zandy again. She would look on her with a love that was pure, the love of a sister in the eyes of God, and they would both be cleansed of their sick desires and live in chaste friendship forever.

But in the light and heat of the day, Brigid wanted Zandy's lips on hers more than she wanted a cool breeze or a drink of water. Zandy's tongue in her mouth erased every thought of God or hell. They rolled in the grass, skin sticking together from the heat, and Brigid forgot her hopes of eternity in the ecstasy of the moment.

The summer felt never-ending, like one long hot day they passed through over and over. The sun rose and Brigid kissed Zandy; the sun set and she grappled with her sins. Father Angus preached over Adelaide's spaghetti and meatballs, and Brigid sat in her chair, the backs of her thighs slick with sweat, thinking about Zandy.

She wanted so badly to be alone with Zandy, more alone than they could be in a park or a library. She wanted to be with

Zandy in a room with a door that closed, to touch her in places she hadn't yet dared. Zandy would let her; Brigid was sure of it. Zandy wanted it as much as she did. If only they could have a sleepover, like other kids did. The thought made Brigid dizzy: a whole night unfurling before them, quiet after the lights went out, sleeping bags to muffle any sound.

In the first week of August, Father Angus left for the day. Brigid didn't ask where he was going; she never did. Adelaide would be at work until early afternoon. As soon as the door shut behind her uncle, Brigid ran to the kitchen, grabbed the phone, and dialed Zandy's number. It was the only phone number she ever called; she had it memorized.

It was Zandy and not her mother who answered, which felt to Brigid like another little miracle, dominoes falling one after another into sweet inevitability. "Can you come over?" Brigid asked in a rush.

She didn't elaborate, but Zandy must have heard something in her voice, because she answered quickly and seriously, "Yes." Before Brigid could say anything else, Zandy hung up. Brigid felt unfolded by the exchange, as though she'd said far more than the words she'd actually spoken.

No one had ever bothered to tell her she wasn't allowed to have friends over when her mother and uncle weren't home. It was too obvious to require speaking aloud. If she got caught, protesting that it had never explicitly been forbidden wouldn't save her. The only option was to not get caught.

Brigid went to the living room and sat in the big armchair that faced the window, watching the street. After a few minutes, Zandy came into view. She wore jean shorts and a Tweety Bird T-shirt twisted into a knot above one hip, the spare fabric held in place with a purple scrunchie. She was walking fast, taking long steps, her face red with the heat. Her dark-blonde hair was unbrushed, glinting with sweat at the hairline. Brigid's chest felt full, as though everything beneath her sternum was swelling, too large to fit.

There was no one else home, but it still felt important to make as little noise as possible. Brigid hurried to the front door and opened it before Zandy could ring the bell. Zandy stood there, her hand half raised, eyes wide and surprised. Her nervous face split into a smile when she saw Brigid.

Brigid beckoned with her head, and Zandy followed her wordlessly into the house. She slipped her shoes off while Brigid closed the door, turning the knob carefully so the latch slipped into place without a sound. It felt as though the house itself was listening, on guard for anything that might break the silence. Brigid walked up the stairs first and Zandy followed, stepping where Brigid stepped, skipping neatly over the squeaky stair third from the top.

Then they were in Brigid's room. Brigid stood in the doorway as Zandy walked past her, then pushed the door shut with a feeling of enormous importance. With that one gesture, she felt she was cutting something off, or starting something new, or both. She stood for an extra second with her palm flat on the door, listening through it for movement in the house beyond. Then she turned to face Zandy.

Zandy was so pretty, Brigid thought. She was smiling again, or maybe it was the same smile that had appeared on her face when Brigid opened the front door. Maybe she'd carried that smile all the way through the silence of the house, just to offer it to Brigid here, now, alone in her room, dim sunlight through the closed curtains.

"Thank you for coming," Brigid said. It sounded silly and too grown-up, but Zandy didn't seem bothered.

"Thank you for inviting me," she said back, and they both giggled. Zandy took a step toward Brigid, and Brigid took a step toward Zandy, and then they were drawn toward each other, falling objects in thrall to gravity.

Brigid had gotten lots of practice kissing Zandy that summer, but this felt like more than a kiss, just as closing the door had felt like more than closing a door. Zandy put her hands on Brigid's waist, and Brigid wrapped her arms around Zandy's shoulders. She could feel Zandy's whole body in a line against hers, not pressed against her exactly, but *there*, thrilling and solid. Suddenly Brigid couldn't stop thinking about Zandy's body, about how it was like hers, how it was different. It had been a tantalizing abstraction before, but today something had changed. She could touch Zandy's body. And she *wanted* to.

But it was Zandy who moved first, who slid her hand up from Brigid's waist, under her shirt, to her rib cage. "Is this okay?" Zandy said, her mouth close to Brigid's mouth, and Brigid heard the words like she was inside them. She was afraid to speak, or maybe it wasn't fear, but she was trembling and the words wouldn't come, so she reached down and grabbed Zandy's wrist and pulled her hand up higher, hoping that would do for an answer.

It worked well enough. Zandy kept touching her, kept kissing her. Brigid felt suffused with a strange heat. She pushed her own hand up Zandy's shirt. Zandy gasped, and their teeth clacked together, but it didn't seem to matter. Brigid's fingers found the bottom edge of Zandy's bra, soft elastic, sweat-damp and slightly cooler than her skin. Where both of their shirts were shoved up, the bare skin of their stomachs touched. Brigid thought deliriously about lying down, about how they could move against each other then. She wanted to nudge Zandy toward the bed but didn't want to stop kissing her to say the words.

Brigid realized she was still running her fingers back and forth across the elastic at the bottom of Zandy's bra, as though it was a border she was afraid to cross. As though Zandy might stop her. But Zandy wasn't stopping her; Zandy had Brigid's whole breast in her warm palm, and that didn't feel like anything, exactly, not so different from Zandy touching her stomach or her shoulder, but it was such a private and forbidden kind of touch that just thinking about it made little tingles of electricity shoot up Brigid's thighs.

She moved her hand up, over the smooth fabric where Zandy was so soft—much softer and fuller than Brigid, not at all like touching her own body. She thought about pulling the bra down, or up, or out of the way somehow, but that seemed too complicated. Instead she ran her fingertips over the thin fabric, tracing circles around Zandy's breast. She didn't quite have the courage to touch Zandy's nipple directly, but she could feel the edges of it, where it tightened and drew the surrounding skin toward itself, and she let her fingers graze over it as if by accident.

Zandy gasped again, her half-closed eyes popping open wide. Brigid froze, her hand still under Zandy's shirt, afraid she'd done something wrong. Zandy stared back at her.

"Oh, wow," Zandy said. "I *really* like that."

Relieved giggles erupted out of Brigid like fizz from a soda bottle, and she leaned forward to kiss Zandy again.

That was how they were standing when Adelaide opened the bedroom door.

Later, Brigid thought about what she could have said, whether there was any lie she could have told that would have convinced her mother, that would have saved her. In the moment, she didn't even try. She just stood there, one arm around Zandy's waist and the other hand on her breast, staring at her mother in the doorway. All the heat and excitement in her body went sludgy and dreadful in an instant. Her sweat felt like ice on her skin.

Adelaide didn't say anything. Brigid didn't say anything. Zandy, looking back and forth between them with confusion and dismay, didn't say anything either, but she stepped back from Brigid and pulled her shirt down over her stomach. The scrunchie that had been holding it twisted up above her hip had come loose; Brigid could see it on the floor, half under her bed, but Zandy didn't ask for it and Brigid didn't point it out to her.

"I," said Zandy after a horrifically long time. "I should go."

Adelaide didn't move to let Zandy through the door, so Zandy squeezed past, pressing her back against the doorframe so no part of her body would brush against Brigid's silent, staring mother. Brigid ached to follow her, to call after her, to beg her to stay, to follow her down the sunlit street and never set foot in this house again, but of course she couldn't. She stayed where she was, listening to Zandy's footsteps on the stairs, the front door opening and quickly closing again. There wasn't even a pause for Zandy to put her shoes on; she must have grabbed them and run out the door barefoot, sneakers dangling from her hands.

The sound of the door closing broke the terrible, frozen silence between Brigid and her mother, and Brigid remembered how to move and speak again. "What are you doing here?" she asked.

Adelaide's eyes narrowed. "I am not the one who needs to explain myself," she said. "How long has this been going on? Are you up here with that—*girl*—every time I'm at work?"

"No!" Brigid gasped. "No, no, this was the only time, I promise. I *swear*, Mom. I didn't—I wouldn't—" Her voice was thin and high. She couldn't breathe.

"Oh, for heaven's sake, calm down," Adelaide snapped. "There's no need to be so dramatic. I made a mistake trusting you, that's all. You'll just have to come with me to work from now on. And obviously you won't be seeing Alexandra again."

The words hit Brigid like a fist. She swayed on her feet, trying not to keen from the pain. Tears burned down her cheeks. But it would be all right, she told herself frantically. She could make it up to her mother; she could earn her forgiveness. "And you won't tell Uncle Angus?" she asked, barely above a whisper.

"If you don't want your uncle to know about something," Adelaide said coldly, "don't do it in his house."

Without waiting for a response, she turned and walked downstairs. Brigid curled into herself, feeling the strength go out of her body as terror surged in. She barely felt it when her knees hit the floor. She just doubled over with her arms tight around herself, where Zandy's arms had been only a minute ago, and sobbed.

Chapter 13

"Do you want to come up here and have dinner with us?" Brigid finally asked. It had been a week since their lunch at Lorenzo's and she was halfway to convincing herself that Zandy wasn't real. No one could be that handsome and magnetic while also being so sweet and funny and kind. A memory combined with a heated imagination born from years of loneliness; that was the only logical explanation.

Brigid longed to see Zandy in person, to ground herself in the planes and curves of her body, the specific gravity of her, the light on her skin and the smell of her hair. She needed it like someone spinning in circles needs the immovable line of the horizon.

There were other reasons, of course, that she yearned to see and smell and touch Zandy—reasons she hoped Zandy shared. They hadn't talked about it directly. For a moment Brigid thrummed with anxiety, fearing Zandy would make an excuse, that it was too soon, or maybe too late.

"I'd like that," said Zandy.

"Really?"

"Why wouldn't I?" Brigid could hear the smile in Zandy's voice. "Are you a terrible cook, Brigid Byrne?"

Brigid laughed. "You can decide for yourself."

"You said us, right?" Zandy asked. "I get to meet Dylan?"

"Yes. You'll love each other," Brigid said. She wondered if it was too soon to introduce them. She hadn't even mentioned Zandy to Dylan, much less broached the topic of sharing dinner. But it was too late to back out now.

When Brigid got home from work, Dylan's bedroom door was shut. Brigid sighed, wondering if her daughter had showered or eaten anything all day. Being suspended from school was only sinking Dylan deeper into herself, letting her sullen silence calcify into a shell around her. Brigid couldn't imagine why Principal Halyard thought this was a useful consequence for hurting Kai.

Pushing the thought aside, she knocked on Dylan's door. There was no response, so Brigid opened the door. Dylan was lying on the bed on her stomach, looking at her phone.

"Hey," Brigid said in a cheerful voice that sounded shrill to her own ears. "Can you come out to the kitchen so we can chat?"

"What did I do this time?" Dylan said grimly.

Brigid shook her head and forced herself to smile, though self-loathing rustled through her like the autumn breeze through the branches outside. What kind of mother was she, she wondered, if her daughter flinched like that at the sight of her? "You're not in trouble," she said lightly. "I just wanted to run something by you."

Dylan looked at her suspiciously, then shrugged and got out of bed. She brushed past Brigid without meeting her eyes and flopped into a kitchen chair. Brigid followed and slid into the seat across from her.

"So," Brigid began.

"I knew it," said Dylan, aggrieved.

"It's nothing bad!" Brigid exclaimed. "I just wanted to tell you we're having company for dinner tomorrow."

Dylan leaned back in her chair, glowering in silence. "My friend Zandy is going to drive up from Denver," Brigid stumbled on. "She's going to have dinner with us—"

"You said that already," Dylan muttered.

Brigid flinched, irrationally stung by Dylan's lack of enthusiasm. Still, she tried to rally. "I'm excited for you to meet her," she said.

"Yeah, right," Dylan replied.

"What is that supposed to mean?" she said. Dylan shrugged. Brigid took a deep breath, trying to remember the breathing exercise her therapist taught her. Breathe in for a count of five, hold for a count of seven—was that backward? She did it again. "Honey, can you tell me why you said 'yeah, right'?"

"I'm not exactly the kind of kid you can brag on," Dylan said. "Like, what are you going to do, show your new girlfriend my suspension paperwork?"

"She's not my girlfriend," Brigid said. A moment too late, she realized that wasn't the part of Dylan's statement she should have objected to first. "And you're an amazing kid. You've been having a hard time this year, but you're getting through it, and that's impressive."

"Yeah, you seem really impressed," Dylan said. "That's why

you've barely spoken to me since I got suspended."

Brigid stared at her. "Are you kidding? You've been locked in your room practically twenty-four seven. I keep trying to talk to you and you shut me out. I mean literally, kid. You shut the door and lock it."

"Because I'm tired of watching you give me that sad look, like you can't figure out how you screwed up this bad but you're sure it's someone else's fault."

"What are you talking about?"

"I'm talking about me," Dylan said. "I'm talking about my whole existence being something you did on a whim, without taking a fucking second to consider how anyone else would feel about it."

"Dylan," Brigid said helplessly.

"Mom, why don't I have two parents?" It was a question Dylan had asked before, when she was much younger, but not with this desperate fury, not with her face white and eyes ringed in red. Not staring Brigid down as though a wrong answer would destroy them both.

"Every family is different," Brigid said, reaching for her earlier, rehearsed answer even though she knew it wouldn't be enough. "I wanted to have a baby, but I didn't have a partner to help, so I went to—"

"That's bullshit." Dylan didn't sound angry. Brigid could have handled anger, maybe. She didn't know what to do in the face of Dylan's immense, overwhelming sadness.

"Why are you asking this now?" Brigid had never breathed a syllable about Gwen, or the controversy surrounding Dylan's conception. There were no photos of Gwen in their house, not even on Brigid's phone. On the rare occasions when Brigid looked Gwen up on social media, she cleared her browser history afterward.

"You used to have a partner, didn't you?" said Dylan. "I was supposed to have two moms. What happened? Why did she leave?"

"That's—that wasn't . . ." How did she know this? Brigid felt sick. The smell of grilled fish. Her favorite blue dress, the one she'd never worn again.

"I bet it was your fault," Dylan sneered. "You drove her away. What did you do?"

Brigid tried not to meet her daughter's eyes, but her gaze flickered that way before she could stop herself. It was enough. Dylan's eyes went wide—in shock, Brigid thought, but also a hint of vicious satisfaction.

"It was me," Dylan said in wonder. "She left because of me? Because you wanted kids and she didn't?"

"Baby, no," Brigid said. "You can't blame yourself for that."

"Oh, my God, Mom! I'm not blaming myself! I'm blaming you," Dylan said. "Did you ever think about how I would feel? I have nobody except you, and a sperm donor I'll never meet. No siblings, no other parent. I don't even have grandparents. You made me to be your whole world, and you expect to be mine, and it's just . . . it's not fair! It's too much pressure." Tears were rolling down Dylan's face now, blurry through the tears in Brigid's own eyes. "And then the second something's wrong with me, you panic, because if I'm fucked up then your whole life is fucked up," Dylan finished brutally.

"You're not fucked up," Brigid said, trying not to sob.

"Yes, I am," Dylan roared. She stood up abruptly, knocking over her chair. "You don't want to see it, you don't want to talk about it, you just want to go off with your new girlfriend and pretend this is a normal family."

"I do want to talk about it!" Tears spilled down Brigid's face, and she heard her voice reach the high, shaky register she hated. "I want to understand what's going on! I want to help, Dylan, please."

"Well, you can't." Dylan turned and left the room, leaving her chair on the floor. Brigid pressed her palm into her mouth to muffle the sound of her sobs.

The day Zandy was coming for dinner, Brigid asked Cypress to run the store so she could get ready. "On Friday the thirteenth of October?" Cypress said incredulously. "Do you know what kind of crowd we're going to have?"

"You'll handle it fine," Brigid reassured them, and wondered whether it was bad luck to have a date on Friday the thirteenth. But she didn't believe in bad luck, she reminded herself.

She cleaned the bathroom, the living room, and the kitchen, started dinner, and cleaned the kitchen again. After a few moments' argument with herself, she tidied her bedroom, too—not that there was any reason Zandy might see it, but since she was cleaning the rest of the apartment, didn't it make sense to do the bedroom too? Skipping it would just be lazy, she told herself as she changed out her sheets for fresh ones.

Then she ventured into Dylan's bedroom. She didn't clean it often; Dylan was old enough to be responsible for her own laundry and vacuuming, and Brigid tried not to intrude on her personal space. But one of the little salad bowls was missing, and Brigid suspected Dylan of appropriating it for a late-night snack of Cap'n Crunch.

She knocked on the door and got no response. Brigid sighed.

Dylan had been napping longer and longer during her suspension, compensating for staying up more and more of the night. She would need to get back on a normal sleep schedule before returning to school, but Brigid didn't want to think about that right now. "Dylan, I'm coming in."

There was a bad smell inside the room—worse than some spoiled milk from a forgotten cereal bowl. It needled Brigid as soon as she opened the door, prickling her nose and making her mouth water, as if trying to wash the stink away. She remembered the time Dylan had forgotten her lunchbox at school over Thanksgiving break and brought it home a week later reeking of moldering celery. How long had Dylan been ignoring this smell? How was she even able to ignore it?

"What is that?" she asked, and when Dylan didn't respond, Brigid finally realized that she was alone in the bedroom.

"Dylan?" She raised her voice and said it again, but there was no answer, no movement elsewhere in the apartment. Where was Dylan? And what on earth was that smell?

She didn't see anything obviously fermenting on Dylan's desk or bookshelf. Brigid knelt to peer under the bed. As soon as she swiped the duvet up, she knew this wasn't the source of the stench—there was no nauseating intensification, only a puff of dust that made her eyes water. But before Brigid could drop the blanket and continue her search for whatever was rotting in here, she caught sight of something sparkling.

What was that?

Brigid reached out, trying not to touch the dust bunnies that crowded the floorboards. Her fingers touched something cold and faceted, something she recognized but couldn't place until she scooted back out from under the bed and drew it close to her face.

It was the rose quartz necklace from the Tenth Muse—still on its black velvet cord, with a sticker saying $19.99 in her own careful handwriting. She hadn't rung that up. She could check with Cypress and Nadine, but she already knew they hadn't either.

"Well, shit," Brigid murmured, staring at the pendant in her hand. Dylan had stolen the necklace, stolen from the store, stolen from her.

And there were more things under the bed, weren't there? Dim shapes Brigid had glanced past while reaching for the necklace, dismissed as schoolbooks or clothes that fell or were shoved under the bed instead of being put away.

Flattening herself on the floor again, Brigid did indeed find several widowed socks, some half-finished algebra homework, and a scarf Dylan had complained about misplacing last week. But she also found candles, a packet of incense, and a deck of tarot cards—things she recognized, things Dylan hadn't paid for.

The rage that burned through Brigid was colder and wilder than she remembered feeling in a long time, mixed with something else in a bitterly intoxicating brew. Shame. She had failed again—she was failing. Her own daughter didn't know right from wrong. Her daughter was a shoplifter, a thief, a liar. How little must Dylan respect her, Brigid thought furiously, to have treated her livelihood this way? Her fingers tingled, her breath came fast. It was almost a high, the heady cross-fade of anger and self-righteousness.

Brigid dug all the stolen items from under Dylan's bed and piled them on top of her pillow, where they couldn't be missed. She had forgotten about the bad smell, about Dylan's mysterious absence, about Zandy's visit. She just wanted Dylan to see the evidence, to face what she'd done. For a moment, Brigid imagined destroying all Dylan's contraband. It would feel so good, shredding the tarot cards and spreading their glossy remains across Dylan's floorboards, a mosaic of violence. She could almost feel the fibers rending in her hands.

But she stopped. Forced herself to breathe. There might be more, she thought—other stashes of stolen goods scattered throughout the room. Before the reckoning, she needed to know the extent of Dylan's betrayal. Brigid stormed over to Dylan's closet and threw it open.

Now, when she'd forgotten to brace herself for it, the heavy stench of corruption hit her in the face, as if a decaying hand had closed over her nose and mouth. The air inside the closet was so fetid she could almost see it, a cloudy gray miasma. Brigid coughed and took a step back, then stopped herself. Her stomach roiled with something worse than simple nausea. She wanted to turn and run from the room, but she forced herself to face the closet again, to step toward it. She needed to know.

The floor of the closet was usually piled with Dylan's shoes, despite the rack Brigid had bought years ago to organize them. Now, however, all the shoes were neatly put away. On the cleared floorboards, someone—Dylan, obviously—had drawn a circle in white chalk, so bright it seemed to float in the closet's darkness.

Inside the circle was horror.

This was where the smell had come from. The rank stench of decay, of abattoir, of clotted blood turning black and foul. There were animal remains inside the circle. At first Brigid had the impression of a single grotesque creature, something so impossible and twisted its death might have been a mercy; but as her eyes adjusted to the darkness, though they swam with tears at the horrific smell, she began to sort fur from feathers and realized there was more than one dead thing staining Dylan's floorboards. She saw the blue-black sheen of a magpie's tail, the light brown fluff of a squirrel, and something so red she could have mistaken it for blood. But there was no fresh, red blood here, only the sludgy fluids leaking from decomposing corpses. The red was a cardinal; it had given the impression of blood spatter because its head was ripped from its neck, feathers strewn over all three small bodies.

Brigid covered her mouth and turned away, fighting down a feeling rising in her throat that might have been the urge to vomit, or scream. She caught a glimpse of white, not the bright white of the chalk circle, but slick and yellowish. Bone, her brain told her. And that wasn't the worst of it. The pitiful little animal bodies, bent and broken and decaying, sickening and tragic all at once—there were pieces of them missing. Gaping holes in what was left of their flesh. Not simply rotted, but torn away. No, she corrected herself, even though she didn't want to: bitten off. Devoured.

She knew if she looked closely at that stretch of bone, she would see teeth marks.

Chapter 14

P lastic bags layered inside of plastic bags. Vinyl dishwashing gloves, peeled off and flung in yet another plastic trash bag once their grisly job was done. A whole roll of paper towels. Two sponges. Bleach, despite the stain it left on the hardwood floor. The fumes stung Brigid's nose, but she welcomed that, wished she could soak her whole body until it burned.

After a trip to the Dumpster in the alley, the carnage in Dylan's closet was nothing but an ugly memory and a bad smell in the air, sour decay still tainting the caustic odor of bleach. Brigid climbed into the shower and ran it hot enough to hurt. Distantly, she expected herself to cry, but no tears came.

She was sitting on her bed wrapped in a towel when she heard the faint sound of the front door opening. Dylan crept through the living room. Brigid sat still, breathing slow and quiet. She heard Dylan go into the bathroom, and then the sound of the tap running, just a trickle. Dylan didn't want to be heard. Dylan was washing her hands. What did she need to wash off her hands? Brigid wondered.

Dylan's bedroom door creaked open, and then a long pause. For the first time in more than an hour, Brigid remembered the stolen goods from her shop. She'd left them piled on top of Dylan's bed, hadn't gotten around to deciding what to do about them before she was distracted by the slaughterhouse in the closet.

Unspeakably weary, Brigid made herself stand up and begin dressing. She remembered, as if it were a detail from a movie she'd seen a long time ago, that she wanted to wear her green sweater with the shawl collar tonight, because it made her tits look good. Stiffly, she pulled it on, barely feeling the soft knit against her skin.

Brigid knew Dylan was at the door of her room before she spoke, but she didn't turn around until her daughter said, "Mom?"

Turning to look at Dylan seemed to take a hundred years. Her daughter's face was pale and exhausted. Earlier, Brigid had been half sick with rage at Dylan's theft and lies. Now she just felt sad and far away. "Where were you?" she asked.

"I went for a walk." Brigid thought about birds and squirrels and the closet floor and the bathroom sink, and she didn't ask where Dylan had gone.

After a pause, Dylan added, "You were in my room," her words rising at the end like a question. Brigid thought she was trying to sound indignant but couldn't quite summon the energy for it.

"Yes." Brigid let the word hang there in the air, like the bleach fumes she could still smell. If Dylan walked away now, she decided, she wouldn't pursue it. At least not tonight. Whatever this conversation was going to be—and she suspected it would be bad—it could wait.

Dylan seemed to be considering the same thing; she swayed on her feet, as though about to pivot. Finally, though, she said, "You invaded my privacy." Again, it sounded hesitant, more like a question than an accusation.

Brigid nodded. "And you stole from me." She didn't say anything about the carrion in the closet, though Dylan must have known she'd found it. She couldn't even imagine how she'd begin.

"I wouldn't have, if you . . ." Dylan's voice cracked, on the verge of tears. "I just . . . I don't know how to make it stop."

"Make what stop?"

She thought Dylan would cry, but she didn't. Instead, she bit down hard on her lower lip. Brigid stared at the glimpse of her daughter's teeth, still so white, so sharp. Were the little corpses she'd thrown into the Dumpster marked in the shape of those lovely teeth?

Something hot and dark flared up inside Brigid: the desire to grab the girl, shake her hard, demand a response. She wanted to rattle Dylan's teeth, her pretty teeth, her tearing teeth, to make them chatter in her head.

"Tell me what you mean," Brigid said. Her voice sounded far away, half an octave lower than she usually spoke.

"I've *tried*!" The words burst out of Dylan in a shriek. "I keep trying to tell you, and you don't listen!"

"I'm listening now, dammit, so tell me what you want to stop!" Somehow, without being aware of her feet moving, Brigid had crossed the room. She stood very close to Dylan now— stood over her, really, the few inches of difference between their heights freshly apparent as Dylan shrank back, dropping her gaze instead of looking up at Brigid. Inside, Brigid's chest buzzed viciously. Her fingers itched to grab, to shove, to dig in hard like claws. Brigid saw fear in her daughter's face, and it gave her an awful sense of satisfaction. Brigid had been scared for so long. Why shouldn't Dylan feel it too?

The buzzer rang. Zandy was here. In thinking her name, Brigid heard the echo of Zandy's voice in her own mind. *I know how hard you're working to give her a better childhood than you got*, Zandy had said. Brigid felt something tearing, an overstretched membrane giving way, collapsing memory into the present. She remembered how Zandy saw her, and how good it felt to be seen that way; and she was suddenly, horribly aware of what Zandy would think *now*, seeing Brigid loom over her terrified daughter. How disappointed she would be.

Brigid took two quick steps back, almost falling over her own feet. "Dylan," she said, and now her voice was higher than it should be, raspy and painful in her throat. "Sweetheart, I'm sorry. I want to help. I just . . ." She didn't know how to end that sentence, what excuse she could possibly give. Now she saw that a tear had escaped Dylan's eye and was crawling down her cheek, leaving a glistening salt trail.

"I'm sorry," Dylan said miserably. She tucked her head lower, as though trying to fold into herself and disappear. Brigid ached to hold her, to comfort her. She had a powerful, visceral memory of Dylan as a child, knees freshly scraped, clambering into Brigid's arms. Brigid remembered the warm weight of her, the hot, slightly metallic smell of her dirty hair, her tears and snot soaking into the collar of Brigid's shirt. If only she could reach back through time, grab that moment in her fist and never let it go.

"Please, Dylan," said Brigid, and then the buzzer rang again. Zandy was outside, waiting to be let in. They couldn't deal with this now. Brigid was still standing here pantsless, in her sweater and underwear. "Sweetheart, will you go let Zandy inside? I promise we'll talk about this later."

Dylan's face hardened into porcelain. "Sure. No problem." The tear track was an errant stain, a spill; the girl's eyes were dry.

Chapter 15

B rigid, fully clothed, greeted Zandy at the door. Zandy hugged her and complimented her sweater and didn't say anything about her wet, unbrushed hair. Zandy herself looked perfect, of course, in jeans that hugged her generous thighs and a crisp button-down shirt the color of cinnamon. She'd brought a bottle of wine. Brigid was quick to open it and down her first glass.

Zandy just watched, intent but quiet, as Brigid gulped the dregs from her wineglass and poured another helping. "Long day?" she finally asked.

"I suppose so," said Brigid. In fact it felt like her day had been much too short—as if everything, the crystal under the bed, the charnel house in the closet, the fight with Dylan, had raced past in a few frantic minutes; as though she'd just woken up and was still trying to get her bearings. She couldn't explain that, though. It was easy to talk to Zandy on the other end of the phone, on the other end of miles of highway. Here, close enough to feel her body heat, to smell her cologne, Brigid couldn't think of the words.

Instead of calling for Dylan, she set the table herself. "I meant to make a salad," Brigid fretted. "I'm so sorry, today just got away from me." Her throat felt thick and hot with tears. She wanted to collapse into Zandy's arms and be hugged and soothed. But Zandy wasn't leaning toward her, offering an embrace. Zandy was at the sink, looking at the view out the window.

"This is gorgeous," she said. Brigid flashed hot with resentment, then just as quickly cold with shame.

Zandy turned around, surveying the kitchen. "What can I help with?" she asked. "You said a salad—want me to chop veggies?"

"That would be great, thank you." As Brigid washed greens and Zandy diced peppers and cucumbers, Zandy chatted aimlessly about her day and her drive, and the grinding tension between Brigid's shoulder blades began to ease.

The salad came together quickly, but Brigid was still most of the way through her second glass of wine by the time it was ready to serve. "Shall we grab your offspring from whatever cave she's lurking in?" Zandy said lightly.

Brigid caught her breath, her heart speeding up painfully in her chest. "No problem," she said stiffly. "I'll just go do that."

She felt like Zandy was looking at her strangely as she walked down the hall. Every movement felt awkward, artificial. How did she usually do this? she wondered. What was walking down a hall supposed to feel like?

For a moment, standing outside the door to Dylan's bedroom, Brigid had to swallow down bile. Her hand was shaking as she raised it to knock on the door, but Zandy probably couldn't see that from the kitchen. The knock itself was steady and clear.

"Yeah," Dylan said from inside, barely audible.

"Dinner's ready," said Brigid. Her pulse was pounding. What if Dylan refused to come out? What if she made some horrible scene in front of Zandy? What if Brigid got angry again—so angry she couldn't control herself?

But after a long, agonizing moment, Dylan said, "I'm coming." Brigid turned away from the door, heaving for breath like she'd just run up three flights of stairs.

Dylan emerged as Brigid was pouring her own third glass of wine and topping off Zandy's barely touched first. "Hi, sweetheart," Brigid said, hoping her voice didn't ring false. "Zandy, this is my daughter Dylan. Dylan, this is my old friend Zandy."

"It's great to meet you," Zandy said, holding out her hand for Dylan to shake. Dylan stared at it for a moment, but then, with a faint smile, she took it.

They settled into their places around the table, and Brigid served the chicken. Zandy asked Dylan question after question, not grilling her, just taking an apparently earnest interest. Dylan didn't exactly light up, but she wasn't as hostile as Brigid had feared; she responded to Zandy's questions with more than a begrudging syllable at a time and even expressed some curiosity about Zandy in return.

It wasn't bad. It was awkward, but there was warmth too, and Brigid could see the possibility of future meals like this. A future with Zandy in it, making goofy jokes, Dylan rolling her eyes fondly. She could see them, all three, finding space for one another in their lives. It felt possible; it felt close.

And yet—the tightness in her chest would not loosen, not completely. She was jumpy, struggling to focus on what Zandy and Dylan were saying, because she was listening for—something else. She didn't know what. She almost heard it, like a sound too low for the ear to perceive, but whose vibrations still ran through her body. Like footsteps, getting closer. Something wrong. She ate without tasting, didn't realize until Zandy pointed it out that she'd forgotten to put dressing on her salad.

Dylan was telling Zandy about her independent study on the life cycle of jewel wasps. "So the cockroach is still alive when the wasp lays eggs in it," she explained. "It's like, a living incubator, and when the larvae hatch they eat their way out."

"That's incredibly disturbing," Zandy said, but she was smiling, encouraging Dylan to continue. Brigid saw Dylan's answering flicker of a smile. It should have warmed her, seeing this connection between them. Instead, her stomach roiled, the bite of salad she'd just swallowed creeping sour up the back of her throat. "Does the cockroach feel it?" Zandy asked.

Dylan's eyes widened. "I don't know! That's a good question. The wasp venom paralyzes it, so it doesn't try to fight back, but I don't know whether the roach can still feel pain. I should look that up." More animated than Brigid had seen her in days, Dylan tapped her fingers on the table thoughtfully. "I wonder how you'd know if a bug feels pain, when it can't move . . ."

"Stop it," said Brigid, too loudly. "This is horrible."

Zandy looked at her in surprise, but then nodded. "I guess it's kind of a gross topic of conversation for dinner, huh?" She flashed a conspiratorial grin at Dylan. "Your mom is too delicate for this, but I'd love to hear more about it when we're not eating."

Dylan wasn't looking at Zandy. Her narrowed eyes were focused on Brigid. "There are a lot of things she doesn't want to hear about," she said darkly.

Zandy opened her mouth to say something else placating, but Brigid cut her off. "You're not eating, Dylan."

Dylan looked down at her plate, where she'd been using her fork to shred the chicken into smaller and smaller pieces without putting any of it in her mouth. "I'm full."

Brigid remembered the mess on the floor of the closet. The visible bone, the mangled flesh. Dylan's long walk. "What else have you had to eat?" she said.

"Do you really want to know?" Dylan sneered.

"Now, hang on," said Zandy.

Brigid shoved her chair back and stood up. Her pulse hammered in her temples. "Do you know what I had to clean off the floor of her room today? Dylan, want to tell your new best friend what you've been doing behind my back?"

"Brigid." Zandy put a hand on Brigid's forearm, and Brigid could feel the strength in her grip. "Please."

Brigid stared down at Zandy's hand, pale and foreign against the green wool of her sweater sleeve. Hot tears stung behind her eyes, and she realized she was on the verge of crying—again? Still? Had she cried already today? She genuinely couldn't remember. "Zandy, I'm so—"

"Oh, I'll tell her," Dylan said, and Brigid snapped her head up to look at her daughter. Dylan was standing too, now, staring across the table at Brigid with fire in her eyes. Her face was so intense, so furious, that Brigid flinched. Zandy's hand on her arm tightened.

"Dylan?" She hated the quaver in her voice as much as she hated herself for flinching. *Never show weakness*, she reminded herself, then wondered where that utterly alien thought had come from. That wasn't how she parented her daughter.

"I'll tell her what I ate," Dylan said, and she sounded strange—both familiar and not. There was something ill-fitting about it, as though Dylan's voice were a musical instrument being played by a beginner. She sneered at Zandy. "You seem like a girl who appreciates a good meal. You want to hear about it? Oh, Zandy, they tasted so good. So *warm*. There's nothing like fresh, hot blood on a cold day."

Brigid's arm hurt where Zandy's fingers were digging into it. Dylan shivered in a grotesque caricature of pleasure.

"I've been hungry for so long. I haven't eaten in *years*. I felt their bones crack in my teeth—have you ever tasted marrow?" Dylan seemed larger than life, imbued with a terrible ferocity that made her small body loom with a force it had no physical claim to. "Ever felt a heart beating between your molars and just—" She snapped her teeth, and Brigid and Zandy both jumped back.

"Dylan, sweetheart, we can figure this out." Brigid's voice was so, so small. "You need help, honey, we can help you."

Dylan's face fell. For a moment, the derision was gone and she was just a confused, upset girl. "How?" she said, in a voice that sounded more like her own. "I've been begging you for help and you do *nothing*. I'm so hungry all the time, do you understand? I'm so fucking *hungry!*" The last word was a scream. The plates and glasses on the table rattled as though Dylan had slammed her hands down on the table, even though she hadn't touched it. Brigid wondered when her daughter had gotten so tall.

"Okay. Okay. You're hungry. Tell me what you want and I'll get it for you."

The laugh that ripped from Dylan's mouth sounded like

thunder and fire, and nothing at all like laughter. "You'll bring me dead things like this?" She gestured to the plate of chicken in front of her, and it tilted wildly, spilling pink scraps of flesh onto the table. "Bloodless and cold and already rotting? Is that what a mother does for her child? Can't you see that I'm starving?"

Brigid's neck hurt. Finally, she realized it was from tilting her head back to look Dylan in the face. Because Dylan was, somehow, high above her. Dylan wasn't this tall—no one was this tall. For a moment Brigid thought her daughter was standing on a chair, and she opened her mouth in reflexive warning—*get down from there, you could fall*—but Dylan's chair was pushed far back from the table, and Dylan was nowhere near it.

Dylan wasn't standing on the chair. Dylan wasn't standing on *anything*. Dylan floated in the air. It couldn't possibly be true, and Brigid didn't want to see it, but it was happening in front of her eyes. Dylan's feet dangled just above the table, not touching it, but the table shook nonetheless. Brigid shook, too.

"So hungry," Dylan groaned. "For so long. She was screaming and you didn't hear her. I try to help, but you just feed me dead things and leave me in the dark to chew my own bones."

Zandy's hand wasn't on Brigid's arm anymore. Zandy was backing away from the table, her eyes enormous, her face gray.

"She?" Brigid asked. "What do you mean, she?"

"How long are you going to pretend you don't know?" Dylan said in that same strange voice. "Do you really not remember me, Brigid? Is it so easy for you to forget? To move on, like I never meant anything to you at all?"

Brigid's knees felt watery. She remembered. Of course she remembered. She'd been here before, looking at a young girl and knowing something else was looking back.

"Please come down from there," she said.

A shudder went through Dylan, and she faltered in the air, as though gravity had tried to reclaim her and almost succeeded. Suddenly, she looked afraid. "Mom," she said. "Why won't you make it stop?"

"I don't know how," Brigid pleaded. "Honey, tell me how."

The fear was gone in an instant. Dylan cackled. "Not so smart as you always thought, are you?" she said. "Take me to the old man. He knows. You can lie to yourself all you want, but *he knows*."

The old man—Brigid knew she meant Father Angus. Serafina had called him that, too. There was no way for Dylan to know about Father Angus. Somehow that, even more than the levitating, made Brigid certain.

Because it hadn't been Serafina who'd called him the old man, it had been the thing inside her. Something far older and more terrible than Father Angus; something he had cast out but not destroyed.

On another day, Brigid would have tossed this explanation aside. She would have laughed at it, pushed it from her mind, written over it with logic and reason.

But tonight, her daughter was hovering three feet above the ground. Tonight the table was shaking when no one touched it. Tonight her adult, reasoning mind was cowering against the wall alongside Zandy, and what remained at the wheel was her child mind, the place where she kept her nightmares, her superstitions, and all the beliefs she'd deny in the clear light of morning.

Tonight, Brigid believed. She believed in the one God, the Father, the Almighty, the maker of Heaven and earth, of all that is seen and unseen. She believed in the devil and the monster under the bed. Her child mind was a vast and ravenous hole, a long slide into darkness, and Brigid had spent the past two decades telling herself that hole was long behind her. Now she saw with stinging clarity that all she'd ever done was cover it up, patch it with plywood and papier-mâché. The hole—and what lurked inside it—was still there. Brigid was still standing on its cusp, toes over the edge. And Dylan had just reached out with nothing but her words and clawed the cover away.

Demons were real. Brigid believed. No—she *knew*.

The dead things in the closet. The crystals and candles under the bed. The air in the small dining room now, trembling against her skin like the promise of a storm, crackling in her throat with every breath she drew. And her daughter in the middle of it all, shadow across the table longer than it had any right to be, blaspheming against God and gravity.

She knew what he would say—the old man. Gray hairs spiking from the bad omen of his brow, his anger all she knew of faith. *Your sins, Brigid.* The rug under her knees, its weft and warp etching themselves deeper into her skin, into the soft shale of her bones. *Reflect on your sins. Name them. You cannot outrun them. You will be judged.*

Here, hovering in midair with a belly full of roadkill, was her judgment. Here was the retribution she had wrought.

"Let her go," Brigid said to the thing in her daughter's body.

Dylan laughed. The laugh was like the scream of an animal being slaughtered, a sound Brigid had never heard but which she recognized in the murky depths of her body. The laugh was like the smell of blood, burning. Brigid wished, for one moment and with all her soul, that she had never been a mother.

The laugh went on and on. Dylan's mouth opened wider and

wider. Her tongue hung out, obscenely pink and wet, twitching and tasting the air like a snake. Brigid realized there were tears rolling down Dylan's face. She wanted to reach out to her daughter, but her hands dangled by her sides, heavy and numb.

Through the laughter, she heard another sound, a moan of deep effort—the sound someone might make while rolling a boulder uphill, or dragging the cross on which they would hang until death. Vocal cords creaking like a gallows. Dylan, locked in mortal struggle, still screaming with laughter and shaking with sobs.

Her tongue. Her tongue extended from her mouth, still twitching, *stretching* as though someone had it in a pincer grasp. The slick muscle flexed, trying to escape, but going nowhere. The pitch of Dylan's moan rose higher and higher, up the scale, from a rumble to a howl. Brigid watched—stared—hypnotized or simply too afraid to move. A drop of blood appeared at the tip of Dylan's tongue. And there was a third sound now. Laughter; screaming; and tearing. A sound like ripping fabric, the rupture of a thousand tiny fibers braided into one violent fricative of destruction. A wet sound.

Blood fell onto the tablecloth like wine poured from a glass. Dylan laughed and cried as her tongue ripped in half from tip to root. Still it reached from her mouth, forked like a snake's, two gory feelers groping out of sync.

Zandy screamed. Brigid screamed. Dylan had never stopped screaming. Her head swayed on her neck as her eyes turned glassy and unfocused. The scream went high and thready as her breath finally ran out, but the blood kept flowing from her tongue.

Brigid forcibly snapped her mouth shut, cutting her own

scream off short. She could panic later. Right now, she needed to help her child.

"Zandy, we have to get her down," Brigid said without looking away from Dylan. Her daughter's face was rapidly growing pale. Blood loss, Brigid thought. Was it possible to bleed to death from a cut tongue?

Zandy moved into Brigid's peripheral vision. She looked ill, but at least she wasn't screaming anymore. When Brigid looked back up at her daughter, the two halves of Dylan's tongue hung limp from her open mouth, instead of straining in the air. Her head lolled forward, hair falling in front of her face, arms dangling. A dead man's float in midair. Brigid knew that when she touched Dylan, her skin would be clammy and cold.

She pushed a chair close to the table and stepped up onto its seat. Beside her, Zandy did the same without having to be told. Almost in unison, they reached for Dylan's hands, drifting back and forth in a current no one else could see or feel.

Just as Brigid's fingers grazed Dylan's palm, Dylan twitched all over, like a hypnic jerk. Her eyes flew open and she stared directly into Brigid's face.

Then she fell from the sky like a gutshot bird, landing on the table in a cacophony of broken china, wilting spinach leaves, and her own blood.

Chapter 16

No matter how hard she thought about it later, Brigid could never remember Father Angus coming home the day she got caught in her room with Zandy. She remembered herself on the floor, shivering and sobbing intermittently; remembered waiting for his arrival like waiting for a storm to break, knowing it would wash her away. She remembered her foot falling asleep from staying curled in one spot for so long, terrified of what was coming but too small and shattered to run. She couldn't remember the noise of Angus's key in the front door, or the echo of his footsteps in the hall. Had she pressed her ear to the floor as her mother recounted her sins? Had she crept down the stairs to overhear them better? Or stood in the same room to bear the shame out loud? Had Angus shouted and sworn about the abomination in his household, or had he gone white and quiet? Brigid didn't know, could never recall.

Whatever she once knew of that day, of the stretch of hours after her mother discovered her with Zandy, it was swallowed by what came next. All she could remember was praying.

She prayed on her knees, in Father Angus's study, where she was usually not allowed even to open the door. Before her was the wooden crucifix, Christ's face carved in horrible, loving detail, his expression somewhere between anguish and rage. When she first knelt, the cross above her was perhaps three feet tall, but it grew in the night, in the long hours of prayer, until the dying God loomed over her twice the size of a mortal man. And behind her, even larger, stood Father Angus.

He didn't strike her; he didn't even threaten her, as far as she could remember. As if in a nightmare, she didn't dare turn her head to look at his face. And she didn't dare rise from her knees.

In her hands was a rosary. It wasn't the rosary Adelaide had given her for her first communion, a pretty thing with beads of amber and glass, golden and light. This one had black stone beads, opaque and irregular, cold to the touch. Between every decade of ten beads was a metal disc embossed with a circle of thorns.

"Pray," said her uncle's voice from behind her.

Brigid held the cross pendant between her thumb and forefinger, the rest of the beads pooling in her palm. Unlike the crucifix on the wall, this one featured no Christ in torment. It was an empty cross—which only then, kneeling in her uncle's shadow, struck Brigid as a terrifying emblem to wear around one's neck; like an empty electric chair, like a guillotine with the hungry blade raised and gleaming. More carved thorns twined around the cross.

"The Apostles' Creed," her uncle prompted.

"I believe in God," Brigid said quickly, then stumbled. It wasn't a long or a difficult prayer, but her mind was blank and numb. Her tongue felt the wrong size for her mouth. She wished for her mother's voice beside hers, keeping pace. Where was her mother? Somewhere else in this big, dark house. Even if Brigid dared to rise from the floor and leave the study, she felt sure she could wander the house for hours without finding Adelaide.

Though he didn't speak or move, she felt Angus's impatience behind her, the danger growing with every moment she hesitated. "I believe in God," she said again, desperately, and then the words were there, unfolding from her tongue, dry and papery but certain. When she finished the creed, she hurried into the Lord's Prayer without waiting for Angus's instruction. Was she hoping he'd be pleased? Impressed? Maybe merciful. Maybe if he saw the intensity of her prayer, the focus of her devotion, he'd see that she'd learned her lesson and this would be the end of it.

Brigid prayed three Hail Marys and a Glory Be, counting off one of the strange black beads with each recitation. Maybe it was the darkness of the room, but they seemed a deeper black than anything she'd ever seen—absolutely flat, no sheen to them whatsoever. She didn't like the way they felt in her hands, either. They seemed to cling to her skin, the way ice sometimes did straight out of the freezer, though they weren't that cold. Irrationally, she feared they would take a layer of skin off her fingertips.

Then she was at the thorn crown marking the beginning of the first decade. Here she stopped, trying desperately to remember what was next. The Mysteries—but which Mysteries was she supposed to be reciting, and what order did they go in?

"No Mysteries tonight," said Angus, and for a moment she was relieved. Then he said, "One Act of Contrition for each decade, instead. And while you're praying it, Brigid, think of your sins."

She squeezed her eyes shut. It wouldn't be so easy, then.

"Your sins," he said, and his voice was softer but somehow more dangerous.

Brigid raked through her mind for the words to the prayer. They came slowly, as though she were dragging them up from the bottom of a well, blackened with slime. "O my God," she said, tracing the thorns with her fingertip, "I am sorry—"

"Heartily sorry," Father Angus corrected.

"Heartily sorry for offending—"

"For having offended thee," he said. "Start over."

The second time through, either she got the words right or her uncle gave up correcting her. When she made it to the end of the Act of Contrition without interruption, she continued straight into the beginning of another Lord's Prayer, but Angus's voice stopped her.

"What are your sins?"

In the secret of her mouth, where he couldn't see, Brigid bit down hard on her tongue. It felt enough like screaming that she was able to stay silent.

"Speak them aloud," he insisted. "Cleanse your soul."

Slowly, painfully, tasting blood, she said, "My sin is kissing Alexandra Mulligan."

"And why is that a sin?"

She wasn't sure what response he was looking for, feared that anything she said might kindle a rage and—she didn't know. What was she so afraid of? He hadn't laid a hand on her. And yet, and yet, his shadow, the grimacing face of Jesus, her bare knees on the red rug. She heard a low pounding sound, as if from very far away. Was it her own heartbeat?

"It's a sin," she said slowly, as if feeling her way out onto a rickety bridge that might collapse at any moment, "because . . . being gay isn't God's plan for us?"

"It's a sin to indulge unnatural desires," Father Angus said. She hadn't heard him move, but his voice suddenly felt as though it was right in her ear, hot and loud and horribly intimate. "You are opening yourself to evil. You allow Satan a fingerhold in your soul, and he will use it to work his way in, slowly but surely. He will spread you open and enter you and use you as his plaything." The words he used made her stomach twist in ways she couldn't quite understand. The words themselves felt violent, violating. For just a moment she remembered Serafina's vile accusations (*bet he fucks you, bet you like it*) but she pushed the thought away in disgust.

"When you look at a girl with lust in your heart," he said, and she couldn't tell if his breath smelled like raw meat or if she was just tasting the blood from her own bitten tongue, "when you desire her body, when you *touch her*—" Brigid clenched her jaw, suddenly convinced and terrified that he would illustrate his words by putting his hand on her shoulder, knowing she couldn't bear the feel of his skin, knowing she'd scream, she wouldn't be able to stop herself and this, whatever it was, would get worse, so much worse.

But Father Angus didn't touch her. He only said, "Each and every time you allow yourself to entertain this fantasy, this *mockery* of the true and godly love between a woman and a man, your soul slips that much closer to Satan's grasp."

"I'm sorry," she said, because he seemed to be waiting for her to say something.

"For every decade, an Act of Contrition, and then confess your sins," said Father Angus.

Brigid nodded. Keeping her head low, she passed the next bead between her fingers and began the Lord's Prayer. Angus loomed over her in silence while she prayed the ten Hail Marys and the Glory Be. At the next crown of thorns, she paused, breathed deeply, and remembered the words to the Act of Contrition. This time she recited it flawlessly. Then, more hesitant, she added, "I'm sorry for my sin of . . ." Brigid tried to remember her uncle's exact words. "Indulging my unnatural desires." She waited for him to correct her, but he said nothing.

All right, Brigid thought. One decade complete, four more to go. Her knees would be stiff and sore by the time she was done. She breathed deeply, straightened her spine, and continued. It was almost a meditation, repeating the Hail Mary over and over until the words barely sounded like words. She couldn't quite get lost in the flow—her fingers kept snagging on the unpleasant surface of those black stone beads, their odd bumps and protrusions jolting her from the monotony, like dreaming of missing a stair and falling hard awake. Still, it was a kind of peace.

Finally, she made it all the way around the circle of beads, back to the first crown-of-thorns disc. She thumbed over its spiked engraving. Her mouth was very dry. There was another prayer she was supposed to say to close the rosary, but she couldn't remember what it was. The Apostles' Creed? No, she had said that one already. Without thinking, she began to turn her head—her neck twinged from bending over her beads—to ask her uncle what came next.

"Another Act of Contrition," he said. His voice was heavy and jarring. It broke through her fragile scrim of calm. Dread returned in a gush, like blood. "And begin again."

Brigid straightened her neck with a jolt that made the twinge worse, staring straight ahead again, remembering with the sound of Angus's voice that she was afraid to look at his face. "Another rosary?"

Her heart was already sinking, but it felt even heavier when he said, "Until I tell you to stop."

She didn't ask again. She didn't turn her head again. She prayed, and she confessed her sins. Every few decades her uncle broke in, although she needed no reminding, to say, "Another Act of Contrition, and meditate on your sin, Brigid." She circled the rosary again, twice, three times, lost count, kept praying.

"What is your sin?" her uncle's voice asked from behind her, low but dangerous as faraway thunder, drawing ever nearer.

"Unnatural desires," Brigid said. Her mouth was so very dry. She wanted a drink of water but didn't dare ask for one.

"And what awaits you if you give in to such temptations, which are hateful to the Lord?" Father Angus spoke each word with savor, luxuriating in the threat, in the certainty of Brigid's damnation.

"Hell," she said, feeling it burn on her tongue.

There was another voice somewhere—not her uncle's voice, not in her ears, but a voice she could hear from deep inside. It might have been Zandy's. It tried to tell her not to listen, that she had nothing to be ashamed of, that nothing as sweet and good as the way the other girl felt in her arms could truly be wrong.

But she couldn't trust that voice. That voice had led her here; it would lead her further astray, to darker places, to deeper pain. A door inside her she usually kept locked now hung open, swaying on cracked and twisted hinges, and beyond that door was the shadow of a girl, starved and chained but still terrible, still beautiful. Brigid remembered how she had looked at Serafina: with awe, with fear, and yes, with desire. She hadn't understood it at the time, but she did now. The evil in Serafina had called out to the evil in Brigid. That was why Brigid had yearned toward her, incoherent as the longing was. Serafina, or the demon under her skin, had awakened something in Brigid; Zandy had tempted it to the surface. The price Brigid was paying now was nothing compared to what it would cost her if she let that wickedness run free.

So she prayed. Every so often she heard that pounding, as if from very far away, and she wondered if it was her heart. She didn't eat or drink or rise from her knees. She didn't know how long she knelt there; the rosary told no hours, and every completion prompted her to begin again, so time passed in a circle of beads, never moving forward.

The rug in Angus's study was soft and dark red. For the first few rosaries, Brigid was grateful for its protection from the hardwood floor. But as the night went on and on, dark and shapeless and impossibly long in the windowless room, she began to ache. Her hips ached, and her back, and her ankles, but most of all her knees. What started as a vague soreness bloomed into a deep scarlet pain, hot where her bare skin stretched between bone and floorboards. The friction grew from irritating to unbearable, and then past unbearable, and every plush fiber in the rug dug into her skin like thorns. And still, she didn't dare move.

Brigid's lips were numb from repeating the same words over and over. Her fingertips felt so tender the carved thorns on the steel discs seemed on the verge of splitting them open. She was aware of all the blood in her body, how close it was to the surface, how easy it would be to spill.

Brigid never noticed herself crying, but at some point she realized she tasted salt on her lips, and heard her voice shaking as if from sobs. Had she wept without noticing? She wondered if Father Angus had heard her. Sometime later, she heard his voice cut angrily through a fog, reminding her of the correct wording of the Hail Mary, and thought she must have briefly fallen asleep on her knees. Her body swayed as though in a high wind; the back of her neck was a knot of steel cable; she did not dare think about her knees. Still, Father Angus told her to keep praying, and so she prayed.

Then, as she finished the Act of Contrition—the words "to sin no more, and to avoid the near occasion of sin" falling from her exhausted mouth like stones—Father Angus said, "That's enough."

Barely hearing him over the sound of her own throbbing head, Brigid passed her dry tongue over her lips and began again. "Hail Mary, full of grace—"

"That's enough," said her uncle again, and if she didn't understand the words, Brigid understood the danger in them. She stopped speaking and waited, trembling. She wondered whether she was cold.

"You've done well to repent your sins," said Father Angus. "You can go now."

Go. A mercy or a curse. Brigid brought her hands to her face to wipe away the tears that had dried hours ago, then gazed in confusion at the rosary she still held, its beads pressing into her feverish cheeks.

"Here," she said, the first word in endless ages that wasn't part of a prayer or a confession.

"Keep it," said her uncle, still unseen behind her. "Pray on it when temptation beckons."

Brigid didn't know where to put it, fumbled for her pocket but couldn't seem to find it, so she wrapped the rosary twice around her wrist. The thorny cross hung down the inside of her forearm, almost parallel to the thick blue vein there. Somehow, even after she'd been praying on them for hours, pressing them in her hot, sore hands, the beads were cold on her skin.

"You can go back to your room," said Father Angus, and she could hear in his voice that it was unsafe to make him repeat himself this many times, but she couldn't seem to construct in her head the series of movements that would bring her to her feet. She placed her hands flat on the floor and tried to push. That was no good. She needed to curl her toes under, she remembered, so she could shift her weight back onto her feet. It was like trying to operate a machine for the first time, based only on written instructions. Her feet were huge and numb and stupid. She didn't know how long ago they'd fallen asleep, bloodless and foreign from bending under her body's weight for so long. Once again, she tried to push herself up to her feet.

This time, the senseless appendages wobbled and twisted, rejecting the instruction she sent. They were wet sand, giving way. They could not hold her. She crashed back to the floor on her knees—*oh*, her knees—

Brigid blacked out, except there was no blackness, only the sick orange of pain, swallowing consciousness.

When the tide receded, she found herself in Father Angus's arms. It was the only time he touched her that night, cradled in his arms like a baby, her legs dangling. She wanted to scream again at the closeness, the bitter smell of his sweat, but she didn't let the sound out. She held it inside and let it ricochet against the walls of her chest. Her eyes stayed closed, her head limp against his shoulder.

Father Angus laid her in bed, but it was her mother who came to her in the morning—the next three mornings, while she sobbed in pain and exhaustion, her knees too swollen to walk and too painful to sleep. Adelaide brought her food and carried her to the bathroom. Brigid didn't see Angus again until she could stand and walk down the stairs under her own power.

For the first day, Brigid was practically delirious, aware of nothing but her own misery. On the second morning, she saw that Adelaide's face was red and raw, as though she'd been crying.

"You told him," Brigid said. "Why did you tell him?"

Adelaide's eyes went wide, then narrow. "How was I supposed to know what he'd do?" she snapped. She slammed a bowl of cereal down on Brigid's bedside table so hard the milk sloshed, then stormed out of the room.

Chapter 17

The hospital room had two cushionless chairs and one window seat, a padded bench that was apparently supposed to double as a visitor bed, though it was much too short and narrow. Outside, the night was bitterly cold with no snow to soften its edges, and the window glass chilled the air around it. Brigid lay on the poor excuse for a bed with her knees tucked up, resting her head on a thin pillow the nurse had brought her. Shivering made her already exhausted muscles ache more, but she couldn't summon the energy to get up and walk to the hall to ask another nurse for another blanket.

Beside her, Dylan was awake. She didn't move or speak, but there was something alert about the way she lay in the hospital bed, angled so Brigid couldn't see her face. In the darkness of the room, a thicker darkness coiled around the girl's small body. There was no way Dylan could see Brigid, yet Brigid knew she was being watched.

Zandy was gone and Brigid couldn't remember her leaving, so she must have fallen asleep at some point, but she felt like she'd been awake all night. Her eyes were dry and raw. She hadn't cried on the way to the hospital, following the ambulance in her own car though the paramedics had offered to let her ride with Dylan. She hadn't cried while the doctor stitched up Dylan's tongue, then the gash on the palm of her hand from a broken wineglass. Zandy stood by Brigid's shoulder, silent and sturdy, her very presence inviting Brigid to lean against her and cry out the horrors of the day, but Brigid couldn't.

After Dylan was stitched and bandaged, pumped full of pain-killers and antibiotics and other people's blood, the doctor had asked Brigid a series of questions about her daughter's injuries. Brigid understood what she meant, why she was asking, and had to bite back laughter. *Is it safe to send her home with you?* the doctor's warm brown eyes asked, and Brigid tried to scream back *please, no, it isn't safe at all.* But she answered the questions in a gravelly monotone and did not fall on the floor by the doctor's feet, begging for help, for relief, for answers. She physically couldn't do it. She was a scarecrow in a field, the steel bar of her spine rusting, her whole body sagging and tattered from rain, but still she could not fall.

Her responses to the doctor's questions were inconsistent and nonsensical, she knew, but she didn't have it in her to come up with a rational explanation for Dylan's injuries. Zandy kept trying to jump in, to smooth over the splintering holes in Brigid's story, but Brigid shook off her interjections. The doctor looked at her suspiciously, and she was right to do so. Brigid was even glad, in a distant way, that someone was paying attention, trying to keep Dylan safe. If only that were possible.

"She fell on the table," Brigid said over and over. It didn't explain what had happened to Dylan's tongue, but what on earth could? *Nothing*, Brigid thought in despair, *nothing on earth.* Something from an entirely other place. Dylan was no help, from the doctor's perspective, simply refusing to utter a word. Brigid didn't know whether it was because of the pain in her tongue or because Dylan—or whatever looked out from Dylan's eyes—was happy to let her mother bear the blame for the injury

The doctor who stitched Dylan's tongue assured Brigid that it would heal without difficulty. "Some people actually do this on purpose," she said with a shake of her head. "Body modification, you know? And the biggest problem they have is that it's hard to get it to stay split. The tongue is extremely good at healing." Brigid had nodded, barely registering the words.

Now, though, they played over and over in her head. Body modification. On purpose. She imagined forked tongues, snakes' tongues, twin prongs of muscle flickering at the air.

Brigid had a sudden, vivid rush of sense memory: her uncle's kitchen, bright sunlight at the edges of heavy dark curtains, the smell of sweat and old carpet, and Father Angus's voice, rolling like waves over the words "the great serpent." Brigid might have been eight or eighteen in this memory; it was grounded in nothing, connected to nothing. "The great serpent has your soul within his coils, he is whispering in your ear with his forked tongue."

Brigid was too exhausted and too afraid to try to fight the truth anymore. It didn't matter what Zandy, or anyone else, thought. Brigid knew what she had seen all those years ago, when Serafina Santoro had been possessed by a demon and her own uncle had cast it out. She knew what she was seeing now.

She knew—though the knowledge sickened her—what she

had to do.

The bags were ready, waiting in the trunk of her car. Brigid had stuffed clothing into backpacks while they'd waited for the ambulance to arrive, barely registering Zandy's look of disbelief. She could wait until morning, but why bother? She was awake now, and so was Dylan. They should move before she lost her nerve.

As she unfolded herself from the bench, her knees twinged with the memory of a long-ago pain. The terrible pillow fell to the floor with a sigh.

Fighting every instinct of her body that wanted to flee in panic, Brigid took slow, careful steps toward the bed in the middle of the room. As she drew even with the head of the bed, she flinched.

Dylan lay just as she had before, except that her eyes were wide open, and so was her mouth. Despite the darkness of the room, Brigid could see her swollen, stitched tongue, hanging over her bottom teeth. A demon stared out from her daughter's face, knowing she saw it. Taunting her.

The thought came into Brigid's mind, for the first time in more than twenty years, that she should pray. She felt the words of the Hail Mary in the back of her throat, almost on her lips. But she swallowed them down hard.

When she opened her eyes, it was just Dylan looking back at her. "There's no one in the hall right now," said Dylan before Brigid had a chance to speak. Her swollen tongue slurred the words, but otherwise she sounded like herself. "We can leave, but we have to hurry. If you wait, they'll try to stop you."

How could she know that? How did she even know Brigid intended to take her out of the hospital, without the approval of her doctor? Brigid asked herself the questions, but they were just formalities. She knew how—or perhaps not how, but she knew *what* was telling her daughter things she had no logical way of knowing.

As Dylan had promised, the hall was empty. Their feet sounded impossibly loud on the floor tiles, but despite how the echoes made Brigid tense, no one came to investigate. Inside the mirror-lined elevator, Brigid avoided eye contact with both her own reflection and her daughter's.

Sunrise was still more than an hour away, and the parking lot was bitterly cold. Brigid shivered in her sweater and jeans. Dylan, still in her hospital gown, didn't seem to notice. When Brigid pulled the backpack out of the trunk and offered it to her, Dylan grabbed the first shirt and pants she found and pulled them on without comment. They drove in silence, but whenever Brigid glanced over at Dylan, she saw that her daughter was wide awake.

As they descended from the foothills into Denver, the flat edge of the horizon came into view, just beginning to turn pale with the approach of dawn. Dylan didn't ask where they were going, even when Brigid exited the interstate and turned onto a residential street, slowing down as though she needed to check the house numbers. In fact, she could pick out her destination from a block away. The house didn't shine like a beacon; it was the opposite, a silhouette of pure darkness, nearly pulsing with the absence of light. Or maybe that was just the exhaustion throbbing behind her eye sockets.

Brigid slowed the car to a shuddering crawl as they drew even with the house, still hesitating to come to a complete stop, as though she feared the car might never move again. Without turning her head, she felt the house in her peripheral vision. No lights glowed on the porch or in the windows, but the building was not empty; it was too dark for that, too malevolent. The lightless windows at the front of the house, four on the first floor and four on the second, stared back at her, flat and empty, making her think of spiders' eyes.

"You're driving past it," said Dylan. The slur in her speech was worse than it had been two hours ago; her tongue must have swollen more.

Brigid thought to ask how she knew that, how she even knew what "it" was, but the question would have been a waste of time. Instead, she stomped hard on the brake. Despite how slowly they'd been moving, Dylan jolted forward and looked annoyed. A brief hum of satisfaction buzzed through Brigid, followed immediately by guilt and shame. She was a bad mother, a bad person. This was her child, her injured, traumatized child—

But Brigid's child didn't know where Father Angus's house was. Brigid's child didn't even know her mother had an uncle. What rode in the passenger seat was a stranger, no matter how much it knew about her.

Dylan was swinging open the door before Brigid even turned the car off. As soon as the girl was outside, however, her confidence seemed to abandon her. She wrapped her arms around herself and finally shivered, turning her head to look up and down the unfamiliar street. Brigid was struck again by how small she was, all skeleton and thin, fragile skin, nothing to protect herself from the sharp October wind.

Swallowing a shudder that had nothing to do with the cold, Brigid stepped close to her daughter and wrapped an arm around her thin shoulders. Dylan didn't look at her, but Brigid felt her relax just slightly—whether from the embrace or simply the body heat, she couldn't be sure. Still, they walked up the front steps together.

Brigid watched her hand reach for the doorbell with distant fascination, waiting to see whether she'd change her mind and run back to the car, flee into what was left of the night. She didn't. She rang the bell. Apparently her body knew, even if her mind had yet to accept, that there was no backing out now.

Brigid and Dylan stood on the dark doorstep for what felt like a long time, waiting. They didn't speak. Brigid didn't ring the bell again. She didn't wonder whether the house was occupied, whether anyone had heard the doorbell ring. It was strange how, beyond a certain point, being terrified felt so much like an otherworldly sense of calm.

The door opened, as she'd always known it would, as perhaps it always had been: opening for her to return. Brigid stared into the widening darkness behind it, like a mouse into the jaws of a cat. The darkness had a shape she knew. The muscles in her legs twitched with the impulse to step back, to turn and run, to grab her daughter and carry her away from this place, but she fought the urge, locking her knees and holding her whole body so still that, for a moment, she couldn't breathe.

Angus Byrne was thinner than he had been, but just as tall; Brigid felt the familiar angle at which her head had to tilt to look at his face, deep in her body's memory. His shoulders sagged unevenly, like the roof of a dilapidated house. His red hair was mostly gone, but he had grown a beard, though even that looked undernourished and scraggly. His eyes were red-rimmed and watery, the skin around them threadbare. He was old; he was frail. Brigid's long-ingrained terror and revulsion was shot through with pity, the way his gray beard was still shot through with veins of deep copper.

Still, when his eyes locked on hers, she felt herself wilt. She was a child, kneeling in a dark room, held in place by the weight of a shadow. She opened her mouth and for a moment the only words she could think of were the Act of Contrition: *O my God, I am heartily sorry . . .*

"Adelaide?" he said. His voice was as thin and crumpled as the skin around his eyes. Behind Brigid, Dylan made a small, startled sound.

Brigid turned toward her daughter, turned her back on the monster of her childhood, though self-preservation cried out against it. "Dylan, are you okay?"

Her daughter stared at the open door, and for a moment all Brigid saw in her face was fear and confusion. Brigid's chest ached as if her rib cage wanted to split open, pull Dylan inside, and protect her. She reached for her daughter, thinking not in words but in images and sensations: *grab, carry, run.* She would take Dylan far away from anything that frightened her. That was Brigid's job.

Then Dylan's face hardened, and Brigid saw the corners of her lips curl up just slightly. A smile of recognition.

Brigid's mind replayed the sight of Dylan hovering above the table, the fleshy sound of her tongue splitting down the middle. She stared at her daughter's face. Dylan was in there still—Brigid had to believe that—but she wasn't alone. Something else looked out from her face, something darkly pleased to lay eyes on its old adversary.

Her hand came down on Dylan's shoulder, and Brigid held tight. To steady her daughter; to steady herself; to keep either or both of them from running. "It's okay," Brigid said. Her voice sounded frayed. Still gripping her daughter, she turned back to face her uncle.

Angus's initial confusion had settled into something too exhausted to be surprise. "Brigid," he said. His voice was the faraway thunder it had always been; even when quiet, it foretold the storm. "My gosh. You've really grown into your mother's face." His eyes, paler blue than they'd once been, shifted to Dylan. "And who's this young lady?"

Brigid stared at him. Had she ever in her life heard him say "my gosh"? Or "young lady"? This man—this deflated, threadbare version of Angus—talked like a kindly neighbor on some old sitcom he never would have allowed her to watch. She didn't know what exactly she'd expected when she knocked on his door, but it wasn't this.

"Hi, Uncle Angus," she said, managing to replace the honorific *Father* just before it slipped out. "This is my daughter, Dylan."

His eyes went wide and, if she wasn't mistaken, slightly soft. "Dylan," he said. "What a pleasure to meet you." Brigid took in her daughter as if she were seeing her for the first time: thin and shivering, with bruises on her face. She couldn't imagine what Angus must be thinking, what his first impression of the two of them must be. She simply didn't have the energy.

"We're having some trouble," said Brigid.

Dylan laughed. The sound was so bright and loud and out of place—and it had been so long since Brigid had heard it—that for a moment she didn't recognize it. This wasn't a bitter laugh, not the sound of something terrible commandeering her daughter's voice to mock her. This was Dylan's real laugh, even with the edge of exhaustion and hysteria pushing it up the scale toward shrillness. Despite everything, Brigid felt a warmth in her chest. That was Dylan. She was still in there. They could still find a way through this.

"Oh, my God, Mom," said Dylan through her giggles, sounding for that one sweet moment like a normal teenager, perhaps one whose mother had just painfully misused slang. "Some trouble? That's what you want to call it?"

Brigid folded her arms. The urge to laugh rose up in her throat, and she let it rise, hoped it would bubble over—but she just didn't have the energy. Laughter fizzled out, settled, like a wave that subsides without breaking. "Feel free to explain it yourself, then." Dylan just shook her head, rubbing her eyes with the heel of her hand. The last echoes of her laugh shifted into an enormous, jaw-cracking yawn, and Brigid got a sudden glimpse of Dylan's tongue. It was redder than it should be, swollen around the neat black stitches that paraded in a tidy line down its center. Along the split, darker red oozed up, like mud bubbling up between railroad ties.

Brigid flinched. Warmth vanished. Her heart was a crumbling stone.

She turned back toward Angus and knew by his face that he had seen it too. His mouth sagged open, then closed hard. His eyes, deep in shadow, grew even darker. Brigid braced herself for whatever would come next: demands for an explanation, dire warnings, perhaps an impromptu sermon on how her own sins had imperiled her daughter.

"You sound mighty tired, young lady," he said. "Why don't you and your mom come inside and get some rest, and in the morning—well, later in the morning," he amended, glancing up at the lightening sky, "you can fill me in on that trouble you're dealing with. How does that sound?"

The question was directed at Dylan, but he never took his eyes off Brigid She could see, there in his sagging, threadbare face, the shadow of the man she had feared so much, a face she recognized from her nightmares as much as from her childhood. She could see it in his eyes, daring her to question his mild-mannered generosity. She knew the kindly-old-man act was flimsy, that it would peel away at the first sign of defiance from her.

But they had nowhere else to go, and what good would it do Dylan to see the wolf beneath the sheep's skin now? All it could do was frighten the girl, make her more resistant to whatever needed to come next. Brigid still loathed her uncle, but she couldn't deny that he was their only hope.

So she looked right back at him, hoping he could see in her face that she knew what he was; that she would never forget it; that she was not fooled. And she said, "Thank you so much. That sounds great."

Father Angus stepped back from the door, holding it open for her. Reflexively, she thought of the old cliche: *Home is where, when you have to go there, they have to take you in.*

Sure, Brigid thought. *That's also a fair description of hell.*

Brigid looked over her shoulder to make sure Dylan was following her, but she couldn't make her daughter go first. She walked through the door. She walked into the darkness. She walked into the house, and her child followed her, and Father Angus closed the door with both of them inside.

PART II

Chapter 18

Brigid woke up not knowing what year it was. She was in her childhood bedroom, which meant she was a child, and her cell phone was buzzing, which meant she was an adult. Zandy Mulligan was calling her, which could have gone either way. She squinted at the caller ID and tried to reconstruct how she was here, but the loud vibration of the phone made it hard to think. "Stop," she whined out loud, hitting the ACCEPT button before she was fully awake. Then she remembered how she was supposed to answer the phone, the manners her mother and uncle had drilled into her throughout her childhood—and they might hear her, she thought in her time-slipped fugue, the walls were thin here. "Byrne residence, Brigid speaking."

"Oh, shit, I woke you up, didn't I?" said Zandy. "I'm so sorry. Are you still at the hospital or did you go home and get some rest?"

"No, I'm . . ." Brigid's empty stomach lurched as the night came flooding back. Dylan's mad words, Dylan's tongue, the long silent drive down I-70 out of the mountains, her uncle at the door. She sat up fast, and her head spun. She was back here. She had brought her *daughter* back here, to the worst place in her life.

"Brigid, you there?"

She took a deep breath and let it out with a hiss between her teeth. "Yeah, I'm here. I'm still waking up. Uh, I left the hospital late last night. Or early this morning, I guess, technically." It wasn't a lie, but she knew it was dishonest. Some half-awake instinct urged her not to tell Zandy where she was.

"How was Dylan when you left?"

Another deep breath. "She was . . . the same. Stable. They said something about doing a psych evaluation today." Still not a lie, precisely, but that wasn't doing much for the prickle of guilt she felt all over, like a rash breaking out on her skin.

"Yeah, that makes sense. Shit, I might need a psych evaluation, too, after last night."

Brigid sat up in bed, suddenly wide awake and nervous. "Zandy, what do you think happened last night?"

The pause that followed was very long; long like a tunnel Brigid might fall down forever; long like a throat that might swallow her. Finally, Zandy said, "I thought I saw some very weird shit."

"You *thought* you saw it." Brigid felt the walls of the tunnel rushing past. "What do you think now?"

"The things I thought I saw . . . aren't possible," said Zandy with difficulty. "So I have to assume I was hallucinating, or something."

"And if I saw the same thing?"

"I can't know that." Now Zandy sounded defensive. "You

didn't tell me what you saw. We weren't comparing notes while it was happening. And anyway—"

"I saw my fucking kid floating three feet off the floor, and then—"

"*And anyway*," Zandy said louder. Brigid felt it like a physical shove, like Zandy clapping a sweaty hand over her mouth, stopping the words she didn't want to hear. "It's absolutely possible for two people to have the same delusion. It's called . . . shit, I don't remember, but I saw it on some TV show."

Brigid wanted to say something scathing in response, but her mouth was dry and empty.

"Last night was really scary, Brigid," said Zandy, gentler now. "Your daughter hurt herself. I may be confused about how exactly it happened, but there's no doubt about that part. We saw her hurt herself, and maybe our minds couldn't handle that. Maybe we had to come up with some kind of story to make sense of those memories."

"How did she cut her tongue?" Brigid demanded. "What, did she just rip it in half with both hands? Did she stick a steak knife through it? Jesus, Zandy, you *saw* it! She was fucking levitating!"

"I know you thought that's what you saw. I thought I saw it, too," Zandy said. Her voice had gone too far past gentle; she was now speaking to Brigid the way a parent might speak to a toddler having a meltdown in public, cloying sweetness badly masking intense frustration. "But it's impossible."

Heat flared behind Brigid's eyes, and she realized she was about to cry. She stuck the knuckle of her left index finger in her mouth and bit down, hard. Pain narrowed her focus to that single point, feeling the serrated edges of her teeth in her skin. When she removed her finger, a crescent of purple bite marks forming on either side of the knuckle, she felt confident she could speak without breaking into sobs. "You know, for a little while I thought there was one silver lining to all this. As horrible as it is, I thought, at least now Zandy sees what's happening. At least I'm not alone." Her voice cracked on the last word.

"You're not alone," Zandy said in that same syrupy voice. "Even if I'm still not clear on what happened, we went through it together. I'm here for you, Brigid. I want you to get the help you need."

"I know what kind of help I need," Brigid muttered.

Zandy took a long time to reply again—long enough that Brigid considered hanging up. Then Zandy said, "Do you mean that story you told me about your uncle?"

"You're right," Brigid said. "What happened last night was impossible. What's happening to Dylan is impossible. If there's a way to fix it, that's going to involve something impossible, too."

"You can't seriously believe," said Zandy, and Brigid waited for the end of the sentence, but there wasn't one. Apparently Zandy couldn't bring herself to say the words, even for the purpose of negating them.

"I'm willing to believe in anything that will keep my daughter safe," said Brigid.

"You think your uncle will keep her safe? Did he keep *you* safe, Brigid?"

The carpet fibers like barbed wire, digging into her knees. The shadow at her back. The Hail Mary on her cracked, peeling lips. "He helped that girl," she said, knowing it wasn't an answer.

"Brigid." A breath. "You haven't called your uncle, have you?"

"No, I haven't called him." No point reassuring herself the words she spoke were technically true. It was a lie. She was lying to Zandy.

"Okay. Good," said Zandy. "Please don't. I know you're pissed at me, Brigid, but please just wait a little while, okay? Don't call him yet. Let me try to figure out how I can help you."

"Okay." Another lie. Brigid's face felt numb.

They listened to each other's breathing for some time. Despite her anger and disappointment and guilt, Brigid was struck by the fervent desire to touch Zandy, to hear her breathing up close, feel it stirring the fine hairs on her skin.

"I'm guessing you'll head back to the hospital this morning," Zandy said finally. Brigid didn't respond, as though refusing to confirm the lie would absolve her from telling it. "Do you want me to come up? I could bring you guys some food. I'm sure Dylan's sick of hospital food by now."

"I don't know what Dylan can eat," Brigid said. "And I think she probably won't be up for visitors today."

She knew Zandy heard the coldness in her voice, the deliberate turning away of the proffered reconciliation. Zandy sighed. "Brigid," she said, ever so slightly admonishing.

Brigid's neck prickled and her face grew hot again. She was so tired of everything she did, everything she *felt*, being wrong. A mother could never get any credit, could she? Doing everything perfectly, without complaint, was just what people expected; they'd never congratulate her, only excoriate her for all the ways she fell short. If Zandy only knew how much she was bending, she thought, how much she was sacrificing, just to keep her daughter safe—

She'd be horrified, Brigid reminded herself, and twice as convinced you're insane. The words came from somewhere so deep inside her she barely recognized it as part of herself—someplace dark and hot and rank with sulfur. You're alone, said her own mind, sounding like a stranger. You've made so many mistakes, taken so many wrong turns, and now you're alone at a dead end in a road you never should have taken. It's all your fault.

Brigid thought about screaming, about throwing her phone across the room, stomping on it until the screen shattered, bringing her foot down in broken glass over and over until her sole was in bloody ribbons.

No, that was foolish, she told herself. Zandy wasn't even in the room. She wouldn't feel the depth of Brigid's rage; she'd just hear a distorted crash and the flat silence of a dropped call. There was no point.

"Thanks for checking in on us," she said instead. Then she hung up and pressed the heels of her hands into her eyes, grinding into the sockets until she saw constellations of her own blood.

It was just after ten a.m. She'd been asleep only a few hours, and she felt it in the back of her neck, the weight of every limb. Brigid wanted to fall back into the twin bed and pull the quilt over her face. She remembered the childhood satisfaction of waking before her alarm and falling luxuriously back to sleep, because there was nowhere she needed to be.

But there were places she needed to be. It was somehow only Saturday morning, though emotional epochs had passed since Friday night. Cypress and Nadine could handle the store; Brigid only sometimes worked on weekends, and no one would miss her if she didn't show up today. Still, she had come to this house—this awful, ugly house—for a reason, and it wasn't to catch up on her sleep.

Brigid swung her legs out of bed, ignoring the phantom ache

in her knees. Nothing was wrong. She was just tired.

The door across the hall—the room that had once been Adelaide's—was closed. Good; Dylan was still asleep. Brigid felt a spasm of reflexive irritation, the desire to knock on the door and ask her daughter if she planned to sleep the whole weekend away, but she reminded herself that Dylan desperately needed the rest.

Still, she stopped by the door and listened. Did she hear Dylan's breathing, deep with slumber? Was that the faint sound of snoring? Was Dylan really asleep, or was she sitting awake in there, thinking unknowable thoughts? Images flashed through Brigid's head: Dylan with her fingers in her mouth, picking the stitches out of her tongue. Dylan floating flat on her back, as if lying on a raft, a foot above the mattress. Dylan crouching by the window, sash pushed up, waiting to dart out a hand and scoop an unsuspecting bird into her mouth.

"Calm down," Brigid said to herself out loud. She carefully turned the doorknob so it wouldn't make a noise, and again time folded over itself. She was a child, creeping into her mother's room after a nightmare, making no noise so Father Angus wouldn't wake.

Easing the door open just an inch, Brigid peered into the bedroom. The dark curtains she remembered were still there, blocking out the bright fall day. Everything within the room was murky shadow, but she could just make out the shape of a body in the bed, the slight rise and fall of breathing. More embarrassed than relieved, Brigid closed the door again.

She walked down the stairs slowly. The house was dark and quiet, all the curtains closed. It might have been empty, but she knew it wasn't.

Father Angus sat at the kitchen table with his back to her. She saw the thin skin on the top of his head, circled in wispy hairs. The shape of his skull underneath was ugly and intimate, something she wasn't supposed to see.

"I made coffee," he said without turning around. "I don't know whether you drink it, but I figured you could use some help waking up."

She should have said *thank you*, but she couldn't make her mouth form the words. Instead, she found the mugs where they had always been and poured herself a cup. She wanted cream, but Angus didn't offer, so she sipped it black.

"Damn, that's strong," she said out loud without thinking. Then she flinched. She had never in her life sworn in Father Angus's hearing.

Instead of scolding her, he chuckled. "Your mother always complained about my coffee too," he said. Still facing away from her, he gestured to the chair beside him. "Want to sit down?"

Brigid walked to the table but stayed standing, looking down at the top of his head. Those errant strands of whitish hair, like mist draping a mountaintop.

"We need help," she said abruptly.

Angus still didn't turn his head or look at her. He took a long, slow sip of the strong coffee, also black. "There isn't much money," he said.

She circled around the table to face him, but he didn't lift his head to meet her eyes. He kept staring—just as he had been a moment ago, but now his gaze was interrupted by her body, and he didn't react at all. He stared at her breasts, his face unchanging. Brigid's neck went hot and she knew she was conceding defeat as she sank into a chair.

"That's not the kind of help we need," she said. Now that she was here, she was reluctant to say the words out loud. Ridiculous—hadn't she already crossed the boundary of sanity when she stepped over that threshold? She couldn't possibly be worried about what this man, this monster, thought of her. Still, her voice faltered.

"What, then?" he asked after a few seconds of silence. "Is it about the girl's father? Who is he?"

Brigid burst out with a laugh, one loud "Ha!" like a single peal of a bell. Her uncle's brow furrowed deeply; Angus Byrne was not a man who appreciated being laughed at.

"Her father?" Brigid asked, feeling more laughter rise in her throat, trying to gulp it back down. "Do you seriously think, after everything, I went out and married some man? Did you think I'd just . . . outgrow it?" This was not the way to begin asking for his help. She knew it from the look on his face. Still, she couldn't stop herself. "Did you think your prayers might have worked?"

Angus's face clouded with anger. Then, suddenly, it cleared. His jaw relaxed; his forehead smoothed. "I'll admit to being old-fashioned," he said, in the same voice he'd used at the door—the voice of the kindly old man. "I tend to assume that children have mothers and fathers. But you're right, I should have known better when it comes to you." He leaned back in his chair. "Where is the girl's . . . other mother? Is she all right?"

Brigid curled her toes under the table, so she wouldn't ball her hands into fists. "There is no other mother. It's only me."

"I see." In his silence, she heard the litany of her sins, her failings, the ways she had let Dylan down. *I detest all my sins,* said her own voice in her head, but she pushed it away hard.

This time Angus didn't break the silence. He just sat there and looked at her, waiting, his breath rasping faintly on every inhale. He wasn't well, the old man. She could see that at a glance. His body, enormous and permanent as it had always seemed to her, was beginning to fail him. Brigid wondered if she should feel pity, or satisfaction, but could find neither.

She couldn't look at him any longer. She looked down into her coffee: black and thick, no light gleaming off its surface. If she unfocused her eyes, it became a hole, a bottomless void.

"I want you to exorcise her," she said into the chasm of the mug, into the darkness where blood moved, unseen.

In her peripheral vision, Father Angus's face seemed to freeze, like a glitching video. Brigid waited. The tiniest ripple spread across the surface of her coffee, from some unseen movement of the air.

"Why?" he finally asked.

"There is something . . . terrible . . . in my daughter," Brigid said slowly. "I don't know anyone else who will believe me."

"Tell me what you've seen," her uncle said. She had startled him into dropping the performance; his voice wasn't warm or affectionate, but at least he was giving her permission to be honest. At least he didn't turn her away, shut her down, as Zandy had. Something inside Brigid cracked like melting ice.

She told him everything: about the rune on the floor, about Kai's blood in Dylan's mouth, about Dylan rising above the table, her tongue splitting in half. She had to double back because she realized she'd forgotten to mention the dead things in Dylan's closet. When she was finished, she finally looked up at Angus. His fingers—thinner than she remembered, fingernails graying—were tented in front of his lips.

"I have never encountered anything like this," he said solemnly.

Brigid took a deep, steadying breath, which didn't help. "I think you have," she said.

"What?"

"That girl, when I was a kid," she said. "Serafina."

His face seemed to still, to smooth. "Serafina," he repeated, a question or a confirmation, she couldn't tell.

"I remember some of the things she said, while she was . . . here." While she was imprisoned, bound, *tortured*, but she couldn't say that to Angus. "She called you the old man. Dylan—what's inside Dylan—it said the same thing. It said, 'take me to the old man.' Dylan's never *met* you, she didn't even know you existed, why would she ask for you?" Brigid was breathing too fast, her face and neck hot. It was the coffee, too strong. Her heart was racing. Angus just sat there, placid as a stone—she remembered the stone beads of his rosary, still and smooth, but with strange angles that worried her skin. "It's the same thing, the same one." She couldn't quite say the word *demon*, though they both felt it, vibrating its inaudible but undeniable frequency in the air. "It had Serafina, and you got it out of her, but you didn't kill it, and now it's got Dylan. It wanted to come here. It's using her to get to you."

Angus lifted his coffee cup and took a long swallow. Brigid mirrored him, strangely disappointed the bitter drink didn't burn her tongue.

"Well," he finally said. "If the demon wants me, it will face me."

Relief washed through Brigid, followed so quickly by terror that she felt dizzy. Black spots laced the edges of her vision, and the horrible coffee surged back up her throat. What had she consigned her daughter to?

"You won't tie her up," she said quickly. "Not like Serafina. You won't hurt her. I'm not leaving her alone with you."

His face gave away nothing, not hurt, not anger. "Which is it, Brigid? Am I your daughter's only hope, or do you not trust me?"

She said nothing. She drank the awful coffee. It tasted a little like penance.

Chapter 19

The door to Adelaide's room—to Dylan's room—was still closed when Brigid went back upstairs, no clear objective in mind besides getting away from Father Angus. His new calm unnerved her. She wanted his help, but she loathed his presence. She'd feel better if he revealed himself as the monster she remembered, towering and threatening, promising hellfire.

Brigid stopped outside the door and listened. There was no sound from inside, no movement, no light under the door, but somehow she knew her daughter was awake. She could picture it, just as she'd known Dylan was awake in the hospital bed the night before: eyes open, bruised face alert, waiting for some signal Brigid couldn't imagine. Brigid stood there for a few moments, thinking about knocking, but she was certain Dylan knew she was out there. If she wanted Brigid to enter, she would say so.

Finally, she returned to her own room, closed the door, and fell face up across the bed. What was she doing here? Why had she lied to Zandy? No one knew she was here, except Angus and her daughter—if Brigid and Dylan never came home, no one would even have an idea where to start looking.

"Fuck," she said out loud, but very quietly so her uncle wouldn't hear. Morbid. Where had that thought come from?

The ceiling above her bed was as blank as it had always been. Apart from the small collection of books and clothing she'd taken with her when she moved out, the room looked exactly like it had when she lived here—that is, it looked like no one had ever lived here at all. No posters or artwork decorated the beige walls. The bedspread was a vague blue and gray pattern that would have looked at home in a hotel.

Brigid had left hardly a mark on this room, though she'd lived in it for twelve years. She had always been afraid to get comfortable, to think of this as her home. As far as she could remember, she'd never bothered to ask Angus for permission to decorate; she must have simply assumed he would say no. The room had never belonged to her. The door didn't have a lock, and if Angus saw it closed, he was likely to open it again, without knocking or saying a word. A constant reminder that she had no privacy, no space of her own; that she was being watched.

The only place in this house where she'd ever felt safe had been Adelaide's room. It didn't have much more decoration than her own bedroom, but the bed was piled with extra blankets and pillows, and there was a big comfortable armchair for reading, and—most important—it *smelled* like Adelaide, like talcum powder and cheap shampoo and the lavender hand lotion she liked. It was a haven, or the closest thing Brigid's childhood had contained.

In fact—Brigid sat up on the bed as the memory came back to her. She hadn't thought about it in so many years. Everything in this house had been shoved to the back of her mind, locked away, off-limits. The restricted archive, where she never gave her mind permission to wander. But now she remembered that her hiding place had been in Adelaide's room.

Every child needed a hiding place; Brigid knew that from the books she hurried through in school or at the library or, occasionally, brought home in her backpack and consumed in hasty glances when her homework was done. Angus didn't object to reading as much as most things a young girl could do for fun, but if he saw her with a book he'd interrogate her about it, making sure it was suitable, that it wouldn't expose her to any ungodly ideas. Even if she answered every question to his satisfaction, he'd still end by suggesting she read the Bible instead. So if she couldn't get away with claiming she was reading something for school—an excuse that got harder to invoke once Angus pulled her out of Twelve Apostles and commanded Adelaide to educate her at home—she tried to do it where Angus wouldn't see her.

But even her sparse, secretive reading taught her that children had hiding places. Some of them were amazing—time-traveling treehouses or wardrobes that opened into Narnia—but many were mundane. Girls hid their diaries, boys the treasures they collected on their adventures. Love letters; stolen cigarettes; Claudia Kishi's candy stash. To Brigid, *what* you hid was less important than the act of hiding something—of having a place, however tiny, that was only yours. Even if you couldn't escape physically, there was a part of you that couldn't be contained, couldn't be crushed, couldn't be forced to kneel.

As a child, Brigid yearned for a hiding place, but knew she didn't dare keep anything private in her room. Angus would find it; Angus would know. So she'd used her mother's room instead.

Adelaide had a small walk-in closet, and when she was little and they first moved into this terrible house, Brigid used to sneak into her mother's room when she couldn't sleep. If she woke Adelaide, her mother would scoop her up and return her to her own bed—at least, after Angus's long lecture on how Brigid was too big to share a bed with her mother. After several nights of that, Brigid hit on an alternative plan. Slowly, on tiptoe, with her pillow cradled in her arms and a blanket around her shoulders like a cape, she would sneak across the hall and into Adelaide's room, then into the closet. She would make a little blanket nest in the deepest corner, half hidden behind her mother's dresses, and there she would curl up to sleep, secure in the knowledge that her mother was between Brigid and the rest of the house—between Brigid and Angus. When she was older, Brigid realized that Adelaide had never been willing or able to protect Brigid from her uncle, but as a child, she simply trusted that her mother's presence was enough to keep her safe.

In the back of the closet, trying to fall asleep, Brigid sometimes ran her fingers through the carpet pile—an awful shade of avocado green by daylight, but in the middle of the night it was soft and soothing against her hands. That was how she found that the carpet wasn't properly attached to the floor in the corner. When she tugged on it, it pulled away from the wall ever so slightly, leaving a little gap. She liked to curl her fingers around the edge of the carpet, feel the transition between soft pile on top and tough plastic underneath. Sometimes she fell asleep with her hand tucked into that little space between the carpet and the floor, like a pocket.

When she decided she needed a hiding place, the loose carpet in the closet was the perfect choice. Concealed behind curtains of hanging skirts, a hiding space within a hiding space, some-where she was almost positive Angus would never look. What had she even hidden there? She tried to remember. A note Zandy had passed her in class one day, though it hadn't contained anything flirtatious. Occasional library books she didn't want Angus to see. Once, grocery shopping with her mother, Brigid had succumbed to an uncharacteristic wild impulse and pock-eted a tube of mascara; upon realizing she would never be able to get away with wearing it, she had slipped it under the carpet. It was comforting knowing it was there, even if using it was impossible.

Brigid sat up. She wanted to check her hiding spot—an im-pulse like the one that occasionally sent her doubling back to her car to make sure she had locked it, or getting out of bed in the middle of the night to check that the stove was off. Some-how, seeing the trivial secrets she'd stashed all those years ago would reassure her, ground her. It would prove she really had lived in this house, that her life had left a mark in some tiny way.

For a moment, as she stood up, the anonymous bedroom seemed to telescope around her, stretching out until the door almost disappeared in the distance. Brigid swayed on her feet, blinking hard, and the room was its usual size again. Her head spun. She desperately needed sleep, and food, but those things would have to wait.

She crossed the hall as silently as possible, instinctively avoiding creaky floorboards despite the years away. The door to Adelaide's room was open now. Brigid's chest thrummed with apprehension about encountering Dylan, but her daugh-ter wasn't in the room. Breathing a guilty sigh of relief, Brigid slipped through the open door. Dylan must be in the bathroom. Brigid would have to be quick, but she'd hear footsteps coming from the other end of the hall.

There was no nostalgia in her own austere bedroom, but here, Brigid was flooded with a surge of emotion she hadn't prepared for. She missed her mother. The room was as tidy as Adelaide had always kept it, the bed carefully made up, which Dylan never did at home. A ghost of talcum and lavender hung in the air, or was that only Brigid's memory? Her eyes were drawn to a spot on the floor by the head of the bed; this was where Adelaide had always left her slippers, lined up neatly with their toes toward the door so she could slip into them as soon as she woke. The carpet there was slightly more worn than that around it, the faintest mark of the woman who had once lived in this room.

Had she died here, too?

The thought hit Brigid for the first time, so shocking it felt like a physical blow—a fist to her sternum, knocking the breath from her chest. For a long, painful second, her lungs spasmed, flailed, forgot what they were there to do. She was drowning, drowning, her chest clenching like an empty fist—

Then it was past, and she drew an enormous, violent breath that hurt her throat. Tears spilled hot down her cheeks. Her nose was running. She wiped it on her sleeve.

She'd never thought about it before—never once wondered, never *let* herself wonder, where Adelaide had died. She didn't even know *how*. All Angus had told her, in that brief awful phone call, was that her mother had died by suicide—"the sin of despair," in his Catholic euphemism. Whatever questions Brigid might have had about the details, she had shoved them away, into the dark corners where she kept all thoughts of childhood and her family and this house.

Now, out of nowhere, she ached to know, needed to know. She turned in a circle, looking around the room as though it might offer up some clue, but there was nothing. Had it been here—an overdose of sleeping pills in the bed? Or down the hall, slit wrists in the bathtub? For all Brigid knew, it hadn't happened in the house at all. Maybe Adelaide had thrown herself in front of a bus, or jumped from a highway overpass. Somehow, though, those theories didn't feel right to Brigid. She thought her mother had died here, in this house. This was the kind of house where people died.

Focus. Breathe. Dylan would be back any second, and Brigid didn't want to explain why she was in tears. She wiped her nose again—on her other sleeve this time—and went into the closet.

The bars where her mother's clothes once hung were empty; she should have been expecting that, but it caught her off guard. Even stripped of all the layers of fabric, all the softness, the inside of the closet felt . . . muffled, somehow. As though air and sound moved differently here, more slowly.

Brigid knelt in the corner. She hadn't bothered to turn on the closet's light, or the one in the bedroom beyond, where the curtains were still closed against the daylight. Here in the deepest recess of the house, it was almost too dark to see. But after a moment, Brigid realized she didn't need to see. The closet was the same; the carpet was the same. Her hands remembered the way to their hiding place.

The carpet in the corner pulled back as easily as it always had—maybe more so. Had it loosened more over the years? She curled her fingers into it, reaching for half-remembered treasures she'd hidden here so long ago.

But instead of the smooth curve of a mascara bottle or the

softening edge of old paper, Brigid felt something thin and hard and cool. Wire? Her fingers skipped from one ridge to another, like rungs on a ladder, and then she knew what she had found. She pulled the spiral notebook out from under the carpet and looked at it in confusion. Was this hers? Had she kept a diary as a child, and forgotten until this moment?

The notebook had a plain royal-blue cover. It was the kind Brigid remembered from childhood back-to-school shopping, piled into shopping carts alongside three-ring binders and boxes of No. 2 pencils. But this wasn't a fresh new September notebook, full of clean narrow-ruled pages ready to be filled with vocabulary words. It bulged with extra pieces of paper, glued to the pages or just shoved between them. Around the slapdash scrapbooking, the notebook had been written in extensively, almost every page filled from edge to edge with words.

Brigid recognized the handwriting on sight, but it wasn't hers. That dense, spiky cursive was distinct to Adelaide Byrne.

She felt around under the carpet again—nothing else. Everything she'd stashed there as a child was gone, which meant Adelaide had found it all and disposed of it. Guilt and shame made Brigid's face hot. She reminded herself forcefully that her mother was dead, and that she was an adult now, long past being punished for passing notes in school or shoplifting mascara.

So Adelaide had found Brigid's hiding place, and decided to make use of it herself. Why? Brigid had never known her mother to keep secrets from Angus, but that was the only possible explanation. Whatever was in this notebook, Adelaide hadn't wanted her brother to know about it. Brigid felt a flush of something like pride. This small gesture of independence was more than she'd realized her mother was capable of. She wished she'd known whatever version of Adelaide lived between these pages.

Carefully, tenderly, Brigid opened the cover onto a nightmare.

HOUSEWIFE MASSACRES FAMILY, the first headline declared. The article was printed out on white paper, not cut from a newspaper, and the photograph that accompanied it was heavily pixelated from overmagnification. Still, Brigid recoiled from the woman in the picture. She was white with a sleek bob, blonde or maybe light brown rendered in pale gray, smiling with her arms around the shoulders of two similarly gray-haired children. Her smile was too wide, cutting into her cheeks painfully. Her eyes looked trapped and screaming.

Brigid tried not to look at the children's faces. She couldn't stand to imagine those innocent, cheerful expressions gone slack with betrayal, with terror, with pain. But she couldn't stop herself from reading the article. In it, she learned that a neighbor had heard screaming and called the police, who arrived to find Tara Crick, thirty-nine, Jordan Crick, forty-two, and their two children, no names or ages given, dead in the bathroom. The two children were drowned in the tub; Jordan, apparently trying to save them, had been slashed multiple times across the face, neck, and hands with his own straight razor. Tara had taken the razor to herself last, maintaining consciousness long enough to write BAD MOTHER on the mirror with the blood from her own wrists. Friends described her as a loving parent, a hardworking PTA member, and a devout Catholic.

Below the article, the page was filled in with Adelaide's handwriting, but Brigid didn't take the time to read it. Instead she flipped to the next printout, this one about a fraternity president who had raped and murdered his girlfriend. The man on the following page had gunned down three strangers in a grocery store.

Murder, rape, assault, suicide—but mostly murder; the notebook was full of it. Brigid's stomach roiled. The closet, once cozy, was now suffocating her. Why had Adelaide kept such a macabre collection?

Too late, Brigid slammed the notebook closed, as though what she'd seen could be trapped between paper. Maybe that was why Adelaide had hidden these articles here—a coping mechanism, a way of sequestering them from her daily thoughts and fears. That explanation didn't satisfy Brigid. Why had her mother sought them out in the first place?

She pressed her hand over her chest, at the base of her throat, where she could feel her pulse galloping. Rubbed her hand over the spot as though her heart were a skittish animal she was trying to soothe. She needed to calm down. Dylan would be back any moment.

Wouldn't she? How long had Brigid been kneeling here in the closet? Her hips and knees twinged. She dragged herself up to standing and almost stumbled as she tried to put weight on her right foot, which had fallen asleep. She'd been in Adelaide's closet for a *long* time—ten minutes or more. Certainly long enough for Dylan to return from the bathroom and demand to know what Brigid was doing in there.

But Dylan hadn't come.

Limping slightly as pins and needles shot through her right foot, Brigid hurried out of the room and into the hall. Again she felt a rush of vertigo, exacerbated by the difficulty of keeping her balance, and braced herself against a wall until the dizziness passed.

She realized she was still carrying Adelaide's notebook. Feeling rushed, as though she would be discovered at any moment, she ducked into her own old bedroom and stashed it under her pillow.

Where was Dylan? At the other end of the hall, the bathroom door stood open and the light inside was off. Dylan wasn't snooping in the master bedroom, either. Downstairs, then. Or—the thought choked Brigid with sudden dread—had she left the house altogether?

She raced down the stairs and swung around the corner into the kitchen, her mouth already open to yell at Angus that her daughter was missing, then lurched to a halt. The shout emerged half formed, a choked squeak that hurt her throat. Dylan was sitting at the table, a mug of coffee in front of her, and Angus was at the stove making scrambled eggs. They both turned to stare at Brigid on her noisy, clumsy entrance.

"Oh," she said, feeling her face go red. "I couldn't find you."

Dylan didn't say anything, just lifted the mug to her lips and sipped.

"We've been getting acquainted," said Angus in his new voice, the one that made Brigid want to chew glass. "It's about the most exciting thing that's happened around here in decades, finding out I have a great-niece."

Brigid had to swallow twice before she could speak. She hated hearing Angus refer to *having* Dylan, laying a claim to her in any way. "She's too young to drink coffee," she said, her voice half an octave higher than it should have been. "And since when do you cook eggs?"

"Lived alone for plenty of years," said Angus mildly, refusing to snarl back at her, which was all the more infuriating. "Before you and your mother moved in with me, and after, too. I know how to fend for myself in a kitchen."

Dylan's eyes snapped to him. "Mom used to live here?" she asked. She was slurring still, her tongue thick and unwieldy in her mouth. Instead of sparking sympathy in Brigid, as she knew it should, the sound made her boil with rage. What Dylan had done to herself made her so *angry*. She knew it was wrong to feel that way, but she couldn't smother the awful heat in her gut. The pins and needles feeling in her right foot wasn't fading; instead it was crawling up her leg, an awful sensation, slightly numb but still unbearable.

"Sure did," said Angus. "She grew up here. Moved in when she was just a little thing." He smiled, as though remembering Brigid's adorable childhood years with an affection he'd never displayed when she was actually a child. "Her mother, too— well, I suppose to you she'd be your Grandmother Adelaide."

"Grandmother," said Dylan in wonder, rolling the word around on her injured tongue. "I didn't know." She looked pointedly at Brigid and took another long swallow of coffee. There was cream in it, Brigid noticed; Angus had probably offered it to Dylan, another irritation when she already felt scraped raw. Pins and needles all over her body, now, skin tingling and sore. "Where does she live now?"

"Oh, dear," said Angus softly. He was scraping the eggs onto a plate with a wooden spatula, but he set the plate down and turned to Dylan. "I'm sorry to be the one to tell you this," he began, and Brigid *felt* it like a jab. Something hot was writhing under her skin. It wasn't pins and needles, it was thousands of tiny legs crawling across her nerve endings.

"Don't," she said quickly.

Angus looked at her, wide-eyed, a caricature of innocence. "Brigid, I think your daughter deserves the truth."

"*Don't*," Brigid repeated, higher and louder. "She doesn't need to know about that. It's just going to upset her."

"My mom doesn't think I need to know *anything*," Dylan said. The venom in her voice made Brigid flinch. It wasn't the strange, wrong-sounding voice of the night before. This was just her daughter, so bitter it seeped into the air around her. "I didn't even know you *existed* until last night. She thinks she can keep me, like, bubble-wrapped, so I never have to find out anything that might hurt my delicate china doll feelings."

"I'm sure your mother is trying to do her best by you," Angus said. "It's not easy being a single parent. I saw how much my sister struggled." He didn't give Brigid so much as a sidelong glance, but she knew what he was insinuating: that Adelaide had been a bad mother and now Brigid was following in her footsteps.

Hatred swarmed inside her, buzzing, squirming against the underside of her skin. How dare he pretend to be sympathetic when all he'd ever done was shame Adelaide and break her down? "Oh, you saw how much she struggled?" Brigid said. "And what did you ever do to support her? To *help* her? Did you even try to *stop* her from—did you even—" Her chest heaved, her skin burned. She couldn't stand it, couldn't stand to cry in front of him.

Finally, Angus turned and looked at her. "I know I'm not perfect, but I helped your mother in the best way I knew how," he said. "I gave the two of you a place to live when you needed it. I gave you a home—one you've come back to after all these years. You've made it very clear you don't think that was enough, Brigid, and I have never demanded gratitude, but you cannot claim that I did not love my sister. I miss her every single day."

He looked so sad. She couldn't remember ever seeing him look sad before. It almost made her believe him.

"So my grandmother is dead?" Dylan asked.

"Yes," said Angus. "I'm sorry. It was thirteen . . . no, fourteen years ago now. Before you were born, I suppose."

"How did she die?" This time the question was delivered, unmistakably, to Brigid. Angus opened his mouth, then closed it again. He shrugged, as if to say *this is between the two of you*. Brigid itched everywhere. She wanted to claw off her skin.

"Please don't," she said again, knowing it was useless, knowing Dylan wouldn't stop, Angus wouldn't stop, between the two of them they would burn her alive from the inside out. "It's just going to upset you."

"No, it's going to upset *you*," said Dylan. "That's all you care about. Why are you so scared to tell me anything? It's *my* family too, I deserve—"

"My mother killed herself," Brigid said. She meant it as a slap to the face and that was how it sounded, loud and startling in the close, dark kitchen. Nevertheless, Dylan didn't flinch or break her gaze. Angus made a very deliberate show of turning away from Brigid and picking up the plate of eggs. He set it on the table in front of Dylan, who ignored it.

"Why?" she asked.

"I don't *know*." It came out furious, almost hysterical, obviously defensive. She knew she was handling this all wrong, but panic and rage had a hold on her and she couldn't see how to get free.

"Well, did she leave a note, or—"

"I don't know," said Brigid again, looking to Angus for help. He opened his mouth to respond, but Dylan didn't give him the chance.

"You don't know?" she demanded. "How could you not know if your mother left a suicide note? Where were you?"

Brigid's mouth gaped, but she was out of words.

"You weren't here," Dylan said, figuring it out herself. "Like, *really* not here. Like, not even talking to her? You just walked away and shut her out?" Brigid's silence was the only answer she could give. She wasn't searching in vain for words anymore; she was trying to smother the feeling crawling up her throat, like a scream, or worse. Anything to make Dylan stop talking, stop saying these horrible things.

"God, Mom, no wonder you didn't want to tell me about her." Brigid thought about clamping a hand over Dylan's mouth. "You think you can just ignore everything you don't like and it will go away"—She imagined squeezing, pinching her nose, watching her face turn purple, watching those hideous accusations shrivel up and disappear—"but it's *fucked*. You cut off your own mother and"—slamming her head against the wall, a crack loud enough to drown out every other sound in the world—"that's probably why she killed herself, isn't it?"

Brigid picked up Dylan's plate and threw it hard. The plate split in half against the wall, then fell to the floor and shattered into smaller pieces. Eggs slid down the old, faded yellow paint in a smear of brighter yellow. The silence in the kitchen was so perfect Brigid could hear them plopping onto the floor.

Dylan's face was as pale as the plate Brigid had just destroyed, her eyes glittery wet. All the heat and fury drained out of Brigid in an instant, and cold shame flooded in.

"Baby," she whispered. "I'm so sorry—"

"Brigid, I think you should leave," said Angus. Brigid flinched at the sound of his voice; she'd almost forgotten he was in the room. "Take a little while to calm down."

She shook her head hard. "No, I'll just—the dustpan is in that closet, right?" She moved across the room quickly, her hands feeling huge and clumsy, her ears ringing.

"No," said Angus firmly. "Brigid, stop. I can clean up the floor." His hand came down on her shoulder, immense and heavy. She pulled away from his touch with an urgency that was almost violence, and heard Dylan gasp at the sudden movement. As if it had indeed been violence. As if she were afraid of Brigid.

"I'm sorry," Brigid said again, not to Angus—never to Angus—but to Dylan. Her daughter didn't answer.

"You should leave," Angus repeated. "I cannot allow you to lash out at your daughter in my home. She deserves to feel safe here."

Brigid looked from Angus to Dylan and back, her heart clawing the inside of her chest like a cornered animal.

"You should leave," Dylan echoed. It hurt Brigid in a deep place she couldn't name, hearing her uncle's words in her child's mouth.

She pulled herself up straight, did not press a hand over her chest to quiet the thrashing beast inside. "Fine," she said. "We'll leave."

The worst part was that Angus didn't even look satisfied; he gazed at her with pity. "I think it would be better if Dylan stays with me," he said, his voice gentler than she had ever heard it. "I don't mean for a long time. Maybe just for tonight, to give you both a little time to calm down. We can talk more tomorrow, if everyone feels ready."

She shook her head. "No. No." There was no panic now, only

a vast, swallowing emptiness. "No, she's not staying here without me." She meant it as a command but it emerged as a plea.

"I'll be fine, Mom," said Dylan. Then—oh, horror of horrors, betrayal of betrayals, the serpent's teeth closed around Brigid's throat—she crossed the room and stood beside Uncle Angus. Under his protection. Under his shadow. "I'll talk to you tomorrow."

"No," said Brigid. "Not with *him*."

Dylan rolled her eyes—such a familiar gesture, a teenage girl annoyed by her overprotective mother. "You lived with him for like a decade, right? I think I can survive one night."

Do I look like I survived to you? Brigid wanted to scream, but she simply didn't have the energy. Instead, in a very small voice, she said, "You have no idea who he is."

Her daughter looked back at her and said, "I have no idea who you are, either."

Chapter 20

B rigid's car flashed a low gas warning around the time she stopped crying. She'd been driving in aimless patterns for more than an hour, not knowing where to go, afraid to put too much distance between herself and Angus's house, because something might happen and Dylan might need her.

Dylan had stayed her sentence of exile long enough for Brigid to dash upstairs and grab her scant belongings. She'd also collected the notebook from under her pillow, aware even in her misery that it would be a mistake to leave Adelaide's bizarre collection where Angus could find it.

Now the notebook was somewhere in the passenger side footwell, along with all the rest of Brigid's things, spilling out of her half-zipped backpack as she swung around a corner at an irresponsible speed. She pulled into the parking lot at Rocky Mountain Lake Park, not caring that her car straddled two spaces. Her eyes were dry and sore, her nose and upper lip raw from wiping on her sleeve. She'd circled the neighborhood a dozen times and come to a stop only a few blocks from her uncle's house. Wasn't that a sad metaphor for her life? she thought. All that time running, thinking she'd escaped, but she'd never gone far. Now she was right back where she'd started. It barely felt like a decision she had made—more like she was being *pulled*, like there was nowhere else she could possibly go. She was a fish that had finally run out her line and was being reeled in. The hook had been set in her flesh so long ago she'd grown around it, forgotten it hadn't always been a part of her body.

Brigid's throat was sore from crying. She found her purse and fished around for a Tylenol. As she dry-swallowed the tablet with a grimace, she wondered whether Dylan was in pain, whether she'd taken anything for it today. The thought—and the realization that it hadn't occurred to her until now—hurt worse than her throat. Her daughter was injured and alone. How could Brigid have just left her?

She found her phone in her pocket. No missed calls from Angus or Dylan, not that she'd expected otherwise. There was a missed call from Zandy, however, along with several text messages. Of course, Brigid thought in exhaustion. She should have expected Zandy to check in, wanting to know whether Dylan was all right, probably offering again to visit them in the hospital.

But Zandy didn't ask about Dylan. *Holy shit B*, said her first text. The next said, *I googled your uncle.* Brigid had to take a long breath and let it out when she saw that. Zandy's next message was *I hope this isn't overstepping but I was stressed out and research calms me down.* Then, *Anyway remember I asked why he didn't work for a church???* A pause of several minutes followed, as though Zandy had been waiting for Brigid's response. Then she'd gone on: *He was defrocked in the 80s.*

Defrocked—an odd, anachronistic word, one that took Brigid a moment to recognize. If Zandy was correct, Angus had been expelled from the clergy. He wasn't a priest anymore. He hadn't been a priest for most of her life, in fact. How could she not have known that? Adelaide must have known, she thought, so why wouldn't she have mentioned it to Brigid?

And what had he done that was so bad the Church would strip him of his priesthood? Brigid thought of the headlines in Adelaide's scrapbook. What kind of man had she left her daughter with?

The last message in the text thread was just a link Zandy had sent. Brigid's stomach twisted as she clicked on it.

It was exactly what she'd pictured—an old newspaper clipping, scanned and digitized, just like the ones in Adelaide's scrapbook. Even pixelated, in black-and-white, and some forty years younger, Angus's face was familiar enough to make her flinch. The photograph had captured him in the middle of what might have been a sermon, his eyes and mouth wide, hands outstretched in an imploring gesture.

But the headline was not at all what Brigid had expected and braced for. CONTROVERSIAL "PUBLIC ACCESS EXORCIST" DEFROCKED OVER TV SHOW, it blared. Below, the article explained that Angus Byrne—whom the reader might recognize from his well-known television show, in which he cast demons out of troubled souls in front of a live audience—had been censured by his bishop for performing unsanctioned exorcisms, as well as for the unwanted publicity this generated for the Church. Father Byrne had argued that since he performed this service for no fee, it did not violate his vows, although many of his followers did choose to make donations as an expression of their gratitude.

When he refused to cancel the show, he was laicized—the term the Church preferred for revocation of holy orders.

The article went on to describe Angus's show, which had apparently aired for close to five years on a public access station in Colorado Springs, and the controversy it had generated. Brigid had been too young to remember the Satanic Panic of the '80s, but she'd read about it, and Angus's show had been perfectly crafted to take advantage of that precarious cultural moment. Concerned parents had dragged their troubled children onto Angus's stage and tearfully recounted the evidence that they were under the sway of demonic influences before Angus placed his hands on the afflicted and invited the audience to join him in prayer. Sometimes the supposedly possessed volunteered themselves. Brigid felt queasy with sorrow and pity, thinking about those people so desperate for help—how Angus had preyed on their fear and uncertainty.

But wasn't she one of those people, too? She had delivered her own daughter straight into Angus's hands when she had nowhere else to turn. How could she judge anyone else for seeking the same solace? Or Angus for offering it?

Many of Father Angus's critics argued that the priest was a charismatic firebrand who used Satanic fearmongering to make a name for himself, when what his followers really needed was psychological help. There had been plenty of outcry from Catholics as well, furious that Angus was sensationalizing their faith, treating exorcisms as entertainment rather than a serious spiritual matter.

But the man had his fans, too. Brigid wasn't surprised—she had seen firsthand how people could be drawn in by his energy, his certainty. She could almost see the studio audience, leaning forward in their seats, sweating and trembling, drawing in a collective gasp as if with one throat when Angus roared, "Demon, leave this child!" Could it really all be true? She believed what she had seen with Serafina was real, but did that mean Angus had truly cast out demons every week for five years? If all those demons weren't real, did Angus believe they were, or was he just an incredibly gifted liar? Was this all a massive, decades-long grift? But then why keep it up after the show was canceled?

The article ended with an impassioned defense of Angus from one devoted audience member. "We come here every week—me, my wife, and our two kids," Jordan Crick was quoted as saying. "No one wants to accept it, but Father Angus is telling the truth. Demons are at work in the world, and ignoring them only allows them to become more powerful."

Jordan Crick. Why was that name familiar? Was he someone she knew? It couldn't be—this article was published when she was a toddler. Jordan Crick would be elderly now, if he was even still alive.

But he isn't alive, Brigid thought. *He died.*

Then she knew why she recognized his name.

Sour panic bubbling up her throat, Brigid scrabbled in the passenger footwell for her mother's notebook. Of course. Jordan Crick, husband—and victim—of Tara Crick. Jordan Crick, slashed over and over with his own razor blade as he tried to stop his wife from drowning their children. There he was, in the photograph next to Tara, glued into that spiral notebook and hidden under a carpet for twenty years or more.

Brigid could all too easily imagine the two of them side by side in Angus's audience, rapt and breathless as they watched the priest expel the forces of evil. Jordan and Tara and their children had gone from part of Angus's audience to part of Adelaide's collection. How?

Comparing the article in the notebook with the one on her phone, Brigid saw that four years had passed between Angus's laicization and the deaths of the Crick family. Angus, Adelaide, and Brigid had been living together in Denver by then—her uncle must have moved back into his parents' home after the Colorado Springs bishop defrocked him. And Tara Crick had committed her atrocities in Phoenix, Arizona. Angus couldn't have been involved in the deaths. Could he?

Brigid skimmed to the bottom of the page in Adelaide's notebook. There were her mother's notes, the handwriting crammed and jagged as it had always been, as though Adelaide were perpetually nervous about running out of space. Brigid had been expert at deciphering her mother's penmanship when she was young—sometimes Adelaide had called on Brigid to read out her own grocery lists or notes she'd left herself. It had been many years, but she narrowed her eyes and saw the tiny letters come into focus.

I remember them. Every week in the audience, cheering and crying and praying. Tara would have been in the aisle like a holy roller if the ushers didn't make her sit down. She scared me back then, or maybe that's not true, maybe I just think that now because I know what she did. I can't remember her ever going onstage but she'd wail and pull her own hair and act insane. Histrionic, I thought, but maybe she really meant it. It must have scared her kids. I used to think it was crazy to bring kids to something like that. I was so proud of myself for being a more responsible parent, leaving Brigid home with her dad. Protecting her. It's easy to be self-righteous when you have plenty of options.

Below that, a line had been scribbled out so thoroughly, with so many overlapping loops of black ink, it had put holes in the paper.

Brigid flipped ahead and found a clipping about the sentencing of Martin De Lucca, a mail carrier who'd forced his way into a house on his route, then violently raped the woman who lived there. The article was sparse on details, but said the survivor had been left "disfigured" by the assault. De Lucca pled guilty and showed no remorse, nor even distress at the prospect of going to prison. Both the crime and the conviction had taken place in Colorado Springs.

He only came to the taping a handful of times. He sat in the back and was mostly quiet, very intense and focused. The last time I saw him, he tried to flirt with me. He was very shy and mentioned that he'd been divorced for a year or two, I can't remember. Not a long time. I think I was the first woman he tried to ask out since. When I told him I had a boyfriend and a child he was so apologetic and embarrassed, but still kind—he said he wished me luck. That he hoped we would have a very happy life together. I liked him. I thought maybe we could be friends after that. I was looking forward to seeing him again, but he never showed up to another show. I think he was too embarrassed about being rejected. Or maybe it had nothing to do with me. Maybe none of this has anything to do with me. Maybe he got what he needed from Angus and that was it. Maybe he never thought about either of us again. He was a sad, divorced, lonely man. Rejection and solitude can turn men into monsters. Maybe it's not connected.

Maybe none of this is connected.

Maybe there is no pattern.

Maybe it's all in my head.

So many of them, all in my head.

Brigid was breathing too fast and shallow, her head swimming. The parked car was heating up quickly in the sunlight, despite the cool weather outside. A spike of pain throbbed up the back of Brigid's neck and into her skull. She was probably dehydrated. With Adelaide's notebook clutched in her fingers, so tight her sweat was beginning to warp her fingerprints into the cardboard cover, she emerged from the car. The bright sun intensified the pain in her head—it must be early afternoon now.

She walked carefully as a drunk across the yellowing grass, sidestepping goose shit, until she arrived at the playground. There, in the corner of her vision, was the massive blue spruce under which she and Zandy had first kissed—no, maybe that had been a different tree, closer to the lake. The good memory warped and blurred, disappearing down a dark chasm of droning prayer, beads between her aching fingertips. So many things waited in that darkness, where Brigid had tried to bury all her worst memories. She remembered Gwen. She remembered falling to her knees over the toilet bowl, vomiting and sobbing all at once, no one to hold her hair back because she'd chosen the thing growing inside her over the woman she loved. Hadn't part of her felt it was right, the kneeling, the suffering—the penance? Didn't she deserve it, vile thing that she was, just like she'd deserved her uncle's punishment, like she'd deserved to lose Zandy all those years ago, like she deserved to lose Dylan now?

Shame soured, curdled into rage, as Brigid stared at that fucking tree, where she'd given in to the sin in her heart, where she'd let the devil sink his claws into her soul. She was losing herself, she'd been losing herself for decades, and it had all started under that tree.

A child screamed, lighting up the pathway of pain from Brigid's neck into the meat of her brain. Whipping around, she saw the child—barely more than a toddler—had fallen from their swing. They lay in the wooden mulch, twisted at an impossible angle, broken like a twig. Light glinted off something—a protruding shard of bone? A man who must have been the child's father stood there impassive, eyes fixed on the empty swing, which still whistled on its deadly arc through the air.

The horror of it, the absurdity, struck Brigid behind her breastbone, resonated somewhere in her throat. She choked—not on bile, but worse: on laughter.

Then the child shrieked again, and the momentary confusion resolved. Brigid was looking at a puffy jacket lying on the ground, sunlight shining off its metal zipper. The toddler was still on the swing, leaning back until their sneakered feet kicked at the clouds, howling with delight.

Brigid shuddered with what she told herself was relief. She stumbled the last few feet to a metal bench and collapsed onto it. The father by the swing set glanced at her, then quickly away. Brigid could imagine what she must look like, unrested and unshowered, eyes still red from crying, clutching a battered old notebook like a life preserver. She wasn't surprised when she heard the man say, "I think we better head home for your nap."

Brigid opened the notebook again. This time she flipped through quickly, avoiding eye contact with Tara Crick, Martin De Lucca, and their cohort of monsters. She skimmed the headlines, the locations and dates, following the pattern her mother had already identified. The crimes were not archived in chronological order—some dated back to Brigid's early childhood, others had been committed after she'd moved out of Angus's house. None, as far as she could tell, predated the airing of Angus's television show. Many of the newspaper clippings were from Colorado Springs and the surrounding area, although there were outliers scattered around the Four Corners states, and a few even farther away.

The crimes were all distinct in their grotesquerie, yet they seemed to run together the more Brigid read. Although the details of each were individually shocking, the particularities smoothed out in the bland, repetitive phrases of the newspaper articles. The accused had no history of violence. The accused confessed readily, in many cases turned themselves in. The accused pled guilty. The accused showed no remorse.

Aside from the apparent lack of emotion on the part of the offender, the connecting thread was the television show. Every culprit and some of their victims had, at least according to Adelaide, attended at least one filming. Under each clipping, for a few lines or several pages, Brigid's mother had written down everything she remembered about the person who went on to commit astonishing acts of violence. It seemed Adelaide had been present for every filming of the show, and had spoken to almost every audience member; her recollection was pristine— unless, Brigid thought, she was making it all up.

Could that be it? Aside from the link Zandy had sent, which mentioned Tara and Jordan Crick, there was no evidence connecting the perpetrators of these horrors to Father Angus's show. Perhaps, in her shock and dismay over the fate of the Crick family, Adelaide had constructed a pattern where there was none, pinning violent offenders from the news over memories of people they vaguely resembled, or making up the stories altogether. Maybe this was how Adelaide had fallen apart at the end, what had eventually led her to take her own life—spinning wild webs of violence and conspiracy, all centering around her brother.

I feel it under my skin, Adelaide wrote. The entries in the notebook were not dated or even delineated by page breaks; one thought rolled into another, separated only by the printed-out articles and photos. Occasional changes in pen color and slight shifts in the angle of the crowded handwriting were the only indication that the whole wild project hadn't been assembled in a single day, one agonizing stream of increasingly fractured consciousness. *Crawling over my bones. I think about them all the time, what they did, what I want to do. It must have felt good. It must have felt so good. When I think it, I feel sick, I try to push the thought down, down, into the blood and the dark inside me, it goes so deep, push it into the dark and the sin, isn't that enough? Isn't that enough? And I don't even know if I'm trying to drown it or feed it.*

Brigid's back and tailbone ached from sitting hunched on the metal bench. The cold of it seeped through her sweatpants and into her bones. Her hands were curled tight, knuckles chapped in the wind that grew stronger as the afternoon stretched into twilight. She should go somewhere—sit inside, get a cup of coffee. There was a public library not far away, the one she'd visited as a child, assuming it was still there. But she didn't move.

As the notebook progressed, the news articles grew less frequent and Adelaide's notes between them grew longer and stranger. There was something inside her, Adelaide believed, something that had infected all the offenders in her scrapbook, driven them to acts of horrific violence. Now it was in her, poisoning her thoughts, and she was terrified of what it wanted her to do—or, perhaps, what she wanted to do.

I think about the blood, she wrote below an article about Desiree Salk, who had driven a school bus across a median into oncoming traffic, killing three children and the driver of another vehicle, but escaping with only minor injuries herself. *Blood like hot water, scouring and cleansing, washing away everything. It hurts the way a scalding shower hurts, and afterward I'm fresh and pure and soft again.* Brigid rubbed her eyes, stinging with the cold, leaking slow tears down her cheeks. She could barely picture her quiet, placid mother writing these words. How frightened and confused she must have been, how desperate to rid herself of these unwelcome fantasies. Had she confided any of this in Angus? Had he suspected? Had he tried to help her at all?

On another page, Adelaide's handwriting was even smaller, as though trying to disappear into itself. Thick clots of ink soaked into the page where the pen had pressed down too hard, leaving drowned and smeared letters. Brigid read the partially obscured words almost despite herself.

I found Brigid. She hasn't even bothered with an unlisted number. She's still in Colorado, just up in the mountains. A two-hour drive, maybe. She opened a store—some witchcraft nonsense for women who think being lesbians and burning incense gives them magic powers. How embarrassing. I wonder if she has a girlfriend. An awful woman she introduces as her wife and expects everyone to indulge her delusions. The worst part is that she's so immersed in the fantasy that all this is okay, that her sin is just a "lifestyle choice." She can't turn her back on it now without admitting that she was wrong, and worse, that Angus and I were right. She's too proud to find her way back to God, and to her family.

In some dark corner, under the loose carpet of her mind, Brigid had long harbored the secret hope that her mother didn't see her as deviant. If it weren't for her uncle, she'd imagined, Adelaide might have supported Brigid, loved her, accepted and treasured her just the way she was. Now, reading the bland spite in her mother's words, that hope shriveled with the pain of a dying muscle, an atrophying limb.

And she just left me with him, Adelaide wrote, her tone shifting in the middle of a line with no discernible change in her handwriting. *If anyone knows what kind of person Angus is, it's my daughter. She's seen what he can do. She might not understand the way I do, she doesn't have all the information, but she knows he's a monster, and she left me here with him in this filthy house. She doesn't love me enough to come back for me. No one does. My parents threw me out; he brought me back, but only so he could poison me for years, then chew on my bones.*

My brother says he loves me, and I want to believe him, because if he doesn't then no one loves me at all. But he leaves me alone in this house that goes on forever, I walk down the halls for miles or days and scream and scream and no one hears me. Yes, I have sinned, God knows! But I have repented for so many years. When will I be pure again? When will my punishment be over? Why do I deserve to lose everyone I love, to scream in the stinking darkness and hear only silence?

On the next page, Adelaide wrote, *I drove up to the mountains today and parked outside Brigid's store. I sat there for hours, watching her arrive and leave. She looks different. She's gained weight. It must be easy to let yourself go when you think you don't care if men want you. She could be so pretty. I used to be so pretty. I looked at myself in the rearview mirror and the skin on my face dried up and peeled away and all I could see was my bones. Beauty doesn't matter, because no one can truly love us but God. He sees what's underneath. He loves my blood and my skeleton and the worms digging tunnels deep in my flesh.*

It went on and on like that for pages, uninterrupted. Sin, sacrifice, and details of what she observed from Brigid's life, interspersed with shame and self-recrimination. Brigid couldn't tell how many times her mother had driven up from Denver to watch her in secret, but one page contained a vitriolic description of Gwen, though Adelaide didn't seem to know her name. Had Brigid ever walked past Adelaide sitting in her car without noticing? Shouldn't she have gotten a strange feeling, an intuition that she was being watched? Adelaide mentioned calling Brigid at work and hanging up when she answered; Brigid had no memory of this either.

I am being hollowed out like a Halloween pumpkin. It has eaten my slippery insides, all my seeds are cracked and chewed, my rind is carved into a smile. I'm empty and rotting. Oh, but I'm not empty, there's something in here and it is climbing climbing climbing up the walls of me, ready to squirm out of my mouth and eyes and all my holes. I don't have much longer. We don't have much longer. It runs back and forth under my teeth. I wake up in the night and it's crouching on my tongue.

Adelaide's panicky descriptions of something growing inside her triggered a vague memory—a story Brigid had heard somewhere, or maybe read in a book. She could almost picture the illustration, a sketchy black-and-white image of a woman's face screaming in a mirror. The woman had scratched an itchy bump on her face, and baby spiders had poured out. Was it real, what Adelaide had written in these pages, this long, confused, terrified suicide note? Had something really been inside her, growing, waiting to hatch, like a spider?

No, not a spider, Brigid thought. She remembered Dylan's school project, the one she'd been explaining to Zandy—only the night before, though it felt like months had passed since then. The wasp that paralyzed roaches and laid its eggs inside their bodies, from which the larvae would eventually eat their way out.

"And then what?" Brigid said out loud. Startled by the hoarse sound of her own voice, she glanced around to reassure herself the playground was empty.

If she accepted Adelaide's claims—if she believed there really was something inside these people, some foreign entity—how did it get there? Was Angus the wasp in this metaphor, paralyzing people with his sermons and threats of damnation, piercing and destroying the part of their brain responsible for self-preservation, writing over their instincts with his own? She imagined tiny eggs, soft globes like caviar, under her mother's skin, little clusters deposited in the crannies between her bones. The image repulsed her, but she couldn't push it away.

What happened when the eggs hatched? Was that what Adelaide was keeping track of in her macabre scrapbook—each infection maturing into an eruption of horrific violence?

Or maybe, Brigid told herself harshly, you're making all this up, drawing connections that don't exist, following a trail of breadcrumbs scattered by a woman losing her mind. Maybe you don't need to dig for the real story; maybe the real story is simply that your mother was paranoid and delusional and she killed herself.

But she'd seen Dylan float in the air. She'd heard the sound her tongue made when it split in half. Whatever was happening to her daughter, the explanation went beyond what science and rational thought could explain. Was it impossible that the same had been true of her mother?

The more unhinged Adelaide's commentary became, the harder it was to read her words. In some places the lines crisscrossed over each other, wandering across the page, doubling back. The letters were smaller and smaller, crowded together illegibly. Still, Brigid couldn't stop reading.

Driving up and down the mountains every day. He never asks where I'm going and when I'll be back. Maybe he doesn't notice because he's gone too. There are more rooms in this house than there used to be and I can never find him in any of them. We go days without speaking, or else he doesn't say anything worth remembering, maybe I'm confused. If he asked I would tell him the truth. I think I would. Or maybe he's asked and I've lied and I don't remember that either.

Brigid's address isn't listed but I followed her home from the store. I know where she lives, her and that tall woman with the ugly haircut, if she wants someone who looks like a man why doesn't she just get a man? They go in and out but it's an apartment building and I can't tell which one is theirs. So many people, crammed in together like rats in the walls, slithering and hissing, I can hear them from across the street.

Brigid flipped another page. Another news clipping—the last in the notebook—stared up at her. Brigid gasped, choked on her own spit, and burst into a fit of furious coughing that brought tears to her eyes. Then she looked down at the notebook again, hoping that what she'd seen had been a random glitch of memory, a flash of pareidolia, that the face gazing out at her would be a stranger's.

But of course it wasn't. Of course the last entry in Adelaide's archive, the dead end of her murderer's row, was Serafina Santoro.

Chapter 21

*T*eenager Convicted of Parents' Murders

    Aurora, CO—Seventeen-year-old Serafina Santoro has been convicted after pleading guilty to the torture, murder, and dismemberment of her parents, Don and Giulia Santoro. The Saint Felicity High School senior told police that she killed her father because he had been molesting her since she was ten years old, and her mother because she had allowed it. A medical examination showed signs of repeated sexual abuse, leaving scar tissue that left the girl infertile. Santoro did not display any remorse or distress, despite claiming she understood the severity of the charges. Medical experts have recommended she receive psychiatric treatment instead of prison time. Her sentencing is scheduled for later this week.

Brigid read the words over and over. Unlike Adelaide's handwriting, they were perfectly clear. Still, it took several readings before she could derive anything from them beyond a vague buzzing noise in her head.

Serafina had been assaulted by her own father, over and over, for years. The same father who had dragged her to Father Angus's house, claiming there was a demon inside her. Brigid tried to remember the man's face, but she could only picture the painting of Jesus on her uncle's wall, twisted in agony.

She had believed—had *known* in her bones—that the older girl was possessed. That Father Angus helped her, *saved* her, when no one else could. That knowledge had slept under the foundations of Brigid's entire life, under her hate and fear of Uncle Angus and his Bible, when she'd run from his house and when she'd returned, bringing her only precious thing, her only daughter, with her. Because no matter how much Angus disgusted her, she'd *seen* him cast out the demon from Serafina.

But what had he done, really? Brigid tried to reconstruct what Serafina had said to her all those years ago, why she'd been so certain there was a demon inside the older girl. Serafina had terrified her, had said awful things. She'd talked about hell; she'd made Brigid feel despicable and dirty. She'd said something about sex, too, something Brigid didn't understand but that flooded her with shame. What had it been? Had Serafina actually threatened Brigid, or had she been trying to tell the younger girl what her father was doing to her? Had she seen in Brigid a potential ally, someone who could slip below the sight lines of parents and priests to get her the help she needed?

Brigid felt shame all over again, icy and new. She pictured the scene again, not a demon tied to that bed but a very young girl. Only a little older than Dylan. *So* young. So afraid. Bound and helpless and desperately trying to escape not just that miserable room but the hell that was her life. And Brigid had misunderstood. Had done nothing. Had believed for all these years that Angus saved Serafina, when in fact he only tormented her, then handed her back to her rapist.

Did Angus know, she wondered, what the girl's father was doing to her? Then she wondered: Did it matter? She felt sure he hadn't asked, had simply taken the parents' word for it that Serafina was possessed. Maybe if he'd asked the girl some questions, if he'd *listened*, he could have helped her. Maybe then she wouldn't have done—whatever she did to her father and mother.

Brigid hoped, whatever it was, that it had hurt.

Below the article were more of Adelaide's frantic half-coherent notes, but Brigid could no longer focus her eyes enough to read them. It was getting dark, she realized. The sun was almost gone behind the mountains; the late afternoon was cold. She'd been sitting here most of the day, she hadn't eaten or drunk anything in hours, and the back of her neck was a lighthouse of pain, sending flashes of agony pulsing up into her skull.

She stood, feeling her joints pop and creak, twisting some of the stiffness out of her back. The notebook slipped from her fingers and fell into the dead grass at her feet. Brigid stared down at it for a long moment, thinking, nonsensically, that she could just leave it there. Then someone else would find it and it would be their problem.

But reality gripped her by the throat and shook her. No, that wouldn't help. She couldn't throw away those pages like abandoning a kitten in an alley. That story knew her scent too well. It would follow her home, claw at her door.

Brigid bent and picked up the notebook again. It felt impossibly heavy for such a slim collection of cardboard and paper, ink and glue. She held it against her chest like a schoolgirl as she trudged back to her car.

Her mind raced. She pictured Nadine's hands shuffling an

oversized deck of tarot cards, images dancing past one another, revising and rearranging, a new story every time. What did
Serafina Santoro have to do with the rest of the clippings in the
notebook? From one angle, it was obvious: she was someone
Angus had tried to help, who had gone on to commit murder.
She fit the pattern Adelaide had identified. But did that mean
what Adelaide thought it meant? Had Angus infected Serafina,
put something in her that drove her to unspeakable violence
three years after they met? Or was the explanation sadder and
smaller than that?

Serafina's life had been devastated, her mind traumatized beyond bearing, long before she'd ever crossed paths with Father
Angus Byrne. Maybe he hadn't done anything besides profoundly fail to help a child in desperate need. Maybe he was
just a charlatan, promising salvation but holding out only empty
hands. Maybe all these stories were the same as Serafina's: broken
people who came to Father Angus for healing and didn't find it.
Maybe, in the end, that was Adelaide's story, too.

Sure, Brigid thought, but *that* many people? What were
the chances of one man—even one who courted publicity—
crossing paths with so many future unrepentant killers? It would
be a hell of a coincidence.

*Oh, and the other possibility is so much more plausible? The one
where Angus is planting demon eggs in people's flesh, or maybe their
souls? That has the ring of truth to you?*

Brigid climbed into the car and slammed the door hard. The
argument raging back and forth in her head was making her
dizzy. Or maybe that was hunger.

She turned on the car, saw the low gas warning, and remembered that she had nowhere to go. It was unthinkable that she'd

drive all the way back to Bristlecone without her daughter, but she wasn't welcome at Angus's house, either.

What had she been thinking, bringing Dylan there? Handing her own daughter over to the man who had terrorized her childhood? Whatever was happening with Dylan—whatever Brigid thought she saw last night—it paled in the light of Adelaide's catalogue of atrocities. Either Angus was useless, or he was poison. Help Dylan? Had Angus ever helped anyone in a way that didn't eventually make their lives worse?

She'd been so sure about Serafina—so convinced that, in that one instance, Angus had been the hero. Her misguided trust in him echoed through the years, warping everything she'd ever believed about herself. No wonder she hadn't realized Adelaide was stalking her. She hadn't realized much of anything.

Brigid took out her phone and dialed Angus's house. She couldn't remember the last time she'd called—had she *ever* called, after she moved out of that place?—but the numbers still appeared at the end of her fingers by muscle memory, playing a ten-note song she'd know until her dying day.

Her uncle picked up after one ring, as if he'd been waiting by the phone. "Hello?"

"Let me talk to Dylan."

There was a long pause. Then Angus said, "Dylan was very clear that she doesn't want to talk to you." His voice was hard, none of the false sympathy he'd performed earlier. That probably meant Dylan wasn't in the room. Or—Brigid's mind unfurled worse scenarios, gory and irresistible.

"What did you do to her?" she snarled.

Angus's stony calm split enough for him to sound surprised. "Do to her? Brigid, I haven't done anything to your daughter.

She's been upstairs lying down for most of the afternoon. With her injuries, I'm sure you agree she needs rest."

"Put her on the phone," said Brigid. She heard the frayed edges in her own voice and didn't care enough to hide them. "I need to hear her voice or I will call the fucking cops on you."

Another pause, and a long sigh. "Let me see," Angus finally conceded. There was the clunk of him setting down the receiver, and then silence. Brigid tried to picture him walking through the house, to count out how long it would take—out of the kitchen and into the hall, up the stairs slowly, gripping the railing to take pressure off his aging knees. Then along the upstairs hall to Adelaide's old room. Was the door locked, or did Dylan leave it open to him? Would he knock, or just throw the door open, as he'd done to Brigid when she was young?

Too much time had gone by. Surely Angus must have made it to Dylan's room and back by now. Maybe something really had happened to her. Maybe her daughter was tied up like Serafina, her lips cracked and bleeding, her wrists bruised in the handcuffs. Brigid jittered her knees against the underside of the steering wheel. He wasn't coming back. She should just drive to the house. She could see the phone sitting off the hook on the kitchen counter, her own voice a tiny vibration, drowned out by the sound of Angus's prayers and Dylan's screaming—

"Mom?" Her daughter sounded groggy and irritated. Brigid sobbed with relief.

"Dylan. Baby. Are you okay?"

"I was sleeping," Dylan said, lisping the *s* with her wounded tongue.

"Okay. Okay. I'm so sorry," Brigid said. "I'm coming to get you and we're gonna go home."

"No," said Dylan sharply. "Don't come. I don't want you here."

Brigid could do nothing but breathe, and that just barely.

"Uncle Angus told me what you said about calling the cops," said her daughter. "If you do that, I'll tell them you're the one who cut my tongue. I bet if they take me away from you, Angus could get custody. Since he's my only other family."

"Dylan, please," Brigid gasped, the words scraping past the knife blade she felt at her throat. "I just need to know you're okay."

"I'm *fine*." Brigid could hear the familiar eye roll of exasperation. This was her daughter on the phone, not some malevolent stranger, and she couldn't decide whether that made it better or worse. "I just need you to leave me alone for a little while."

"For how long?" She hated the pleading in her voice. She was the adult here, she screamed at herself from some distant corner of her mind; she needed to put her foot down, take back control.

Except she had never had control. Not really. She was only mourning the loss of its illusion.

"I don't know," said Dylan. "I'm still really mad at you. And I want to get to know Uncle Angus without you hanging over my shoulder telling me he's evil. Maybe tomorrow, or a few days. I'll call you when I'm ready for you to come get me."

"What about . . ." Brigid didn't know how to finish the sentence. What about the other thing, the poison inside Dylan? What about whatever Adelaide had felt creeping under her skin, whatever Angus had done to all those people in the scrapbook?

"You brought me here so he could help me," Dylan said. "Maybe he can. If not, I'm no worse off."

Handcuffs, bruises, Tara Crick's children floating motionless in the bathtub—"You don't understand," Brigid said desperately.

"No, I don't," Dylan said, "because you never explained it. You never told me anything about him, and now you've missed your chance. I'm hanging up now, Mom. Don't call again."

"Wait!" The word came out as a scream. She was afraid it was too late, but then she heard Dylan breathing. The gratitude Brigid felt was pathetic, but she seized the opening anyway. "I need to hear from you every day. Just to make sure you're okay. Just . . . you can call me and say 'I'm fine' and hang up, that's it. And then I won't bother you. I promise."

Dylan considered that for long moments. Finally, she said, "Don't pick up. I'll call and leave a voicemail."

"Every day," Brigid reminded her.

"Yeah. Every day."

"I love you, Dylan."

But there was no one on the other end. Her daughter had hung up.

Chapter 22

When Zandy answered the phone, Brigid was still crying. Waiting until she stopped crying to call might have
meant waiting forever.

"I'll explain when I get there, but can I come to your house?"
she asked through sobs and sniffles. "I'm in Denver and I don't
have anywhere else to go." She knew explaining what she'd
done, where Dylan was now and why, would make Zandy angry,
but she didn't have the energy to worry about it. She certainly
didn't have the energy to come up with a convincing lie.

"Brigid?" Zandy asked, sounding startled.

"Yeah, it's me. Or the completely fucked-up version of me,
anyway."

Zandy made a sound that wasn't entirely convinced it was a
laugh. "Okay, bring the fucked-up version of you over here." She
recited an address, maybe a mile away. "Have you had dinner?"

Brigid's laugh was even less recognizable. "No. Breakfast or
lunch either."

"You haven't eaten since yesterday? Shit, is the hospital food really that bad?"

"I haven't been at the hospital," Brigid said. "It's . . ." She trailed off, not certain how to finish.

"Sounds like a long story," Zandy said carefully. "Don't try to tell it on an empty stomach. Can you find your way here?"

"I'm at Rocky Mountain Lake."

"Okay. Door's unlocked."

It occurred to Brigid, driving toward Zandy's house according to the decades-old map in her head, that she should be self-conscious. She and Zandy were on the precipice of dating, or they had been until that morning; showing up on the other woman's doorstep exhausted, unshowered, wearing the clothes she'd slept in, and on the verge of physical and mental collapse should be triggering all her deepest insecurities. Brigid added that to the long list of things she might get around to worrying about tomorrow.

Zandy's address was a 1950s ranch house of blond brick, ubiquitous in this neighborhood, with a small garden bed gone fallow for winter. True to her word, she'd left the door unlocked. Brigid entered hesitantly, and at the sound of the door, Zandy yelled, "In the kitchen!" Brigid followed her voice and the smell of garlic into a small, brightly lit kitchen, where Zandy stood at the stove. Emotions flashed across her face when she saw Brigid—shock, worry, maybe anger—but they were gone just as quickly, and Brigid felt her shoulders relax a little. She wasn't off the hook, she knew, but Zandy wasn't going to make her talk about it until after dinner.

"It's not as fancy as what you made last night, but it's what I could throw together," Zandy said. "Have a seat." Too exhausted to perform the role of gracious houseguest, Brigid obliged without argument. Zandy grabbed bowls and plates from the cabinet and served Brigid macaroni and cheese, along with a slice of garlic bread on grocery store sourdough and a glass of tap water. Brigid groaned as salt, fat, and warmth sank into her depleted system. The butter was real and the mac and cheese hadn't come from a box. She ate voraciously, in silence. Zandy took her cue from Brigid and ate without speaking, although more slowly. When Brigid's bowl was empty, Zandy rose without a word and filled it again.

Finally, Brigid sat back in her seat. Her stomach cramped from eating too fast after a day of emptiness. Her headache, if anything, was sharper without the hunger pangs to drown it out. Still, she felt the best she had in . . . hours, at least. Maybe since the night before.

"You're a fucking saint," she said.

Zandy nodded in agreement. "Am I allowed to ask now, or would you like to get drunk first?"

"Tempting," Brigid said. "But I think a hangover on top of everything else might actually kill me. You can go ahead."

"Okay." The careful, placid expression fell away from Zandy's face like a veil, revealing deep anxiety underneath. "Where's Dylan?"

Brigid told her.

She didn't tell her everything—the story looped and meandered, doubling back on itself and leaving things out, as disorganized as Brigid's mind—but whatever she left out, it wasn't for the sake of making herself look better. She skipped over Adelaide's notebook; that was her mother's secret, not hers. Telling Zandy about it would have been like inviting her to rifle through Adelaide's underwear drawer. But otherwise, Brigid was as honest as she could remember how to be.

She couldn't look at Zandy's face as she spoke. Instead, she stared at a piece of ice in her water glass. When Brigid began her story, it was a crescent the size of her thumb. By the time she was finished, it was barely a sliver.

"That's a lot to deal with," Zandy eventually said, when she was sure Brigid was done.

"I fucked up so bad," Brigid said, barely above a whisper. "I really thought he could help her. I was so desperate, and now she's there with him, and I don't know how to get her back."

"I'm so . . ." She heard Zandy's voice tremble and crack, and she realized that her grace period was over; Zandy was going to scream at her for being a fool and a liar, throw her out, tell her never to come back.

Brigid made herself raise her eyes. She saw that Zandy's were full of tears. "I'm so fucking sorry, Brigid."

Brigid's eyes widened. "You're sorry? You're not pissed at me?"

"Sure, I'm pissed," said Zandy with a shrug. "You lied to me, and you didn't let me help when I wanted to, and you definitely made some questionable judgment calls." Despite how mild it was compared to what Brigid had been thinking about herself, she felt a hot spike of anger at the criticism. How dare this bitch who didn't even have children tell her how to parent? Brigid swallowed the feeling down. She'd known Zandy would have words for her, she reminded herself. She could take it.

"But," Zandy went on, "I can be mad at you and still care about you. Still want to help you."

Spinning from anger to pathetic, desperate gratitude so quickly made Brigid's headache worse, but she didn't care. "Thank you," she said quietly. "Fuck, just . . . thank you."

Zandy got up and walked around the table toward Brigid, holding her hands before her, palms out, as though approaching an unfamiliar dog. "Is it okay if I hug you?"

Brigid burst out of her seat and threw herself into Zandy's arms. Zandy was quick to squeeze her tight, and Brigid clung to her like a drowner to a buoy. After the last few days, Brigid knew better than to think she was cried out—tears were an inexhaustible resource. For now, though, her eyes were dry, even as shudders like sobs shook her body until her teeth rattled together.

"I'm here," said Zandy. "I've got you." She didn't say "it's okay," and Brigid was grateful for that.

After a long time, her stomach aching from dry sobs, Brigid pulled back slightly. Her lips grazed Zandy's jaw, and she didn't even know whether she'd done it on purpose. Zandy tensed but didn't pull away. Brigid stayed where she was, no longer leaning into Zandy but still pressed close, her face in the crook of Zandy's neck. Zandy smelled good. Not fresh and cologned as she had the night before; now she smelled like home cooking and a hint of sweat, and mostly like good, human warmth. Brigid pushed her face deeper and inhaled, then touched her lips to Zandy's skin again, this time with intention.

"Brigid," Zandy said.

"Zandy." She turned her head just enough to speak the words directly into Zandy's pulse point, the tender skin below the hinge of her jaw. No, there was no cologne there, she was almost positive—but just to make sure, she flicked out the tip of her tongue to taste. No cologne, no bitter floral flavor, just salt and skin. Zandy's hands tightened on Brigid's shoulders, neither pushing in or pulling away. Brigid pressed her open lips to the spot as she licked over it again.

"You've had a really emotional day," said Zandy.

Brigid sobbed again, or laughed, or both. "Yeah."

"Sure this is a good idea?"

Now Brigid did pull back enough to look Zandy in the eyes. She enjoyed the angle at which she had to lift her chin to do so; it felt good to be smaller than Zandy in every possible dimension. It felt safe. Not because Zandy would keep Brigid safe, but because Zandy was safe *from* Brigid. She was big enough and strong enough that Brigid, fucked up as she was, couldn't possibly hurt her. Somewhere in the back of her mind, Brigid knew this conviction might not stand up to scrutiny, so she didn't subject it to any. She simply enjoyed it.

"I know my judgment has been shitty today, but this isn't the first time I've thought about fucking you," she said.

Zandy's eyes went wide, then soft. Her hands slid from Brigid's shoulders down to her waist. "Me either," she admitted. A faint smile flickered at the corners of her mouth, and she tucked Brigid's hair behind one ear. "Brigid Byrne. You've been under my skin for so long."

Brigid should have had a reply to that—something sweet, something romantic, something that let Zandy know the feeling was profoundly reciprocated—but instead she just kissed Zandy. It didn't feel at all like kissing her at thirteen, but at the same time, it felt like they were picking up exactly where they'd left off. They both had garlic breath and neither of them cared. Zandy's tongue was gentle against Brigid's, almost careful.

Brigid didn't want to go slow and careful. She didn't want time to *think*. She grabbed the back of Zandy's neck and dragged her deeper into the kiss. Zandy caught Brigid's energy and returned it with eviscerating focus, swallowing her gasps. This was what she wanted, the clash of tongue and teeth, sweat and heavy breathing, hands under clothes, fingernails and hidden skin. She wanted to be all body, no thought. To crash against Zandy like the sea against stones, shattered by her own violence, transformed into foam, carried away on the wind.

She wanted Zandy to be naked. By the time the thought was fully formed in her mind, she already had Zandy's T-shirt yanked up around her armpits and her fly half unzipped. "Hang on, hang on," Zandy said, taking charge and pulling the shirt over her own head. Above her gray sports bra, but hidden beneath the collar of her shirt, Zandy's chest was tattooed with a black-and-gray cacophony of wings, eyes, and intricately connected wheels—an angel after the biblical description. Beyond that, she was all soft skin where Brigid wanted to leave teeth marks.

"Let's—bedroom," Zandy said. Her face was irresistibly flushed, and Brigid felt warmth rising under her own skin in reply.

"Lead the way."

They broke like a wave over Zandy's bed. Brigid felt like she had something to prove, like every touch and kiss and moan was part of—not her penance, because she delighted in every second of it, but still an offering she was making in exchange for her lies and her mistakes. Zandy tried to meet her ferocity at first, but after a few minutes that almost felt like wrestling, she went soft, yielding. She let her body become the altar on which Brigid offered everything she had.

Zandy was receptive, but not passive; she urged Brigid on, first with words and then whimpers and finally with deep moans and sighs. She wanted more and Brigid gave her more, and more, until she had her hand inside Zandy up to the wrist. Brigid had never seen a woman get so wet. She licked the tang of Zandy from her own skin, right where they were joined, using her tongue to soothe where Zandy was stretched taut between pleasure and pain.

"Oh God, oh God, oh God," Zandy chanted as Brigid curled her fingers infinitesimally.

"Don't," Brigid whispered. "Please. Say my name."

Zandy sobbed and obeyed, and Brigid sucked hard on her clit, and then Zandy was coming. Brigid felt Zandy's orgasm from the inside, sweeping her up like tornado winds, and cried out as if she were coming, too.

Afterward, Brigid collapsed on the pillow, the storm within her exhausted at last, as Zandy sucked her to a gentle swell of an orgasm that went on and on like a sunset. Then she crawled up the length of Brigid's body and slipped an arm under her head, looped the other over her waist. It had been years—all the way back to Gwen—since Brigid had fallen asleep in bed with a lover. For a few hazy minutes she worried she'd lie awake all night, unable to relax into Zandy's warmth, the slow simple melody of her breathing. She was still worrying as she slipped into sleep.

When she woke, there was no disorientation. She knew where she was, even though thick, viscous darkness filled the room. The panic that struck her in the instant her eyes opened was for a different reason—one she couldn't immediately identify.

Then she did. Zandy wasn't breathing. The only sound in the room was Brigid's own gasps, shallow and too fast. And her hands—

She had woken from a dream. Not a nightmare, she remembered that clearly. It had been a *good* dream, intensely pleasurable, even sexual. Already it was dissolving like cotton candy, she could barely grasp its imagery, let alone its narrative, but she knew she had been *tearing*. Digging into . . . something soft, something her waking mind didn't want to name, with her teeth and fingernails. No, her claws. In the dream she had claws.

And in waking life, her hands were covered in something. Something beginning to cool, but still warm. Something sticky. Something wet.

"Zandy," Brigid whispered, as though afraid someone might overhear. "Zandy, are you awake?"

There was no answer. She'd known there would be no answer. She'd rolled over in the night, so she was right on the edge of the mattress, no longer skin-to-skin with Zandy. The space separating them could only be a few inches—the bed wasn't that big—but reaching her (wet, *unclean*) hand across the chasm felt like the work of an hour.

Finally Brigid's fingertips brushed skin. Zandy's arm, she thought, the skin dry and warm—though not as warm as it had been earlier. The heat of her dissipated into the air. How could Zandy be so cool when Brigid was sweating, soaked?

She prodded gently, but Zandy didn't make a sound. Brigid shook her harder, wincing at the thought of the—*whatever* it was—smearing from her hands onto Zandy's clean skin. Still no response. Brigid moved her hand to Zandy's chest, telling herself she was just trying to wake her, telling herself she wasn't searching for a pulse.

Warm. Warmer than skin. Warm and wet and sticky, all over Zandy's unmoving chest. Brigid sucked in her breath but otherwise made no sound. The slippery, clotting, unnameable *some-*

thing must have spilled all over Zandy's beautiful angel tattoo, and that thought made Brigid's guts twist. How had Zandy slept through—whatever this was?

Her hand moved higher, through the substance (she didn't know what it was, *she didn't know*) painted over Zandy's chest. Her hand moved up to Zandy's neck.

Into her neck.

Into the gaping absence where a chunk of flesh should have been. Stumbled into it like hitting an unseen pothole, and the same jolt ran through her body, startling her bones. It was warmer there—inside. Brigid curled her fingers and felt strange ridges, torn edges, layers of soft and tender matter never meant to be touched.

"Zandy," she whispered again, though she wanted to scream. She licked her lips. They tasted like blood.

Blood. The word had crept up on her, evaded her defenses, and now it was here, between her fingers, coating Zandy's chest, streaming from the wound in her throat, staining her sheets. As soon as she named it, she could *smell* it, metal tang filling the air. Zandy was *bleeding*—but even as the realization struck, it corrected itself. Zandy had *bled*. The blood under Brigid's hands was no longer flowing. It was pooling, seeping, beginning to dry. Zandy wasn't bleeding, for the same reason an empty cup could no longer be described as spilling.

Zandy wasn't breathing, because her last breath had slipped out through the hole in her throat.

Brigid pulled her fingers out of Zandy's neck very carefully, trying not to brush the edges of the wound. She wiped her hand on the sheets. Then, slowly, as quietly as possible, she pushed herself up to sitting and swung her legs over the edge of the bed.

Her eyes had yet to adjust to the darkness; she crept, unseeing, through a featureless abyss of black, in what she hoped was the direction of the door.

Blood on her hands. Blood on her lips. Her tongue searched the back of her teeth, found a tough, gristly tendril. Brigid swallowed and wished she hadn't.

Your sins, Brigid.

In her dream, she had felt so good.

Finally, she touched a wall. She bit back a gasp of relief and flattened her palm against the cool, slightly rough surface. A wall would lead, eventually, to a door. Brigid reached out to both sides, searching for a frame, a knob. Instead, she found a light switch. Her questing hand pushed it up before her mind processed what she was touching.

Brigid couldn't stifle her scream as yellow light flooded her eyes. She whirled around, back flat against the wall, terrified to face what the light would reveal.

"Wha . . . fuck?"

Zandy struggled to sit up in bed, one arm flung over her eyes to block out the sudden, harsh brightness. "Bridge?" Her voice was sludgy with sleep, but otherwise normal, moving easily through her whole, unbroken throat. The angel stared with all its eyes from her chest, no scrim of blood to cloud its vision. The sheets were as clean as recently fucked-on sheets could be.

Brigid screamed again, not as loud, just a high breathy rasp of air.

"Brigid, what happened?" Zandy said more clearly, her eyes focusing. "Are you okay? Is it Dylan?"

Summoning all her courage, Brigid looked down at her hands. They were trembling, but clean.

Zandy started to get out of bed. Brigid shook her head hard, as though trying to clear away a circling cloud of gnats. "No, I'm sorry, it's nothing. Just a nightmare. I'm so sorry." She looked around—oh, there was the door—and found the light switch again. She clicked the room back into darkness. It was normal darkness now, full of faint shapes and shadows, not the depthless black of empty space. In it, she heard Zandy sigh, then settle back into her pillow.

"Are you sure?" Zandy asked, but Brigid could hear that she was already halfway back to sleep.

"I'm so sorry," Brigid whispered again. She stood there, naked against the wall, for a long time before she finally left the room.

Chapter 23

"Brigid! I found her! She's on the phone."

Waking up the second time was harder and much more confusing. After leaving Zandy's bedroom, Brigid had curled up on the living room couch, still naked, licking her lips frantically to convince herself she didn't taste blood. She hadn't expected to fall back asleep, nor realized when she did.

Now, her neck hurt and her eyelids felt sticky as she tried to understand why Zandy was at such a strange angle. When Brigid managed to unbend her neck and sit up, Zandy assumed a more familiar vertical orientation. She was still, inexplicably, holding a phone in Brigid's face.

". . . Dylan?"

Zandy sucked in air. "Shit, no, I'm sorry, I didn't mean to make you—no, it's that girl, you were telling me about her. I thought if I could track her down, she could tell people what he did. I don't know about the statute of limitations, but if she wanted to press charges—"

Brigid realized there was a blanket in her lap, one that hadn't been there when she fell asleep. It was dawning on her that Zandy had been awake for quite some time. Zandy was also wearing sweatpants and a tank top, while Brigid was still naked. Flushing, she pulled the blanket up to her armpits. "Who's on the phone?"

"Serafina," Zandy said. "Serafina Santoro." She began to say something else, about how she'd tracked down the phone number for the inpatient program, but Brigid didn't process the words. She grabbed the phone, suddenly terrified Serafina had hung up while she was still struggling her way out of sleep.

"Hello?"

"This is Serafina," said the voice on the other end. It was soft, high-pitched, a little hoarse, as if not often used. It didn't sound at all like the Serafina from thirty years ago, confident and sonorous, as if resonating from the depths of the underworld. Or was that the embellishment of Brigid's memory?

"Hello," Brigid said again, stuck in a groove somewhere between past and present, forgetting how to move forward.

"Can I help you with something?" Serafina, the new Serafina, didn't sound impatient or perturbed. She sounded utterly placid, as if she would calmly wait as long as it took for Brigid to compose herself.

"I'm not sure," Brigid confessed. "I'm sorry, this is strange. What did Zandy say to you?"

"She didn't say her name was Zandy. She said that someone I used to know was trying to get in touch with me. She didn't tell me your name, either." The tranquility in her voice was beginning to disturb Brigid, to shade from unfamiliar into eerie. Serafina's tone didn't change when she said, "If you're a reporter, I'm not interested in speaking with you. I've said everything I need to say about my parents."

"I'm not a reporter," Brigid said quickly. A mug of coffee appeared in front of her, and she glanced up to see Zandy retreating to the kitchen. Some part of Brigid's mind that was still waking up enjoyed the way Zandy's ass moved in her sweatpants. "I'm, um, I don't know if this will mean anything to you, but I'm Angus Byrne's niece?"

If she'd thought this revelation would ripple the surface of Serafina's calm, she was disappointed. "Oh, yes," said Serafina. "The priest. I remember him. I think I remember you, too. You lived in that house, right?"

"Yes," said Brigid. Zandy set a cardboard carton of half-and-half on the coffee table, and Brigid poured it liberally into her mug. There was so much she wanted to say, to ask, but the only words she could find were "I'm so sorry."

"You're sorry you lived there?" There was no mocking in Serafina's voice, merely the desire for clarification.

"I'm sorry I didn't help you," Brigid said. "I saw what he was doing to you, but I didn't understand. I thought . . ." Shame burned in her face, down her bare chest under Zandy's blanket. "It's so stupid, but I believed him. He said you were possessed by a demon and he was exorcising you, and I believed him. I let it happen."

"Oh," said Serafina. "No, I wasn't possessed. I was pregnant."

Brigid didn't flinch. She did the opposite: her whole body went perfectly still. Even her pulse seemed to slow, giving her space to process the words.

"You were pregnant?" she finally repeated, although she knew she hadn't heard wrong.

"By my father," Serafina went on. Her voice was still even, as though describing a movie she'd seen a long time ago. "He said I must have been whoring around. My mother pretended to believe him. They wanted me to get an abortion, but I refused. I don't know which of them came up with the explanation that I was possessed. My father was the one who tracked down that priest from the TV show. Your uncle, I mean."

"Did he—Angus," Brigid said. "Did he know?"

"I don't know what my parents told him. I told him several times, about the pregnancy and about my father. He said it was the devil using me to lie." The lack of anger or grief in her voice made Brigid feel dizzy.

"What happened to the baby?" Brigid asked.

"Oh," Serafina said, and now she did sound faintly sad—the distant sorrow of someone who must break bad news. "There was no baby. I had a miscarriage."

Blood on the mattress. Brigid remembered now. Her fingers were cold. She finally took a sip of the coffee Zandy had made. It was perfect.

"It might have happened either way," said Serafina in that same neutral voice. "There's a lot of scar tissue inside me from what my father did. But I've always thought it had to do with all those days being tied up, not eating. I think it was your uncle's fault I lost my pregnancy. And I'll never be able to have another."

Brigid remembered seeing the body of the young girl—the girl she was still struggling to connect to the mellow, placid voice on the phone—tense and shudder in her bonds, then collapse. She'd been so sure she had witnessed the casting out of a demon, the exact moment when Serafina was left alone in her body. What had the girl said, all those years ago? *She's mine,* Serafina had told Father Angus. Brigid had thought it was the demon speaking.

"I'm so sorry," Brigid said again. She was crying, hot and quiet and slow. Zandy came back and stood in the doorway. Tentative, afraid to ask but feeling somehow that she must, Brigid said, "Was your baby a girl?"

"I never had an ultrasound, so I couldn't say for sure," said Serafina. "I don't even know how far along I was. But I thought she would have been a girl. I felt it."

"I have a daughter," Brigid said. It felt like a confession. Like another reason she should apologize. How dare she have a daughter, a living breathing angry complicated beautiful perfect girl, when she'd watched Serafina bleed hers out onto a bare mattress in a stranger's house?

"Oh" was all Serafina said. She didn't ask any questions. Maybe she couldn't bear to—maybe it was too painful to hear about someone else's child. Brigid went on anyway.

"I'm scared for her," she said. Absently, she noticed Zandy finally stepping through the doorway and coming to sit on the couch beside her. "I'm afraid my uncle is going to hurt her."

"Did he hurt you?" Serafina asked.

"Not like that," Brigid said quickly. "Not like—what happened to you."

Serafina hummed. "That's good," she said. "I remember thinking he might be, back then. You seemed so scared. But maybe I was just projecting." There was no accusation in her voice, no lingering sorrow or anger, but Brigid still felt condemned. Serafina had been so completely alone, and Brigid had done nothing to help her.

"The crazy thing is, I brought her to see him because of you." Brigid laughed, high and humorless. Serafina didn't. "Because I thought he had cast a demon out of you, and I wanted him to do the same for her."

"Oh, no," said Serafina, the way she might have corrected someone who slightly misspelled her name. "I wasn't possessed until after my parents brought me to Angus."

"Excuse me?"

"I wasn't possessed then," Serafina repeated, her infinitely patient tone unchanging. "He didn't exorcise me. It was only after the miscarriage that I got possessed by a demon."

"What?" Brigid sounded like she'd had the wind knocked out of her, and maybe she had. "You . . . how?"

"I can't explain how," said Serafina. "I've thought about it a lot. Maybe the miscarriage created a vacuum inside me, and the demon was drawn into that emptiness. But it's also possible that it was in there all along and I didn't become aware of it until after I lost the pregnancy."

"What do you mean you were possessed?" Brigid asked. Beside her on the couch, she felt Zandy stiffen. "I mean, how did you know?"

"I could feel it," Serafina said. Was it Brigid's imagination—trying to read emotion into a voice so totally neutral, like searching for shapes in clouds—or did she now sound almost wistful? Almost as though, whatever had happened to her or whatever she'd imagined, she wanted it back? "It was inside me. I could feel it growing under my skin. Not like being pregnant—this was different." She paused, reflective, then added, "I used to think I felt like a beehive. Like there was something moving around inside me, and it was so alive."

"How do you know it was a demon?" Brigid asked. She thought of Adelaide's notebook, all her cramped, hasty notes about things crawling over her bones. It must be a common delusion, she told herself. Like those people who thought they had threads in their skin.

"I don't, really," said Serafina. "I just called it that because it was evil. Or it was drawn to the evil in me. It was a sort of symbiotic relationship. It ate all my bad feelings—all my shame and sorrow and self-hate. I used to blame myself. It's very common with children who are abused like I was. That's what the demon fed on. I used to think it loved me, because I fed it so well, but maybe it couldn't. Maybe it was just drawn to food by instinct. Do you think bees love flowers?" She didn't sound like she really expected an answer, but she still paused for a few seconds, as though Brigid might want to offer one anyway. Brigid had nothing to say.

"Anyway, one day it had finally eaten up all the shame in me, and then it was gone," Serafina concluded.

Brigid had a horrible feeling she knew what day that was. She suspected, if she searched through Adelaide's notebook, she could find the exact date. "Did . . ." She cleared her throat, suddenly embarrassed to be asking this in front of Zandy, but she made herself speak the words anyway. "Did your demon kill your parents?"

"No," said Serafina quickly. "Well, not exactly. It was something I'd wanted to do for a long time—years before I met your uncle. It was what I needed, to be free of them. My demon helped me see that. And after I did it . . ."

Brigid was afraid to ask, but she needed to know. "You felt better?"

"There was one moment when I felt the worst in my whole life," said Serafina. "All the guilt and regret and disgust hit me at once, and I hated myself so much I thought I might die, and then it was just gone. And the demon was gone, too."

"Oh," said Brigid. Zandy was staring at her, waiting for an explanation, but she held up a finger: *just a minute.*

"I never told anyone," said Serafina. "Everyone thinks I'm crazy, and they wouldn't believe me. And it doesn't matter, anyway. I don't want to make excuses. I'm not ashamed of what I did." From anyone else, that claim would have sounded defensive if not outright false, but from Serafina, Brigid believed it entirely. "If I explained, it would sound like I was trying to blame someone else for their deaths. I don't want to do that. I want people to know it was me."

"Why are you telling me, then?" Brigid asked.

There was a long pause. "I guess because I hope your daughter will be all right," Serafina said eventually. "And because I think you might believe me."

Brigid was crying again, or still crying. "Thank you," she said.

"It was nice to talk to you," said Serafina, which was impossible, yet she obviously meant it.

"Wait," said Brigid. "Did you ever do anything strange, while you were possessed?"

"You mean besides killing my parents?" said Serafina, and for the first time it occurred to Brigid that this woman might have a sense of humor.

"She floated," Brigid said helplessly. She refused to look at Zandy, refused to see what her face was doing in response to this preposterous claim they both knew was true, but she also couldn't help looking at Zandy, so she closed her eyes. "My daughter. She rose up off the floor, she levitated. It was—very strange." Zandy exhaled hard, the way someone does when they are not quite laughing. "And then her tongue split in half."

"Oh," said Serafina."

"Strange like that," Brigid said. She was pleading, she heard it in her voice, and it was the same plea Serafina had made to her thirty years ago, the one that had frightened her so much because she couldn't understand it: please, please tell me I am not going through this terrible thing alone.

"I didn't float," said Serafina, and Brigid's heart sank. "I threw up teeth, though."

"Teeth?"

"Baby teeth," said Serafina. "I threw them up. A perfect set, all twenty of them. I picked them out of the toilet and kept them in my jewelry box. They were my daughter's."

It could have been a lie, of course, or a hallucination. There was no way Serafina could produce those teeth now, or prove they'd ever existed. And yet Brigid believed her. She could see the teeth, jagged little pearls, sinking to the bottom of the toilet bowl. They were as real as the stitches in Dylan's tongue.

Brigid ended the conversation, offering rote pleasantries that Serafina didn't return, and hung up the phone. She could feel Zandy's presence like a huge, humming question mark beside her, desperate for an explanation, but Brigid sat in silence for a long time. She needed to get things straight in her own mind before she said them out loud.

Brigid thought about Serafina and Dylan and Adelaide and Tara Crick. She thought about things crawling under skin, and about children floating in a bathtub. About her mother making notes in secret, and Angus performing exorcisms on live TV. She thought about Dylan's jewel wasps.

It was simple and ugly and obvious, if you ignored the fact

that it was impossible.

"It eats its way out," she said quietly. Zandy was looking at her, but Brigid couldn't make herself look back or she'd lose the nerve to articulate her discovery. "It gets inside of people and it feeds on all their darkest thoughts, and it grows there, like some kind of larva. And it makes them do something terrible—so it can feed on that, too."

She expected Zandy to tell her she was being ridiculous, but Zandy only said, "What does?"

"I don't know," Brigid admitted. "But it has to do with Angus. I think he's . . . putting it in people, somehow. Infecting them."

"With a demon." Zandy tried to keep her voice neutral, but unlike Serafina, it cost her audible effort. Brigid ignored this.

"I don't know what to call it. I don't think it has a name. Serafina called it a demon. She says it ate the evil inside her. All her bad feelings about her horrible childhood, everything her father did to her. She . . ." Brigid swallowed hard. "It sounded like she was grateful to it."

"Jesus," Zandy muttered. "So you're saying, instead of exorcising people, he's actually the one possessing them?" Brigid started to respond, but Zandy cut her off. "How does that explain Dylan, then? Because she was acting weird before yesterday, but you said she hadn't met him until last night."

"I don't know. I don't know." Brigid's body felt electric, lit up with crackling energy, and at the same time queasy with terror. "Maybe he can do it from a distance? Maybe . . . shit, maybe he's been in touch with her already," she realized. "How hard would it be for him to find her, if he went looking for me?" Not hard at all, she knew from Adelaide's journal. Maybe Angus and Dylan had been talking in secret for months, Angus patiently plying the girl with the promise of connecting to the family she'd always wanted, all the time waiting for his opening.

She remembered Dylan saying, *Tell the old man.* She'd thought it was evidence of the demon inside her daughter, the same one that had claimed Serafina—but she'd been horribly wrong about Serafina. Maybe, all along, she and her daughter had been pawns. Maybe Angus had been calling the shots this whole time.

And she'd delivered her daughter, her Dylan, right to his door.

"I have to get her out of there." Brigid lurched to her feet, not caring that the blanket fell away and left her naked. "I have to get her—"

She flinched when she felt Zandy's hand on her arm. "I know, Brigid, but we need a plan, okay? You can't just run over there because you're freaking out." She didn't say, "That's how you got into this mess in the first place, you idiot," but Brigid could feel the implication. She thought about picking up the half-full coffee mug and slamming it right into Zandy's face. Instead, she turned away, covering her hot face with her hands and trying to slow her breathing.

She didn't want to hurt Zandy, she told herself. None of this was Zandy's fault. No. The person she needed to hurt was Angus.

"You can't just show up and drag her out of the house," Zandy was saying. "Dylan threatened to call the cops on you, and we have to assume she's serious. How can we get her out of there without making her panic?"

Heat flared in Brigid's chest. She felt it like it was happening again, Dylan throwing her out, Dylan choosing Angus over her. Dylan didn't understand—she had no idea how hard Brigid had worked to keep her safe, to protect her from the poison in their bloodline. Brigid needed to make her understand. But first, she needed to get her back.

Brigid was alive with swarming energy, buzzing from the inside. Zandy was still talking but Brigid couldn't focus on her words. Something about strategy, about being careful, planning their next move.

They didn't have time for that. The knowledge writhed under her skin. She looked down at her arms, her hands, almost expecting to see something bursting out. It was all Angus, had always been Angus, and he had set her up. He had tricked Dylan somehow, fooled her into thinking he was her savior. She was brainwashed. The longer Dylan was near Angus, the deeper the poison would sink. They didn't have time for elaborate schemes. Brigid had to get her daughter *out*. If that meant kicking down the door and dragging Dylan out by her hair, honestly, that sounded pretty good. At least it would give her something to do with her useless trembling fucking *hands*.

"Brigid, did you hear me?" Zandy said. "I think we should call—"

"I need to go," Brigid interrupted. "Where are my clothes?"

She found them on the floor of Zandy's bedroom and dressed in a hurry, briefly putting on her bra backward before she realized and fixed it. The whole interminable time, Zandy *kept* talking. Finally Brigid turned to her and held up a hand.

"I'm going back to my uncle's house and getting my daughter," she said. "Do you want to come with me or are you staying here?"

Zandy's face fell. "It feels like you're not listening to anything I'm saying," she said.

Fuck, *this* was why Brigid hadn't dated anyone in so long. Fucking lesbians always wanting to talk about their feelings.

"No, you're right, I'm really not," she said. "I don't have time. I have to get Dylan."

Zandy put out a hand to touch the one Brigid still held up before her, gently lacing their fingers together. "I know. I know you're so worried about her. I am, too, but if you just show up and bang on the door, she's not going to—"

In her pocket, Brigid's phone rang. She yanked her hand free of Zandy's and grabbed it. The caller ID said DYLAN and although Brigid vaguely remembered that her daughter had said to let it go to voicemail, she hit ACCEPT before the second ring was finished.

"Dylan? Honey? Are you okay?"

There was a pause, then a sniffle. Everything in Brigid constricted: her heart, her stomach, even her bones. "Mom?"

"Baby." Her legs gave out; she sank to her knees on Zandy's bedroom floor. "What's wrong? What happened?"

"Can you come pick me up?" said Dylan. There was no mistaking the tears choking her voice. "Uncle Angus . . ." She tried to whisper, to swallow the sounds of her hiccups and sobs. "He's really weird, Mom. He's freaking me out."

The study. Christ looking down from the wall in agony. Red marks of the carpet fibers on her knees. "What did he do?"

"I'll tell you later, but can you please come get me now?"

"Of course. Of course, sweetheart, just come out front and I'll—"

"No, I'm in my bedroom. He was . . . I'm scared to come out."

Brigid bit down hard on her bottom lip to keep a scream of rage from escaping. With the hand that wasn't holding her phone, she slammed her fist down on her thigh. *Fucking* Angus.

She'd make him pay for whatever he'd done to her daughter. What Serafina did to her parents would seem like a trip to Disneyland after Brigid was finished with Angus Byrne.

All she said was "Okay, baby. I'll come inside and get you. I'll make sure it's safe."

Dylan sniffled again. "Just hurry, Mom."

"I love you, baby," said Brigid, but once again, Dylan had already hung up.

She stood up to find Zandy standing too close, again—and this time she was between Brigid and the door. "What's going on?" she asked.

"It was Dylan. She's scared, she's crying, she needs me to come get her."

Instead of stepping aside, Zandy frowned and stayed where she was. "Did she say anything else? It seems a little—"

"Zandy, get out of my way," Brigid said very quietly.

Zandy's voice got louder as Brigid's got quieter. "What do you think Angus is going to do if you burst into his house with your guns blazing? I just want you to stop and think about this, Brigid, just for one second!"

Brigid was out of words. She grabbed Zandy by the shoulders and pushed hard. Zandy had easily three inches and fifty pounds on Brigid, but she was taken by surprise—and Brigid was running on terror and rage. Zandy lost her balance, stumbled backward, and might have gone down if she hadn't slammed into the doorframe with one shoulder. She yelped with pain. Brigid felt her lip curl in a snarl of satisfaction.

"Brigid," said Zandy. There were tears in her big golden-brown eyes, and she was flushed from her cheeks down to her neck. Brigid was struck all over again by how beautiful she was, but it didn't matter. She walked past Zandy, out of the room, out of the house.

Chapter 24

A midst everything that happened the day before, Brigid had never stopped to fill up her gas tank. She didn't notice the warning light flashing until her car sputtered to a stop, a little over a block from Angus's house.

"Fuck," she muttered. She wrenched the steering wheel to the right so the car would coast into the parking lane before it gave up altogether. It made it most of the way, though the back left wheel was still sticking out dangerously into traffic. "Fuck, fuck, *fuck!*" She punched her steering wheel with both hands and screamed so loud it hurt her throat.

But she couldn't sit there sobbing in her useless car while her daughter was waiting for her help. Brigid jumped out and ran. She realized after only a few strides that she'd left everything behind—her purse on the passenger seat, her keys in the ignition—but she didn't turn around. None of it mattered. It didn't matter that she hadn't tied her shoes before she left Zandy's house, that the laces slapped frantically at the pavement as she pounded down the sidewalk. It didn't matter that a driver honked at her and yelled "fucking crackhead" out the window when she lurched into the street without looking. Nothing mattered except getting to Dylan.

By the time she stumbled up Angus's front steps, she was gasping for breath, partly from exertion and partly because she'd started crying again. She took a moment to wipe tears from her face before trying the doorknob. Unsurprisingly, it was locked. Brigid didn't bother with the doorbell; Angus would either ignore it or turn her away.

She hadn't had a spare key to this house in years—Adelaide had slipped one into her suitcase before she left home, but when Brigid found it she dropped it in the trash. She would have cursed herself for that now if she had the energy to spare.

But there was another option—dim, buried in the recesses of her brain. She circled the house, entering the backyard through the gate that was never locked. The key to the back door was, as she'd hoped, still under the flowerpot with the fake poinsettia, though both the pot and the plastic flower were grimier than she remembered.

Through the glass panes of the door, Brigid peered into the kitchen. She didn't see Angus, but if he was nearby—in the hall, or in his study—there was a good chance he'd hear the door. She unlocked and opened it as silently as possible. There was no sound from elsewhere in the house, no footsteps moving her way. Was it possible Angus wasn't even here, that he had gone out on some errand? Brigid hoped, but knew better than to count on it.

Brigid slipped her shoes off—it was actually a good thing she'd never tied them, it was foresight—and held them dangling by the laces as she crept through the house in sock feet. There was no sign of Angus in the hall or the living room. The door to his study was closed, but Brigid thought the room seemed empty. There was none of that ineffable sense that someone was inside, breathing.

At the bottom of the stairs, she stopped to listen again. Her heart banged furiously in her chest. The door to Angus's room was the first one in the upstairs hallway. It was closed, but unlike the study door it seemed closed with intention. Brigid felt instinctively that Angus was behind that door, and if she went up the stairs, he would hear her.

You're being ridiculous, she scolded herself. What did it matter if Angus knew she was here? Dylan wanted to leave, so there was nothing he could legally do. Brigid knew better than anyone how frightening Angus could be to a child, but he was an old man with no power over either of them. *He can't do anything*, she reassured herself. *We can just leave.*

But she couldn't quite convince herself to say it out loud.

As silently as possible, Brigid crept up the stairs. She held her breath as she placed one foot on the carpet directly in front of Angus's bedroom door. She more than half expected the door to fly open at any moment, for her uncle to stand there, backlit and terrible, trapping her in his shadow.

Beneath her weight, the floorboard let out a tiny creak, barely more than a sigh.

"Who's there?" came Angus's voice from behind the closed door. It wasn't the thundering demand Brigid feared, but a tremulous whisper. He almost sounded afraid.

Confusion froze her in her footsteps. "Brigid, is that you?" Angus hissed the words as though he was afraid to speak any louder. Brigid's voice felt frozen, too, cowering in her throat, terrified to move.

"Who's out there?" demanded Angus again, louder this time, attempting bravado. "I will not fear the terror of the night, nor the arrow—"

"Be quiet, it's just me," Brigid tried to whisper. As soon as she heard her own voice disturbing the thick silence of the hallway, it was like a crack in ice she hadn't realized was holding her weight. The damage was done.

Her daughter's voice responded instantly, loud and clear. "Mom! Mommy, help me!"

Brigid forgot all about her confusion and Angus's fear. She lurched forward, past the bathroom and toward the other end of the hall. Adelaide's door—no, it was Dylan's door—stood open, and that was strange, wasn't it? Because Dylan had said she was hiding in there, too afraid of Angus to make her way downstairs. But that didn't matter as Brigid nearly flew through the open door, then stumbled to a stop again.

Dylan lay in a heap on the floor. Her arms were twisted over her head as if in self-defense, and the first thing Brigid saw was her hands. They were half curled into fists, but several of her fingers stuck out at odd angles, crooked and red and swelling. Bruises ringed Dylan's wrists. The fingernails Brigid could see were cracked, some bent back or ripped away entirely. Dark blood oozed from the damaged nail beds, dripping into Dylan's hair, onto her forehead. A small but spreading pool looked almost black against the soft gray carpet.

Brigid was on her knees beside her daughter before she knew she had moved. She grabbed Dylan—more roughly than she should—and dragged her into her lap, cradling Dylan's head.

Dylan stared up at her through eyes that seemed to be having trouble focusing. One side of her face was red and purple, swelling out of shape. Her pupils were different sizes. Her lip was split and bleeding; another cut spilled blood from her left eyebrow down the side of her face. She breathed heavily, and it sounded like it hurt.

"Baby, baby, sweet girl, are you okay?"

"Mom," whispered Dylan. "Is he still here?"

Flames licked scarlet up Brigid's throat. Her mind had gone blank for a moment, but now she was swept up in the flow of linear time again. Dylan was hurt—Dylan had been hurt—someone had hurt Dylan. And of course, that someone was Angus.

She'd kill him. It wasn't a decision she made so much as an outcome she now saw was inevitable. It hardly had anything to do with her at all; she was merely the vessel through which fate would flow. Looking at her daughter's beautiful, injured face, Brigid understood for the first time how much violence she was truly capable of. She would suck Angus's eyes from their sockets. She'd flay him with her fingernails and teeth.

Dylan coughed, then cried out in pain as the motion disturbed some wound Brigid couldn't see. Tears swam in Brigid's own eyes in response. "Okay, love, you're going to be okay. I'm just going to—" Her phone wasn't in her pocket. She reached for her purse before realizing that was gone, too. With rising dismay, she remembered running from the car, leaving everything lying on the passenger seat.

No time to panic. She swallowed it down. "Baby, where's your phone? I need to call an ambulance."

"He—" Another pained, wheezing breath. "Heard me. Took

it." Brigid remembered her daughter's quick, hushed goodbye, and realized it must have been the phone call to her that drove Angus to this extreme. Shame swelled in Brigid's throat, choking her. This was her fault, all of it. He wouldn't have touched Dylan if Dylan hadn't called her. He couldn't have touched Dylan if Brigid hadn't brought her here.

No time. No time for regret. She would make it up to Dylan when she could write her apology in Angus's blood. In this moment, she had to get her daughter help.

"I'm going to go downstairs and make the call," Brigid said, keeping her voice steady despite her tears. "I'll be right back, okay? I promise. Can you get up and lock the door behind me?" Dylan shook her head, whimpering with pain from the movement. "Okay. That's okay. I'll just close it. He won't come back." She hoped it was true, hoped Angus at least had the sense not to touch Dylan again while Brigid was in the house. Her heart beat so hard her chest hurt. "And I'll be right back, baby. I'll stay with you until help gets here."

Dylan shook her head again, licked her swelling lips as though in prelude to speech, but Brigid couldn't stay still long enough to hear what she would say. She lifted Dylan's head and shoulders and slid out from underneath, then lowered her daughter back to the floor as gently as possible, hating herself when Dylan winced anyway.

The room pitched around her as she got to her feet, and she felt the same rush of vertigo she had the day before, the sense that the room was suddenly larger than it should be, the door too far away. Which door? For a moment, there were two of them.

Brigid shuddered as a wave of nausea rolled over her. She

took a step toward the two identical doors, and as her foot hit carpet, the double vision resolved, the vertigo receded, and the room looked the way it was supposed to.

Behind her, as she closed the bedroom door, she could still hear Dylan trying to speak.

The hallway yawned in front of Brigid, looking longer than it had in years. It reminded her of being a child, so small, trying to get up the nerve to cross this dark chasm in the middle of the night. She was prepared to throw herself at Angus like a rabid dog if he got in her way—her fists were clenched in anticipation, so tight she could feel her knuckles turning white—but he was gone, the door standing open on his now-empty bedroom. Maybe he'd realized it was in his best interest not to let Brigid get her hands on him. She didn't know; it didn't matter. She *would* find him, and he would hurt for it, but right now the important thing was getting help for Dylan.

Brigid raced down the stairs, her feet thundering, like she'd never dared to do as a child. She almost hit the wall coming around the tight curve at the bottom of the steps. Something in the front hallway tugged at her attention—out of place, wrong, not how she remembered it—but she pushed it aside. Nothing mattered but getting to the kitchen, to the phone, getting Dylan help.

The cordless phone was on the counter by the stove, exactly as Brigid remembered from her childhood, the same off-white plastic. When the receiver almost slipped from her grasp, she realized her hands were sweating.

How long had it been since she'd made a call on a landline? The dial tone sounded foreign, strange and scratchy. Brigid dialed 911.

There was no ring on the other end. Just that same long, low, slightly distorted dial tone.

Brigid lowered the phone, stared at it in her hand as if waiting for it to explain itself. It didn't. She held it to her ear again. Dial tone. Deep breath. She punched in the familiar number and waited for the ring, but it didn't come. Just the endless, grating drone.

"Fuck. What the fuck." Brigid was breathless again, gripping the receiver until her knuckles ached. The phone wasn't disconnected—she could still hear that dial tone, a horrible sound, had it always been this ugly? Like the edge in Dylan's voice when she whined as a child, that high-pitched grating noise that Brigid felt in her teeth. She punched in the number again, knowing it was useless, but still, when she heard the unbroken dial tone again, she slammed her fist down on the counter and screamed.

"Mom?" Brigid jolted at the voice—not coming from upstairs, but from the phone. It was faint, almost drowned out by the awful dial tone, but it was definitely there.

"Dylan? Dylan, is that you, sweetie? Are you okay?"

"Ma'am?" said the voice again. Not *Mom*, but *Ma'am*. She felt foolish at having misheard, though the voice was still so quiet, buried in that hellish whine, almost inaudible.

"Hello," said Brigid. "Is someone there?" Nothing now, beyond that droning sound—but it couldn't be the dial tone, because there was someone on the other end of the call. Maybe there was something wrong with Angus's phone? It was plausible; the thing was at least thirty years old. A loose wire rattling somewhere inside could explain the buzzing noise, which seemed to slide around the more she listened to it, up and down the scale, louder and softer—not like a dial tone at all.

Brigid hoped the sound was just in her own ear, that the operator could hear her better than she could hear them. Still, she shouted into the phone with all her strength. "I need an ambulance! My daughter is hurt!"

"Ma'am." She could barely hear the voice through the static, the roar, whatever it was. She pressed the receiver into her ear so hard it hurt, and she thought she heard the distant operator say, "Are you sure?"

"Please." Brigid's voice came out breathless and weak. She tried again, summoning the strength to shout. "Please send help. My uncle attacked her—"

"Are you sure?" said the operator. Their voice was clearer now, even through the grinding, drilling white noise. It sounded like a woman's voice, high and musical. "Are you really, really sure?" Not just musical; teasing.

"What?" Brigid asked. The hum got even louder. How had she ever thought that was the dial tone? It was horrible. It hurt her ears and made her skin crawl. She could barely focus on what the operator had said.

"Mom," said the voice from the phone. Brigid's heart dropped. She'd been right the first time. It had been *Mom*, not *Ma'am*, all along. "Are you sure Uncle Angus hurt me?" Dylan sounded like she might burst into laughter at any moment.

"Baby, are you okay? Are you still upstairs?"

The drone was unbearably loud, as though some horrible machinery were grinding directly against Brigid's eardrum. "Are you sure it was Uncle Angus?" Dylan asked. The buzzing sound got louder—it was so familiar, Brigid *knew* that sound, she'd be able to name it if she could just have enough quiet to *think*. She pulled the receiver away again and stared at it in her hand.

Something was strange about her hand. Her knuckles were swollen and split, as though she'd been hitting something. Flecks of drying blood freckled her skin.

"Are you sure it wasn't *you?*" said Dylan's voice from the trembling receiver. Was the phone shaking or was it only Brigid's hand? She couldn't speak, couldn't respond to the horrible, impossible thing her daughter was saying, because her eyes were caught on the phone, which was strangely warm and heavy in her hand, and—yes—*moving* of its own volition, shuddering, *buzzing* against her palm. One of the holes in the receiver seemed to twist, to change shape and widen, like a gaping mouth. Like her own mouth, trying and failing to form words.

No, it wasn't the hole changing shape. Something was coming *out* of it. Brigid wanted to drop the phone in horror, but somehow the signal didn't make it from her brain down to her fingers, which clung as tight as ever to the thrumming, overheating plastic. Whatever it was seemed to extrude, like liquid dripping somehow upward, a moving, squirming shadow. At first it had no form, just texture and movement. It uncurled, like a tiny finger reaching out. Brigid saw a flash of yellow and still didn't understand. Then she saw its wings and realized what the humming sound had been all along.

She threw the receiver to the kitchen floor in disgust. It hit the tile and shattered, and a cloud of wasps boiled up from the plastic shrapnel. Even through their vicious buzzing—even over the sound of her own screams—Brigid could hear her daughter's voice, still impossibly clear from the broken remains of the phone receiver on the floor. Dylan was laughing.

Chapter 25

The first sting just felt hot, for a moment. A strange warmth right below the joint of her thumb, as though she'd been splashed with water not quite hot enough to scald. Only when she looked down and saw the wasp crouching on her hand did Brigid feel the heat brighten into shocking pain.

Brigid slapped the wasp away, but there was another one there already, stinging her wrist. Then another in the crook of her elbow. On her collarbone. On her cheek, just below her right eye, the pain delirious in its intensity. She sobbed and ran.

Wasps poured after her, out of the kitchen and into the hallway. The buzzing, the screaming, whited out all thought except of escape, and Brigid raced toward the front door, except—

It wasn't there.

Impossible, insane—but there was no door. The front windows were where they belonged, heavy curtains drawn as always, and between them was an expanse of blank wall. Its dainty floral paper was just as faded and shabby as the rest of the wall, could not possibly be newly installed. An unfamiliar armchair, hideous mustard-gold velveteen, would have blocked the door if there still was one. *That* was the anomaly that had caught her eye before.

She couldn't stop to make sense of it, the wasps were at her heels—at her elbows, her calves, everywhere. With one shriek of frustration, Brigid kept running, turning hard into the living room. At its far end, it opened onto another hallway that would take her back to the kitchen, and if she outran the wasps it would only be to catch up with them again. Stupid, stupid, she should have gone back up the stairs, back to Dylan, but she was already past them; turning around would mean diving back into the wasps.

But—the laundry chute. A narrow vertical tunnel, it ran from the second floor all the way down to the basement, where the washer and dryer were installed, so the family could drop dirty clothes and sheets straight into the laundry room instead of carrying them down the stairs. Each floor of the house had a cabinet door in the wall that opened onto the chute. On this level, the door was in the back hallway, just past the living room.

When she was little—until Father Angus put a stop to it—Brigid had figured out how to climb the laundry chute, bracing her hands and feet on opposite sides to scoot up and down. Could she do that still?

Hope gave her a burst of speed. She exploded out of the living room and into the hallway, the buzzing of the wasps not far behind her, but maybe far enough. And there was the cabinet door, right where it should be.

Brigid slammed it open so hard it bounced off the wall. Her heart pounded frantically as she spent precious seconds yanking herself up onto the narrow sill of the hole in the wall, scrabbling for a handhold in the darkness beyond. She twisted around to sit on the sill with her legs hanging down into the hallway. A wasp, leading out from the swarm, landed on her bare foot. Brigid kicked reflexively—it stung her just above the arch of her instep, but she barely felt it—and yanked her legs up. Leaning back into that musty black chasm to brace her body weight against the opposite wall, she got her feet under her and began to stand. Then she realized the cabinet door was still hanging wide open. With her feet now inside the chute, pressed to either side of the small doorway, she reached into the hall to grab the door and slam it shut.

Darkness surrounded her. The miserable drone of the wasps was not silenced, but at least it was muffled.

Brigid's breathing began to slow. Adrenaline ebbed, and the places where she'd been stung—her foot, her hands, that awful point on her cheek—burned and throbbed. She felt dizzy too, nauseated, and she couldn't tell whether it was from the venom or the panic.

It didn't matter, she told herself as her mind cleared. What mattered was Dylan. Dylan was injured, waiting for her, trusting in her mother to help. Or was she? Which was the real Dylan—the bruised and bloody girl on the floor upstairs, or the one who had giggled over the phone line? How much of the last fifteen minutes had been real? Was Brigid imagining things, just as Zandy had said all along?

In the dark, she tried to focus her eyes, to see her hands on the walls of the chute. She could see only the vaguest shapes, and even that might have been her imagination. When she flexed her fingers, she felt the wasp stings pulse, each one a hot red overgrowth. But she didn't feel sore knuckles, broken nails, flecks of someone else's blood clinging to her skin.

Her hands were in front of her and she believed they were real. She had to trust that, to trust *something*, didn't she? Here was the evidence: she had not beaten her daughter, but she had been stung by wasps.

How long had they been living there, inside the phone? she wondered. It must have been a long time—there were so many of them—and yet she felt the wasps hadn't been there at all until she'd picked up the phone. They were real; she prodded gently at the sting inside her elbow with the forefinger of the other hand and hissed in confirmation. But they had come from *her*, somehow, all the same. Without meaning to, she had *put* them there.

Through the ceiling, Brigid heard her daughter scream.

Her legs flexed of their own accord, pushing her body upward. As she reached full extension, her feet lost their grip on the smooth wall of the laundry chute and for a heart-stopping moment there was nothing holding her in place. Brigid was falling into a darkness she knew stopped one floor below her— already far enough that a bad landing could break her legs—but sudden terror convinced her it might go on forever, that she might fall and fall and never hit the bottom, and all the while she would hear Dylan screaming.

Her arms pistoned out, jammed into the walls on either side, and with a painful jolt to both her elbows, Brigid came to a halt. She walked her feet up the walls until her legs were once again holding most of her weight.

It came back to her quickly, the way she'd climbed the chute as a child, one foot and one hand on either side of the gap with her body balanced between. She was heavier and more cautious now, though, and the going was slow. Her thighs and shoulders ached almost immediately, and she was sweating furiously in the unventilated laundry chute. She kept having to stop and wipe her hands on her thighs so she wouldn't lose her grip again. Every second seemed to last ages. She listened desperately for another sound from upstairs, half terrified of hearing Dylan scream again and half hoping she would, because at least then Brigid would know she was alive and conscious.

Despite all the impediments, after a few minutes Brigid was sure: this was taking too long. She should have reached the second floor by now. Unless she was sliding back down with every upward crawl, losing as much height as she gained, there was no way she hadn't already covered the distance. For a moment, she had the awful, delirious thought that she had gotten turned around—that she was suspended head down in the chute. But no, that was impossible; she felt the trickle of sweat down her back, inexorably pointing where gravity led.

Brigid craned her neck upward, searching for a line of light, however faint, that would reveal the upstairs cabinet door. She saw nothing but an expanse of black, stretching into a distance impossible to gauge. A new fear bubbled up. She had missed the door somehow. The chute continued upward forever, with no hope of escape.

In a queasy rush, it occurred to her that there was no way she could be climbing the chute the same way she had as a child, arms and legs akimbo. Her wingspan must be two feet longer than it was back then. She should be wedged in the narrow space, arms trapped at her sides, if she could fit inside the chute at all. *What the fuck was going on with this house.*

Trying to swallow another sob, Brigid braced her feet again, pushed upward, shifted her hands. When she planted her left hand, the wall *gave* underneath it, and the shock almost sent her plummeting down to the basement.

Wedging herself in place with her knees locked, Brigid caught her breath. The wall had shifted when she pushed against it. For a moment, she didn't understand, and then she did. She'd found the door.

When she pushed again, the door moved only slightly—warped over the years and stuck in its frame, perhaps. Brigid slammed it with the side of her fist and it popped open. The lip of the opening dug painfully into her stomach as she wriggled through it. With one final kick against the back wall of the laundry chute, Brigid tumbled out and landed in an awkward heap in the second-floor hallway.

It looked wrong. She knew it as soon as she got to her feet; wrong in the same indefinable way the foyer had been wrong, before she'd realized the door was gone. She took a step and realized the floor was smooth hardwood, not carpeted, but that wasn't all. Looking to her left, she saw that instead of the stairs she knew, this hall ended in a wrought-iron spiral staircase, beautiful and dangerous and absolutely impossible.

There are more rooms in this house than there used to be, and I can never find him in any of them, Adelaide's voice whispered in her mind.

At the far end of the hallway, next to the door to Adelaide's room, hung the full-length mirror that had been there since Brigid's childhood. Her own reflection staggered toward her from within it, wild-eyed and wild-haired, face misshapen from the venom in her cheek. She looked like a ghoul.

A ghoul who kept walking, even though her swelling cheek

was making the vision in her right eye go slightly blurry. The door to Angus's room was closed now, but not locked. Brigid opened it and cried out in dismay.

Unlike the hall and the stairs, the bedroom looked perfectly familiar. Painfully familiar. There were folding chairs against one wall, and no sheets on the mattress. Brigid glanced to the window and was barely surprised to see a night sky swirling with snow, though an hour ago she'd been outdoors in the bright October morning.

This was exactly the way the room had looked when Angus had exorcised Serafina, and of course, in the center of it all, Dylan was handcuffed to the bed. Unlike Serafina, though, she wasn't struggling or cursing. She lay still, serene but alert, her bright, open eyes turning to Brigid as she entered the room. The bruises and blood were gone from Dylan's face, and Brigid suspected they'd never been there to begin with.

"Hi, Mom," said Dylan cheerfully. Even the slur from her injured tongue seemed to be gone. Brigid wondered for a moment whether this was another misdirection, a mirage of her healthy, unbroken daughter to distract her while the real Dylan wept and bled somewhere in the house, unheard. But when Dylan smiled, Brigid could see the stitches in her tongue. The pain just didn't seem to be bothering her as much anymore.

Father Angus was nowhere to be seen. "Where is he?" Brigid demanded. She knelt and fumbled with the cuffs binding Dylan's wrists to the bedposts, but the knobs at the top of the posts were too wide to force the cuffs over. "Dylan, baby, did you see where he put the key?"

Dylan gazed up at her, no urgency or fear in her face. "We can't leave yet," she said. "Not before it gets here."

She didn't say *he*, she said *it*. Brigid's fingertips went cold. "Before what?"

"It's almost here," said Dylan. "It's been waiting a really long time. She stopped it before, but now it's started again."

"What are you talking about?" She yanked on the cuffs as though that might help. Dylan winced at the pressure, and Brigid stopped. The pain in her hand and cheek was tremendous. "Honey, please think. Did you see him put the key down? We need to get out of here before Angus comes back."

"Oh, it will be a while before that happens," said Dylan. Her voice sounded strange, as if someone were borrowing it, just as it had sounded before her tongue split. "He's taking the long way around, just like you did."

How could she know that? Brigid didn't bother to ask. "He's dangerous," she said. "We need to get away from him. These weird things that have been happening—he did it all."

"Well, yes and no," said Dylan in that same slightly wrong voice. "It is his fault, but it wasn't entirely his doing. I'm afraid some of the blame must fall to me."

Finally, painfully, Brigid understood. *Me* didn't mean Dylan, it meant someone else speaking from Dylan's mouth. Not Serafina's demon; someone who understood Brigid intimately, or once had. Brigid felt like a fool. How did she ever fail to recognize that voice, which for so many years had been as familiar as her own?

It was her mother. It was Adelaide.

Chapter 26

B rigid crouched by the head of the bed, bringing her face level with her daughter's. She leaned close, so their foreheads were almost touching—so she could feel the furious warmth of Dylan's skin. She forgot about the handcuffs, about the wasp stings, about Angus. "Mom?" she whispered. "Is that you?"

"Don't make me spell everything out for you, Brigid," said Adelaide's exasperated voice in Dylan's mouth. "It's tedious." The scolding was more familiar and instantly recognizable than any maternal tenderness ever could have been, and the tears that flooded Brigid's eyes were some dizzying mix of relief and love and a child's indignation at being rebuked.

"I'm sorry," she said instinctively. Then she shook her head. "No, that's not—I'm not sorry, I deserve an *explanation*. What are you doing to my daughter?"

Dylan's mouth pursed in an expression so shockingly evocative of Adelaide it made Brigid shiver. "She's *my* granddaughter, you know. I can't believe you never even bothered to tell her about me. Are you so ashamed of your own family?"

"I . . ." Brigid faltered. "I was trying to put it behind me. Everything he put me through, feeling like you wouldn't protect me. I didn't want to burden her with all that."

Adelaide rolling her eyes looked exactly like Dylan rolling her eyes. "Ever the martyr," she said. "You had a roof over your head, enough to eat, no one ever hit you. Do you have any idea what *our* parents were like? Let me tell you, kiddo, you had it pretty easy."

Brigid's happiness at hearing her mother's voice again was quickly souring into a more familiar emotional bouquet of frustration and futility. Adelaide was not one of the mother goddesses Brigid hung on her store walls, infinitely wise and nurturing. Even dead, she was petty, bitter, and self-centered. "What do you want? What are you doing to Dylan?"

"Protecting her," said Adelaide, "just like she asked me to."

"Asked you? She never even met you," protested Brigid.

Adelaide sighed as though Brigid had once again forgotten to scrub behind the toilet. "I know you saw the protection spell, Brigid."

The rune on the floor of the shop, like a hole into some vast blackness. Dylan huddled and sobbing. Of course that was where all this had started. "How did she . . ."

"She asked for help, and I came," said Adelaide. "She's my granddaughter. She needed protection."

"From Kai Shriver?"

"From Kai. From you," said Adelaide. "From my brother."

"No, wait." Brigid wrapped her hand around Dylan's wrist, digging into the hard steel of the handcuff. "She wouldn't need protection from him if you hadn't brought us here in the first place. You were the one who said you wanted to see the old man. Dylan didn't even know he existed."

"You think you were protecting her by lying to her? By hiding where you came from?" Adelaide's sneer twisted Dylan's face. "You're so afraid of anyone knowing anything about you, even your own child. Do you have any idea how lonely she is? You're the only family she knows, and she doesn't know you at all."

"Don't," Brigid said. Her lungs felt tight. Her wasp stings pulsed with pain. "Don't try to tell me how to raise my daughter. I've done everything I possibly could to keep her safe." Her fists clenched in the blanket at the edge of the mattress, knuckles going white. "I tried to keep her away from this—this fucking hellhole you dragged me into."

"But you brought her right back here, didn't you?" said Adelaide. "As soon as you had nowhere else to go." She smiled up at Brigid with Dylan's beautiful smile, Dylan's perfect face that Brigid loved more than her own life. Brigid fought the urge to slap her. "You're not as different from me as you'd like to think."

"Bullshit," said Brigid. "Bullshit!" As overwhelmed as she was by the turmoil of rage and fear and sorrow, she still felt a childish thrill at the rebellion of using this kind of language in front of her mother, in her uncle's house. "I brought her here because you were hurting her. You got her suspended from school, you cut her fucking *tongue* . . ." She fought the urge to cry. If she cried, Adelaide would say she was too emotional, that they could have this conversation when she calmed down. "Those things I found in her closet—you were making her eat *roadkill*. How was any of that protecting her?"

"Well, how was I supposed to know?" said Adelaide with familiar indignation. "I had no idea sharing her body would be so exhausting. In case you're not aware, Brigid, I'm *dead*."

Brigid's fists clenched so tight the mattress shifted in its frame. "I fucking know that!"

"Hmm. Well, you didn't come to my funeral, so I wasn't sure the news had reached you," Adelaide sniffed, and despite herself Brigid felt a pang of guilt. "At any rate, it turns out that a dead spirit in a living form has very specific nutritional requirements."

"Like roadkill?"

Adelaide gave her a long-suffering look. "They weren't *roadkill*, Brigid. I ate them when they were still alive."

Brigid's hands hurt from clenching her fists so tight. She wanted to lash out, to throw things and smash things and put her fist through walls. She wanted to grab Adelaide by the hair and snap her neck in one violent shake. But it was Dylan's hair, Dylan's neck. She couldn't hurt her mother without also hurting her daughter. "What about her *tongue*, Mom?"

"We were both trying to speak at once," Adelaide said. "Have you ever mentioned to your daughter that it's rude to interrupt her elders?"

"Of course you'd find a way to make it my fault. And the wasps, the hallway, all of it? Why did you do all that?"

"I don't know anything about wasps," said Adelaide indignantly. "That must have been the demon."

Brigid shrieked with something that sounded almost like laughter. "There's a demon, too! A ghost *and* a demon. Why didn't I think of that?"

"You did think of that, Brigid. That's why you're here," Adelaide reminded her. "Or did you stop believing in demons sometime in the last forty-eight hours? Right around the time it became easier and more convenient to blame everything on your mother?"

"Blame everything—this is insane. You're possessing her!" Brigid half expected her mother to interrupt and call her hysterical. She felt hysterical. "What, did you leave the door open and a demon wandered in too?"

Adelaide pinched her mouth shut and turned Dylan's face toward the wall. Brigid remembered from her adolescence that when Adelaide went silent in the middle of a conversation, it usually meant she was embarrassed and didn't want to acknowledge it. She thought back to the notebook.

"Oh," Brigid said as she put it together. "The demon is yours. That's how it got into Dylan—it hitched a ride with you."

"How was I supposed to know that?" Adelaide snapped, still not looking at Brigid. "No one ever told me, this is what happens when you die possessed. I didn't know it would . . . *stick*, if it wasn't finished with me."

"What do you mean, wasn't finished?"

Although Adelaide refused to look at her, Brigid could see the hard set of her mouth in profile, the determination not to waver, not to cry. It was a rare expression on Dylan's face, and Brigid realized her daughter didn't usually try to hide how she was feeling—at least not at home. How had she never noticed it before, the precious gift of her daughter's trust?

"You found the notebook," said Adelaide. "You already know what it does. What it didn't get the chance to do, with me." Her jaw worked, and Brigid was almost certain she was biting the tip of her tongue, worrying the wound there, using the pain to hold back tears.

"What the hell is *it*, Mom? Don't tell me it's a demon—that's just an easy word for something you can't explain. I should fucking know, after the last few days. Tell me what it *is*."

Adelaide drew in a deep, shuddering breath and blew it out hard through Dylan's teeth. "I don't understand it perfectly myself, but I see it more clearly now that I'm dead. The best I can explain is that it's a parasite. It makes a home inside of you and then it . . . feeds on your shame." Her arms twitched against the handcuffs as though trying to scratch an itch she couldn't reach. "I could never see it, but I could feel it inside me. Or them. I was never sure whether it was one or more than one. Like the Holy Trinity."

Brigid crossed her arms tightly, telling herself she didn't feel a crawling sensation under her skin. "What does it want with Dylan?"

"The same thing it wanted with me. Well, *want* is the wrong word. I'm not sure it has a mind, really, not like a person does. It just . . . eats."

Adelaide paused for a moment. "It eats?" Brigid prompted.

Still speaking to the wall, Adelaide went on. "It eats shame. It finds people who are full of shame and brings it to the surface. Digs for it, makes you feel as much as you can stand, and savors it. And then digests it, I suppose, and turns it into something else."

This time Brigid knew Adelaide was waiting for her to speak her line, like dialogue in a play. The question popped out anyway. "Turns it into what?"

"Hate," said Adelaide. "Anger. Violence. You saw the clippings. It turns pain into poison, and just . . . excretes it into people's brains, until they do something horrible."

Although Adelaide wasn't looking at her, Brigid dropped her eyes anyway, staring down at her own hands. They were both red and puffy with the wasp venom, the right more swollen than the left. She couldn't look at her mother when she said "Killing yourself wasn't horrible enough?"

In her peripheral vision, Brigid saw Adelaide glance over at her, then quickly look back at the wall. "I didn't kill myself."

Brigid flinched in surprise. "What? Angus said—"

"No." The muscle in Dylan's jaw was tight. "I was driving too fast. On my way home from . . . it doesn't matter."

"From stalking me," Brigid said sharply.

Adelaide didn't respond immediately. After a long moment, she said, "I was driving fast. In the mountains. Roads I didn't know well enough, and I was upset and distracted, because . . . well, it doesn't matter why."

This, again, was Brigid's cue to ask. It frustrated her, being shoved back into this role, having to pry information out of her tight-lipped mother. Somewhere in the back of her head, she thought, *Fuck this. I can walk away and leave her handcuffed here. I bet she'd be more excited to share her thoughts after a day or two of rubbing her wrists raw and pissing in the bed.*

But those were Dylan's wrists, not Adelaide's. Brigid swallowed the anger. It tasted like blood. "Why were you upset, Mom?"

"I wanted to talk to you," Adelaide said. "The guilt was eating me alive, Brigid. I was ashamed of what you'd become, I was ashamed of letting you go, giving you up to a life of sin."

"That must have been so hard for you," Brigid said bitterly. "Having such an embarrassing daughter."

"Yes, and maybe you can relate, since I was so mortifying

you didn't mention my existence for twenty years," her mother snapped back. "But I thought if I talked to you, if we could find a way to reconcile, whatever was happening to me might stop."

"But you didn't," said Brigid. "You didn't talk to me. I didn't even know you were there."

"No," said Adelaide. "That's true. I was going to—I believe I did have a plan. A speech, even, although I don't remember it now. I was thinking about it all the way up the mountain. And then I parked in front of your building, and I opened the car door, and I looked down and saw there was a knife in my hand."

"A knife," Brigid echoed.

"A big kitchen knife with a black handle," said Adelaide. "It was beautiful. Elegant. Not one of the ones from our house. I don't know where it came from, but I think it was in my hand the whole way, because my fingers were sore from holding it. I didn't want to put it down. I couldn't put it down. And then I realized that I had another plan, too, and I'd been thinking about it just as much as the first one. Practicing it over and over in my mind. All the details. Where I'd cut you first, and how deep." Her voice got quieter and quieter as she spoke. "And how long it would probably take you to die. Because I didn't want it to be over too quickly."

Brigid turned, braced one hand on her knees and the other one against the wall, and vomited onto the carpet between her feet.

She wiped her mouth with the hem of her shirt, then straightened up. Her mind felt sludgy. She needed to clean the mess. Remembering the linen closet in the bathroom, she turned toward the bedroom door.

"Don't," Adelaide said quickly. "If you leave the room, you

might not be able to find your way back."

Brigid thought of the laundry chute that seemed to go on forever, of the incongruous spiral stairway. Slowly and carefully, she crossed the room to Angus's dresser. The top right drawer had a stack of undershirts in it, old and worn. It felt wrong to look at them. She didn't want to see any soft thing that had touched his skin, stained and washed and faded and stained again.

She grabbed two and threw them down on the floor over the puddle of vomit. It immediately began to soak into the threadbare fabric, bile yellowing the already yellowed cotton.

"I couldn't put the knife down," Adelaide repeated. "And I had two very clear ideas of what I wanted to do when I got out of the car, but obviously I couldn't do them both. I sat there for a long time trying to make up my mind, getting more and more confused. It was like . . ." She took a deep breath and exhaled shakily. "A little like when Dylan got hurt. Like there were two of me fighting with each other. And I did feel—it wasn't my tongue, but I did feel like something was tearing. Inside me."

"Am I supposed to feel sorry for you?" Brigid was startled by the harshness of her own voice. "That it was so painful for you, trying not to kill me?"

"I'm not telling you how to feel, Brigid," her mother said. For once, she sounded more weary than annoyed. "I'm just telling you what happened." She paused, as if steeling herself. "Eventually, I put the knife through my hand."

"What?" Brigid coughed out the word. "Why?"

"I can't explain it," said Adelaide. "It was something I could do. It didn't hurt you. And it was enough to snap me out of whatever else was going on, to get me moving again, so I could drive back home."

"But you didn't," said Brigid. "You, what, drove off a cliff instead?"

"Not on purpose," said Adelaide. "I was so confused, and so tired. And the steering wheel was slippery."

Brigid took a deep breath, waiting for that revelation to . . . she didn't know what. Unlock something inside her, she supposed; unknit some scar tissue deep in her heart. Soothe the lingering pain of her mother's suicide and her own failure to stop it. Adelaide's death had been an accident. If she looked at it from a certain angle, it was almost heroic, even: she had sacrificed herself, albeit unintentionally, to keep from hurting Brigid. Shouldn't that come as a relief?

Maybe it would, eventually. Right now all Brigid could find inside herself was fear for Dylan and rage at what Adelaide had done to her, accidental or not. "So the demon—the parasite or whatever it was, it died with you," she said. "And then it came back with you, too."

Adelaide nodded. "I believe it still needs to complete its life cycle. It's been waiting all this time. And now . . ."

"Now you and it need to get the hell out of my daughter's body," said Brigid.

Adelaide pursed Dylan's lips. "What I've been trying to explain to you, Brigid, if you would take a moment to listen, is that I don't know *how*. I felt Dylan calling for help with the protection spell, but I can't tell you *how* I felt it, or what I did to answer the call. I just wanted to be with her, and then I was. I don't know how to leave. And even if I did leave, the parasite is in Dylan now. It's feeding on *her*, not me. If I'm removed from her body, I don't know if it would come with me this time."

Brigid had probably known that, on some level, from the

moment Adelaide started talking. Still, her heart sank.

"Is that why you wanted to come here?" she said. "Because you thought Angus could take it out? Did you ask him when you were alive?"

"Well, no," said Adelaide, finally turning to look Brigid in the eye. "My brother was never really an exorcist. I know that now. I knew it for longer than I wanted to admit when I was alive, too. He was a charlatan—worse than a charlatan, really, because he didn't just fake exorcisms. He took people who were perhaps mentally disturbed, but otherwise healthy, and he put something *in* them that made them do horrible things."

"How?" asked Brigid. "Why?"

"He doesn't know he's doing it," said Adelaide. "Of course he doesn't—he has no idea what happens to people when he's done with them. It would never occur to him to wonder."

"Then how?"

"It's in him too," said Adelaide. "The demon, or the parasite, whatever you want to call it—but his is different. It's older. And it doesn't just eat and digest and die, like it does in the rest of us. It doesn't eat at all." She sneered. "He doesn't have anything for it to eat, anyway. He's never felt shame in his life."

"It doesn't eat?" Brigid repeated doubtfully.

"Did you know that some female octopuses can go years without eating while they're tending their eggs?" said Adelaide. "Dylan was reading about that in school. I think this is like that. Angus . . . whatever is in Angus, all it does is lay eggs."

The image of a clutch of slimy eggs oozing under her mother's skin popped into Brigid's head again, and her disturbed stomach threaten to revolt. Adelaide saw her revulsion and added, "They're not literal eggs. Not physically. But it's a form of reproduction. I can't be sure whether he does it by touching people or talking to them or some other way. Somehow, he . . ." She shrugged, the gesture aborted by her chained arms, unable to find the right word.

"Implants," Brigid suggested with a grimace.

"That sounds right," said Adelaide. "He implants them."

"It's like a queen bee," said Brigid. "The only one in the colony that can reproduce." Absently, she reached up to brush a fingertip over the wasp sting under her eye. Just the slight pressure sent a thrill of pain that blurred her vision, and she choked on a gasp.

"Maybe," said Adelaide.

"But I still don't understand," said Brigid. "Why are we here? You said Angus doesn't know how to take demons out of people, so why bring us to him?"

"They only do it once," said Adelaide.

The words didn't immediately make sense to Brigid. Still, the swirling sensation in her stomach intensified. She was beginning to suspect that vomiting again was inevitable, but she continued to fight it. "Who only does what?"

"Everyone he infects—they do one horrible thing and then it's over," said Adelaide. "I've looked them up on Dylan's computer, the people from that notebook. All the ones whose names I can remember. Most of them are still alive, but not a single one has done anything else violent, at least not enough to make the news. A few of them have been released. They have normal lives—they're happy."

Brigid remembered Serafina, her eerie calm. She hadn't seemed happy or normal; she'd seemed lobotomized. "I'm not sure that's true," she said slowly. "Anyway, why does that matter?

What does it mean?"

"Really, Brigid." The impatient tone was back, but there was something else underneath it—a reluctance, maybe even a fear. There was something Adelaide didn't want to say, and she was hoping Brigid would put it together for herself.

"They're happy after they rape someone or drown their children? Stab their parents?" Brigid shook her head. "I don't see what you're getting at." Except the more she spoke, the more she did. Pieces were falling into place, making a picture Brigid didn't want to see.

"It didn't finish with me," said Adelaide, slow and crisp, pronouncing each word carefully. "Now it's in Dylan. I don't know how to remove it unless it finishes. Unless it completes its life cycle."

Brigid bit her lip and said nothing.

"That's why I wanted you to bring her here," said Adelaide. "Because if she's going to hurt someone, it should be Angus."

"Absolutely not," said Brigid reflexively.

Adelaide wrinkled Dylan's forehead in confusion. "You hate Angus. You were ready to rip his throat out half an hour ago. You haven't spoken to him in more than a decade. Why would you care if he died?"

"I don't care about him." An oversimplification, probably, but good enough for now. "I care about Dylan. You want to kill him, in *her* body, and then just leave us to pick up the pieces? Let her go to prison for the rest of her life? That's your solution?"

"At least it would be over," said Adelaide, but her voice faltered. Her endless confidence, her certainty that she knew best—or her ability to fake it convincingly—was finally cracking. Brigid wished she could take satisfaction in it. "At least it wouldn't be inside her anymore. She wouldn't have to carry that pain."

"Have you ever talked to one of those people?" Brigid said. "The ones you think are happy? I have," she went on before Adelaide could answer. "Remember Serafina Santoro? I'm sure you do. She had a miscarriage right here where you're lying. What would have been her baby—it bled out onto this mattress. The stain is probably still there under this sheet."

"I'm surprised that bothers you," said Adelaide. Her scorn sounded forced; underneath it, she was shaken. "Aren't modern women like you supposed to believe it's not a baby, just a clump of cells?"

"She didn't have a choice," said Brigid. "She couldn't ever have another one, did you know that? Angus took that away from her, and you helped him, because you watched it happen and did nothing. And now you want to tell yourself that she's happy, because she hasn't killed anyone else since she dismembered her parents? Are you fucking serious?" Brigid's fists were clenched, she realized, skin stretched too tight over her swollen wasp stings, pulse a throbbing misery underneath. She shook all over. "She's *broken*, Mom. She hasn't killed anyone else because she's lost the ability to care about what happens to her. It's like a part of her brain was scooped out. No." She cut herself off, took a deep breath, forced her voice down an octave. "No fucking way I'm letting that happen to my daughter."

"Well, feel free to share your better suggestion," said Adelaide. Once again, Brigid could hear the doubt beneath the derision.

"Do you realize I might have had a chance to think of a better plan by now if you'd told me what was going on?" Brigid snapped. "Instead of just assuming you knew best, and putting my daughter in danger because you're too proud and stubborn to ask for help?"

Adelaide was silent for a long moment. She stared up at the ceiling, tears welling in her eyes—Dylan's eyes. "None of this was supposed to happen. Ghosts, demons—none of this should even be real. How could I have known?"

Though she didn't want to, Brigid felt a sudden wave of sympathy for her mother. She'd failed to protect Brigid from so much suffering—and now she'd put Dylan in harm's way—but there was no denying that Adelaide had suffered, too. She'd never really been in charge of her own life, always swept up in the wake of someone bigger and more powerful, and it seemed that hadn't changed even after her death. Tentatively, Brigid reached out a hand and rested it lightly on Dylan's shoulder—not rubbing, just a touch, hoping understanding could pass through her fingers.

Dylan's head whipped around faster than Brigid would have thought physically possible, teeth bared in a horrifying grin. Brigid recoiled, but not fast enough. Dylan's teeth caught the pad of her middle finger.

The pain was so stunning and intense that, for a moment, the world went white. Brigid staggered back from the bed, clasping her injured hand to her chest. By instinct, she almost stuck the wounded finger in her mouth, to suck like a paper cut—but this was no mere bead of blood. Red streamed from where her fingerprint had been, from where her finger was now not quite the right shape.

For a moment, the room was silent, neither Brigid nor Adelaide making a sound. Brigid stared at the manic grin on her daughter's face. The scrap of skin was still visible between her front teeth, and Brigid had the brief, absurd thought that she could take it back, sew it on again, that the damage could be undone. Then, with a dramatic slurping sound, Adelaide sucked the bit of flesh through her teeth and swallowed it.

Chapter 27

Brigid didn't scream. What would be the point? Every part of her body felt like a scream; every breath felt like a scream; every word spoken in the room felt like a scream. Her daughter's body handcuffed to the bed was a scream. She was bleeding a scream down her palm, dripping down her wrist, a puddle of scream spreading across the floor. Her throat was raw with all the screams she hadn't released.

The pulsating, grinding pain in her fingertip made the wasp stings fade to a gentle hum. She turned and stumbled toward Angus's dresser, staggering and almost falling. Despite the flow of red from her maimed finger, she knew she couldn't have lost enough blood to make her lightheaded; this must be shock, garnished with exhaustion.

Brigid grabbed another worn-out undershirt, hoping that, despite the stains, it was clean enough. Using her good hand and her teeth, she ripped a strip off it, then wound it around the end of her finger. Blood began to seep through the cotton immediately, spreading like a slow explosion.

Turning back to Adelaide, Brigid said through gritted teeth, "For a minute there I actually thought you wanted to help."

"I do want to help!" Adelaide whined in a childish tone that was nothing like how Dylan had actually sounded as a young child. "But I'm hungry, too. Dylan's hungry. Do you want us to starve?" She bared her teeth and stuck out Dylan's patchwork tongue. Brigid saw that the tender muscle was bruised down the middle, a mottled purple that spread out from the black dotted line of the stitches.

"I want you to get out of my daughter's body and leave us alone," said Brigid.

Behind her, the door burst open. Angus stood in the doorway, holding a Bible and a small glass bowl. His face was grayer than usual.

"Hello, brother," Adelaide said, smiling at him with blood in her teeth.

Angus glowered at her and held out the Bible. He said something Brigid couldn't understand. After a moment, her exhausted brain identified it as Latin.

"That's just the Our Father," said Adelaide. "Is that the only Latin you remember? You really are getting old."

"Angus, you need to get out of here," said Brigid. "She wants to kill you."

He turned on her with a scowl so baleful it would have brought her adolescent self to tears. Even the Brigid of two days ago might have quavered at the rage in his eyes. Now, though, he was nothing. He was slack and empty. A scarecrow stuffed with Bible pages.

"You brought the girl to me for help," he said. "You were

right. She needs it. There is something in her—something unholy." The look on his face was strange, not quite anger. Brigid couldn't place it for a moment. Then it clicked into place. Of course she didn't recognize his expression; she'd never seen Angus terrified before.

It made her laugh, despite her horror and rage. Finally, finally, the man who'd haunted her nightmares all these years was facing one of his own. "What did you see?" Brigid asked, remembering Dylan hovering over the table with blood gushing out of her mouth, Dylan curled in pain on the floor. Did whatever was warping her mind crawl through Angus's too? Or had he seen something real? What could have frightened him as much as her daughter's suffering and her own helplessness frightened Brigid?

He set his mouth in a hard line. This Angus she recognized— the one who would not be swayed, who was *doing this for your own good*. Reflexively, Brigid circled the bed, putting her body between Angus and Dylan.

"You have failed to protect your daughter," he said, low and cold. Brigid tried to steel herself but knew her face gave away how much the accusation hurt. "You are too corrupted by your own sin and pride to save her. The least you can do for her now is not stand in my way." He set the Bible on his dresser and dipped his fingers in the bowl of water. Then he flicked it toward Dylan where she lay on the bed, splashing Brigid's face in the process.

"I purify this child with holy water," he intoned. "I consecrate her body and soul unto the Lord our God."

"You really believe in this nonsense, don't you?" Adelaide said. "I always wondered. You think you're a genuine exorcist. I can't decide if that makes it worse or better."

"Demon, release this child!" Angus shouted. "You have no power here!"

"Angus," Adelaide sighed. She shook her head—Dylan's head—sadly, and in the gesture Brigid saw the perennial disappointment of an older sister with her little brother. "Angus, Angus, Angus."

Angus's jaw went slack. "You're not her," he said. His skin looked even thinner than usual. Brigid imagined she could claw straight through it like tissue paper, peel it from his head to reveal a perfectly dry skull underneath. "You lie, and you serve the Prince of Lies. My sister is dead."

"She wants to kill you," Brigid repeated. "You need to leave. I called 911 before. I'll lock the door and stay with her until the ambulance gets here. If you want to leave the house—if you can—be my guest." She still wanted him to pay for what he'd done, to Serafina, to Brigid herself, but that desire paled before the need to protect Dylan. She could not let her daughter, or anything wearing her daughter's body, kill Angus.

"You didn't call anyone," said Adelaide, rolling her eyes. "Don't you remember?" Of course Brigid remembered—Dylan's laughter, the hideous buzzing, the pain sharpening to a red point. But she'd hoped. She'd hoped that on the other side of what she heard there was a real voice, a real world, someone who would send help.

"Zandy knows where I am," she remembered out loud. "When she doesn't hear from me, she'll come. Or she'll call someone."

Angus looked hopeful. Adelaide laughed. "Zandy," she said in a mocking drawl. "Your new girlfriend, right? Unless you've chased her away already with your anger issues and your delusions and your refusal to trust anyone." Brigid gritted her teeth.

"It's too bad," Adelaide said. "Dylan wants another parent so much. She's desperate for you to find someone—anyone—so she doesn't have to be trapped alone in that sad little apartment with you. If only you weren't so hopeless at relationships, she might have a chance at a halfway normal life."

"You're helping a lot by possessing her and making her eat squirrels," Brigid retorted.

"Zandy isn't going to come looking for you," said Adelaide. "She's going to be so relieved that she doesn't have to deal with you anymore. Honestly, Brigid, you're exhausting—all the drama, all the insistence that your problems are someone else's fault. No one's ever good enough for you. I was a terrible mother. Dylan is a terrible daughter. Everyone always disappoints you and you never forgive them for it."

"Dylan isn't a terrible daughter," Brigid said, tasting stomach acid. "Dylan is amazing. She's never disappointed me. I never held her to impossible standards like the two of you did to me."

"I never asked you for perfection," said Angus, his voice thin. "All I ever tried to do was lead you to forgiveness. You've rejected God at every turn, but it's not too late for you, Brigid, it's never too late—"

"Angus, please shut up," said Adelaide.

Angus pointed to Dylan's body with a trembling finger. "That is not my sister," he said. He seemed to be getting some of his strength back. His spine straightened, and his voice took on an echo of the resonance Brigid remembered. "That is not your mother. Adelaide committed a grievous sin and I pray every night for her soul to find peace, but she cannot walk in this world. This is an impostor."

"You were the one who broke Dad's reading glasses," said Adelaide. "I kept my mouth shut, even when he held me over the top of the stairs. I always kept my mouth shut for you."

Angus fumbled for the Bible he'd set down and held it in front of him, as if for protection. "If you are my sister—*if* you are," he said, and then there was a long silence. Brigid could hear herself blinking.

Finally, Angus said, "Why did you do it?"

Brigid ran through possibilities in her head, wondering what he most needed explained. Was he asking why Adelaide had brought Dylan and Brigid here? Why she'd possessed Dylan in the first place? But Adelaide understood the question immediately.

"I didn't," she said. "I didn't mean to die."

"You left a note," he said quietly. "I found it on the kitchen table, after the police called me. Not all of it made sense, but there were some things you said over and over. That you couldn't live like this anymore. That you hoped Brigid would forgive you."

"You never told me that," said Brigid.

"You never asked," said Angus. "You never wanted to know a thing about how your mother died. You were just relieved she was gone."

"That's not true," Brigid protested.

"You didn't come to her funeral," he said. "You didn't send flowers. You didn't say *anything*." The words burst from him in a sudden cascade of anger. "She was my sister, Brigid. I know you think you're the only one in this family who can feel anything, but I love my sister. I miss her every day. I read that note until the paper wore through."

By the time Angus finished, he was breathing hard, and Brigid was horrified to see he had tears in his eyes. "Oh," she said softly, feeling wilted and obscurely embarrassed. "I just—I didn't think about it, I guess. I was so scared of you. I was afraid of what would happen if I came back."

"Afraid of me? Of an old man whose sister had just died?" He scoffed and shook his head. "Why am I always the villain in your stories, Brigid? Is it so much easier than looking at your own sins?"

What are your sins, Brigid?

Brigid's mouth tasted horrible. She spat on Angus's carpet, both to relieve the bitterness and to enjoy the look on his face. "You'll never admit to doing anything wrong, will you?" she said. "You've never said 'I'm sorry' in your life."

"That's not true," he said in a gentle tone that fit him like a borrowed suit. "Brigid, I'm sorry that the devil has such a hold on your heart. I still want to help you find your way back to God."

Brigid took two steps forward and punched him in the face.

It hurt her hand, made her wasp stings scream. She felt the impact all the way up her arm and into her jaw. The vision in her right eye, already blurred, went pure white for a horrible instant. But her left eye was enough to watch Angus stagger back and slam into the dresser, sending holy water sloshing over the edge of his little glass bowl.

"I need you to shut the fuck up," she said. "I'm so tired of your fucking voice. I know you never get tired of hearing yourself talk, but the rest of us aren't that lucky."

Angus cupped a hand over his cheek, already turning bright red. Brigid was disappointed to see that she'd missed his nose.

Adelaide cackled with laughter.

"Saint Michael the Archangel, protect us in battle," Angus gasped. "Be our defense—"

Adelaide's laughter rose higher and higher in pitch, drilling into Brigid's eardrums, until it sounded more like a scream. She writhed on the bed, pushing her feet into the mattress so her hips lifted. Dylan's body twisted into a deep backbend. Her shoulders strained at unnatural angles as her screaming filled the air.

"May God rebuke him, we humbly pray," gasped Angus.

Dylan's head was nearly upside down now, her face rapidly turning red. She opened her mouth wide again and bared her teeth at Angus. "Come closer, little brother, I'm so hungry," she snarled.

"Please stop," said Brigid.

"I'm glad you're finally learning your manners," said Adelaide from Dylan's arched and distended throat. "Maybe I didn't completely fail as a mother after all."

"What do you want?" Brigid demanded, hearing her voice go shrill. "What are you doing? You came because Dylan asked for help, but—look at this! You're hurting her."

"I'm helping her more than you ever have," Adelaide said. "I'm trying to help her understand. She wants to know about her family. She wants to know why her mother is the way she is. You just want her to shut up and cooperate."

"Isn't that all you ever wanted from me?"

Adelaide laughed. She kicked Dylan's feet up in the air like a gymnast doing a walkover. Her whole body stretched out in a vertical line, toes almost brushing the ceiling. Her hands weren't holding her weight; they strained in midair, wrists flexing and turning at the end of the handcuff chains. "All I want from you is to get out of my way and let me have him," she crooned, smiling a horrific upside-down smile from between her arms.

Angus stepped forward again. "Deceiver," he hissed. "I will not be so weak as to fall to your lies." He grabbed the bowl of holy water and held it out toward Dylan. "Leave this child! Release her innocent soul!"

"No," said Brigid. "You don't have any idea what you're doing."

He didn't seem to hear her. Instead, he began reciting Saint Michael's prayer again, grabbing for Dylan's ankle at the same time, trying to drag her back down onto the bed. Adelaide snapped her jaws at him, and he flinched, but didn't stop his intonation of the prayer.

"Where is Dylan?" Brigid said. She said it only to herself, and only she heard. Her daughter's face was twisted almost beyond recognition, trying to catch Angus's flesh in her teeth. Meanwhile, Angus continued to pray, ignoring everything but his own words.

He wanted to save Dylan. Adelaide wanted to defend Dylan. Brigid wanted to protect Dylan.

But where was Dylan? What did Dylan want? When was the last time anyone had asked her?

The room was full of noises: shouting, prayer, that horrible high-pitched cackling. Voices everywhere, but none of them Dylan's. Cacophony, threaded through with terrible silence.

"Be our defense against the wickedness and snares of the devil," Angus chanted.

Hopelessness surged up Brigid's throat and poured down her face, hotter than tears. The worst fear of any mother had to be losing her child. Dylan was right in front of her, except she *wasn't*, and Brigid had no idea how to find her. How to bring her back.

"Baby," Brigid said, "I'm so sorry." She reached out her hand as if to touch her daughter, but couldn't quite make herself cover the distance.

As Dylan flailed in the air, something slipped from her back pocket and fell onto the bed. It gleamed, a shimmer of light distorted by tears. Brigid blinked hard and looked again. In a valley of rumpled blanket lay a black disc, glossy as water in moonlight.

It was the obsidian mirror from the Tenth Muse. Brigid remembered Dylan's stash of contraband, the crystals and cards under her bed. This hadn't been among them; Dylan must have pocketed the mirror days ago, left it in a pair of jeans discarded on the floor. Who knew how long it had been lying there before Brigid scooped up the pants and threw them in a backpack, rushing to get her daughter to the hospital.

What did the obsidian mirror do? Brigid tried to remember what Cypress had said to Dylan. *See beyond the surface of things. Understand the truth.* And something else, something about how to use it. *A lot of magic is just symbolism.*

Brigid leaned over, staying clear of Dylan's teeth, and grabbed the mirror. Adelaide was twisting in a slow circle in the air so that Dylan's arms twined around each other, elbows creaking unnaturally. Angus continued to chant and sprinkle her with holy water. He didn't have a glance to spare for Brigid until she reached out and lifted the glass bowl from his hand. Even then, he gaped at his empty hand for several seconds before it dawned on him to look for the person who had taken it.

By then, Brigid was down on her knees on the floor. She dipped her fingers in the bowl as Angus had, and flicked the drops across the smooth black surface of the mirror. But maybe that wasn't enough. She upended the bowl. Water poured out in a clear stream, spilling over the sides of the mirror and onto the carpet.

Angus loomed over her, shouting, demanding. Brigid couldn't focus on what he was saying. She flung the bowl away, across the room, and heard Angus scrambling after it—she didn't need it anymore.

Was she supposed to say something? Magic was about words, wasn't it—that was what she'd gleaned from Cypress and Nadine and her customers over the years. You needed the ingredients, the props, but it was words that shaped your intentions, like a mantra while meditating. Something to focus your mind and channel your power. It wasn't so different from a prayer—just with more moving parts.

Brigid was no more a poet than she was a witch, but she'd gone to Catholic school for eight years. So maybe she knew something about symbolism, and maybe she knew something about prayer. She unwrapped the strip of rag from around her finger and swiped the gory cotton through the water on mirror's surface. "My blood is her blood," she said. "Help me find Dylan. Show me how to get her back."

The strip of undershirt she'd used as a bandage soaked up the water, and as it did, her own dried blood melted off it in trickles of red. Brigid worked the cloth in a circle around the mirror's surface, like polishing smears off a window, except she was leaving the smears, not erasing them—swirls of her own blood spreading across the black. The more she wiped, the more it seemed she was rubbing the blood *into* the mirror, not cleaning it away.

"Help me find Dylan," she said. More water fell onto the mirror as she struggled uselessly to clean it—oh, tears, she was crying again. It all swirled together, blood and tears and holy water. Could she see her own reflection, streaky and indistinct as though drifting through lightless depths? She lifted the mirror, cupped it in her hand, angled it to try to catch the light.

Yes, there was her face. It seemed to shift under her gaze, to move and pulsate, the flickering candlelight making strange shadows dance around her eyes and mouth. Brigid leaned closer. The swollen sting under her eye appeared to be throbbing as the light wavered across it.

But that wasn't right. There were no candles in this room. The light wasn't moving—her own face was. Her flesh was writhing, undulating. No, that still wasn't right. Something *underneath* her flesh. Something that had been there for a long time—for decades—but she hadn't been able to see it until now.

Some living things can lie dormant in their larval form for years, even decades, before they finally emerge. Adelaide wasn't alone in her infestation. Whatever was within her when she died—whatever was in Dylan now—it was in Brigid, too.

She was crawling with it.

Chapter 28

A ngus was still shouting. Brigid stood up carefully, cupping the obsidian mirror in both hands. It surprised her how warm the stone was—warm from her blood and her tears. Warm as skin.

She laid the mirror on the bed, just below where Dylan's hair cascaded down, coppery split ends not quite brushing the mattress. Adelaide, upside down in midair, craned her neck to see what Brigid had set there, but Brigid didn't focus on her. Not in this moment. She needed to get Dylan back, and she would, but first . . . but first. It had all become clear when she looked into the mirror. She knew what she needed to do.

Brigid turned toward Angus. His face was dark with fury, white foam flecking his lips as he shouted at her, cursing her pride, her sin, her stubbornness. She heard his words as though they were coming from very far away. The buzzing was louder. The sound of small things moving underneath her skin, a shushing whispering layered sound, shimmering at the edge of her hearing, almost but not quite like voices.

"You refuse to humble yourself before the Lord, and see what it does to her!" he bellowed, shaking his finger at Dylan. At least the girl—or Adelaide within her—had finally fallen silent, focused only on turning and twisting to get a better glimpse of the mirror's moonless sky. "You have brought this evil into your house and you're too proud to let me cast it out again. Shame on you, Brigid, *shame on you.*"

"Shame," Brigid said. "What do you know about shame?" She remembered what Adelaide had said, about the parasite in Angus, the queen, living without sustenance for all these years, because what it fed on was nowhere to be found in Angus's soul. The wordless whispering was louder and more insistent. "Have you ever felt it? Or do you only pour it into others?" She circled toward the door as she moved toward him, making him turn, putting himself between her and the bed.

"I know that God can free you from your shame," Angus said. "Please, Brigid, surrender to Him and let Him guide you."

"I have a better idea," said Brigid.

She hit Angus in the chest with both hands. He stumbled back, caught the backs of his knees on the mattress, and fell across the bed, arms flung wide in a pose Brigid distantly recognized. Before he could push himself up, Brigid jumped onto the bed, planting her knees hard on his thighs. Angus yelped in pain. Brigid grabbed his face in both hands and grinned down at him.

He was terrified, and it felt *good.* He wasn't even trying to throw her off. His body underneath her was a rag doll, weak with dread. It made her feel enormous and powerful. She wondered whether he had felt this exhilaration when he'd forced her to kneel and pray the rosary; if the thrill of control had rushed through his veins, fueling him, keeping him awake all through that awful night. She could see tears in Father Angus's eyes. The buzzing in her head sounded like laughter now.

"You want to know something about my shame?" Brigid said. "Let me tell you. Do you know what I've felt most ashamed of in my entire life?"

Father Angus opened his mouth to answer her. She'd known he would. It was so easy. Nothing could ever make him believe she wasn't in dire need of his opinion, his wisdom, his sermons. He should have kept his mouth closed, but that wasn't in him. He had to tell her what he thought he knew. He couldn't let her think for a moment there might be a question he couldn't answer.

When Angus opened his mouth, Brigid opened hers. Wide. Wider. She stretched her jaw until the corners of her lips cracked and bled. The buzzing sang a glorious crescendo, and she felt them coming.

In the mirror, she'd seen them wriggling below the skin of her face; now they were in her throat. Neither of these materializations was precisely accurate, Brigid knew. They were her mind's metaphors for something that was real, but not physical; something in her body that wouldn't show up on an MRI or under a microscope. And yet she could feel them—every writhing one of them—surging up her esophagus toward the light. For a moment, it felt like they would choke her. She tried to scream, but there was no room for the sound, or maybe they absorbed it all.

Larvae, white and wormlike, each one an inch long or more, poured from Brigid's gaping mouth and into Father Angus's. Some of them spilled onto his face and down his cheeks and chin, landed on the bedspread and twisted their fat little bodies from side to side, not knowing which way to go. A few clung to his lips and crawled across his face, feeling for another way in. One wriggled into his nose. But most of them surged straight down, past his finally silent tongue and into his throat.

The flood of maggots went on and on. Brigid desperately needed to take a breath, but she couldn't; her whole body was an endless spasm of expulsion. Her stomach heaved, her throat clenched, and the infestation gushed out of her like a fountain. She saw a muscle working in Angus's jaw, trying to close his mouth, but it was too late. The pressure was like a fire hose, forcing his lips wide.

At first the larvae that Brigid ejected were sickly off-white, but as the deluge went on they took on a pinkish tinge, then darkened to red. It wasn't a bright, fresh red. It was the red of old blood, sticky and clotted. These grubs were fatter, some of them almost as wide as they were long. They looked swollen, ready to burst. These, Brigid understood, were the ones that had been inside her the longest, that had eaten the best. They had gorged themselves on the darkest parts of her until their bodies distended with it. One landed on Angus's chin and popped like a water balloon: an awful wet noise, a dark smear.

Angus's face was flushed almost purple, his eyes bulging. Brigid knew he wasn't really suffocating, any more than she was. The larvae were real, but they did not occupy any physical space. Neither of them was unable to breathe. Still, Brigid felt the ache in her lungs, the fear that came with it, and she saw the same in Angus's face. Was it too much? Would this kill him—kill them both?

Finally, with a violent cough, Brigid sputtered the last few maggots—so overstuffed they were nearly spherical, nearly black—into Angus's mouth. As she did, she became aware that her arms were trembling with exhaustion. On the verge of collapsing, she shoved herself sideways so she'd roll onto the bed instead of landing on Angus's chest.

Something hard and heavy crashed into the back of her head. Brigid flinched away from the impact and ended up curled on her side, her forehead pressed against Angus's shoulder, smelling his sweat and fear, while the heavy thing sprawled on top of her.

It took her a moment, struggling to get her breath back, to realize that the heavy thing was Dylan—or Adelaide. As though all the magic had gone out of her in the same moment that Brigid expelled her infestation, the girl had fallen in a heap on the mattress.

Was Dylan hurt? Was she breathing? Had she landed on her head? Brigid pushed herself upright, out of the confusion of limbs, while Angus rolled the other way, coughing and dry-heaving. She rushed to cradle her daughter's body, as much as she could with Dylan's wrists still cuffed to the headboard.

"Dylan," she cried, forgetting about Angus and her aching throat and the horrible taste in her mouth—so much worse than when she'd only vomited. "Are you okay?"

Brigid saw Adelaide staring up at her. Then a strange transformation swept over Dylan's face. It was as if she watched Adelaide sink beneath the surface and Dylan, who had been submerged, rise up to greet the air again. The features didn't change, even the expression barely shifted, but somehow Brigid knew it was her daughter looking back at her.

"Mom," said Dylan. "What the hell is going on?"

Brigid snorted a tearful laugh. She was weak, she was drained, she was wrung out like a rag, but she felt *light*. She looked into her daughter's tired, thin, beautiful face and remembered joy. "I promise I'll explain everything, but it's still complicated right now. We need to find the key for these stupid things." She slipped a finger between Dylan's bony wrist and the metal of the cuffs. The skin there was red and irritated, with bruises darkening beneath. "How did you come back?"

"I saw myself in the mirror—or she saw me in the mirror, I guess," said Dylan. "And it was like we both remembered who I was." Brigid felt under the pillow as she talked, then leaned over to look under the bed. No key. "She's still in here, though, Mom. She doesn't know how to leave. I don't know how to make her leave."

"Okay," said Brigid. "We can figure it out. But we have to get out of here first, before he—"

She heard Dylan's gasp—louder than a gasp, like trying to scream while inhaling. Brigid leapt to standing faster than she would have thought possible, adrenaline coursing through her depleted body. Before she turned, she already knew what had scared her daughter.

Angus was getting to his feet. He moved slowly, ponderously, as though dragging heavy chains behind him. His face was still red, his eyes bulging, though he no longer appeared to be struggling to breathe. A few stray larvae still dangled from his lips, his cheeks, flailed for their lives on the collar of his flannel shirt. More were smeared across his skin in streaks of watery reddish-black, too thin and too dark to be mistaken for blood.

And his eyes—his eyes swelled out like blisters, too big for their sockets. They twitched from side to side, settling on nothing, and Brigid wasn't sure he could see at all. He *shouldn't* be able to see. Not with his eyes like that, livid with dark red fluid, drowning out the whites so his pale blue irises floated on a scarlet sea. Dark shapes roiled beneath the surface, like blood clots but *alive*.

Shame. That was what the larvae had eaten, what they sucked from Brigid like leeches, what made them swell almost past their skins. That was what she had poured into Angus, emptied it from her own system in one brutal purging.

What had Adelaide said? Angus had never felt shame before, not in his life. He was full of it now. Brigid could *see* it. She could see it catching up with him, the shame of her whole lifetime, all she'd felt—all *he* had made her feel.

It was his now. Not accruing in layers over years and decades, but all at once. Brigid could have talked until her voice was gone, explaining to him how he'd hurt her, how he'd destroyed Adelaide, how he'd damaged Serafina and Tara and all of them, and it wouldn't have made a difference. He was brilliant at blocking out what he didn't want to hear. No matter how she begged, he wouldn't have listened, wouldn't have understood.

But this was different, now. It was inside his body. He couldn't shut it out.

Brigid watched, in awe and horror and no small bit of satisfaction, as it drove him mad.

"Monster," he said, swinging his arms wildly and connecting with nothing. She stepped out of his reach, and he didn't follow her, still couldn't seem to focus his eyes. Or perhaps what he saw was not before him, but within him. "Demon. *Beast*. May God rebuke—oh, God . . ."

"Mom?" said Dylan nervously.

"God," said Angus. "Jesus. Our Father, who art in Heaven.

Blessed art . . . no. I remember it all. She was screaming. Now I lay me down . . . Oh, God. It's so heavy, how do you stand it?" Tears rolled down his face, but they were black and greasy.

Brigid remembered what Adelaide had said, about the parasite inside Angus, queen of a hive of misery. How it could live for years without sustenance, starving for its offspring's survival. Brigid understood. What else was a mother for, after all? It was easy—or if not easy, at least simple—to follow the violent logic of evolution, to sacrifice your own body so that another might thrive, to waste away in silence while the one you loved more than yourself grew strong.

But if that starving mother were suddenly presented with a banquet, she would feast until she was sick.

Brigid knew how this story ended, the same way as Serafina's and Tara's and dozens of others glued carefully into Adelaide's notebook. She had known it the moment she threw Angus down on the bed—no, the moment she saw her face in the mirror, squirming like rotting meat—no, maybe even before that. As soon as she'd returned to this house. Maybe as soon as she'd held Dylan's infant body in her arms, blood still drying in the baby's hair, staining her copper peach fuzz redder.

Red. All these stories ended in red. On the mattress between Serafina's legs. Tinting the water in the Cricks' bathtub. Adelaide's notebook was blue, but its pages overflowed with red. *Black and white and red all over*, Brigid thought, and almost laughed.

Angus was going to kill her.

That was the inevitable outcome, the only one that made sense. And thinking it, watching her uncle claw the air in search of her, didn't touch Brigid's joy.

She still felt it, that lightness lifting her up from under her sternum. Her shame was gone. Not stoked to an obliterating explosion, the way it had happened to Serafina; just returned to the place it always belonged. Brigid felt none of the passive acceptance she'd heard in Serafina's voice. She still had her anger, her grief. The past was not erased, but it wasn't hers to carry anymore. If she died now, she could do it without regrets.

As long as she knew Dylan was safe.

"We humbly rebuke—no. We humbly—defend . . ." Angus gagged and coughed. "Adelaide? Adelaide?"

But Dylan wasn't safe, not yet, not while she was in the room with Angus, black sticky trails glistening on his sunken cheeks. He stumbled forward in a Boris Karloff lurch, shouting fragments of prayers. Brigid stepped out of the reach of his searching hands, trying to stay quiet, to not give away her location. The key. She needed the handcuffs key.

Not on the bed, not under the bed. Nothing on the dresser top but the ring left by the bowl of holy water. Surely the key was still in the room somewhere. Brigid winced as she pulled out a drawer. Slow and careful as she moved, the wood still scraped, and Angus swiveled in her direction like a scenting hound.

Brigid rummaged frantically in the bottom of the drawer, hoping desperately for the cool edge of metal, but all she found were socks and splinters. Angus lumbered toward her. She ducked out of his way. His grasping hands found the handle of the drawer she'd left open, closed around it, and yanked. Socks spilled onto the floor.

"Cast into hell . . . into hell," Angus stammered. Suddenly his voice broke, and he was crying—not just the steady trickle of those dark tears, but weeping like a child, hiccupping and sniffling and sobbing. He wiped his nose on the sleeve of his flannel shirt, leaving a streak of what looked like black mucus. In his other hand, the drawer hung by its handle, like a lunch box dangling from a schoolboy's grasp. "Adelaide," he called out again, and even his voice sounded like a child's. "Adelaide, where are you? I'm scared. Adelaide, rebuke him!"

He turned again, following a sound Brigid couldn't hear. Now he was looking away from her and toward Dylan, who lay stiff on the bed, her face pale, her lips a thin line. Dylan's eyes begged Brigid for help. Urgently, Brigid pressed a finger to her lips as she nodded.

The drawer full of undershirts hadn't been fully closed when Brigid raided it before. Now she slid her hand carefully into the gap, watching Angus without blinking, trying to keep her breathing slow and silent though she wanted desperately to gasp for air. Her fingers groped through the stack of shirts to find the bottom of the drawer.

"I'm sorry I'm sorry I'm sorry," whined Angus in that same childish voice. "I detest all my sins!" He jerked his head back and forth, as though trying to follow a conversation that only he could hear. "Leave me alone!"

Brigid's arm stuck in the gap between drawer and dresser and could go no farther. She tried pulling it out to turn the other way.

The drawer jolted open with a faint, but perfectly audible, screech.

Brigid didn't even have time to flinch. Angus turned fast and hard, swinging the sock drawer out at the end of his arm. It caught her heavily in the shoulder and sent her flying. The floor seemed very far away. As Brigid fell, she saw Angus's filthy face, his crimson eyes finally focusing on her. Over his shoulder was Dylan, straining to sit up as the handcuffs held her back, her mouth opening on a scream that had yet to reach Brigid's ears.

Brigid slammed into the floor on her left side. In the same moment, Angus brought the sock drawer crashing into her right ribs. She heard and felt something break, but the flare of pain was so sudden and sickening she couldn't tell which side it was on.

Angus stood over her, blackened froth flying from his lips with every breath. Brigid closed her eyes and moaned. When she opened them again, she saw the handcuffs key, shining so bright it could have been spotlit. It must have been in the sock drawer all along. Now it lay on the floor just inches from her outstretched left hand.

She reached for it, but Angus reached too, and he had the advantage of no broken ribs. He got there first.

"Brigid," he said. Her stomach twisted to hear her own name in that bizarre, childish whimper. "Don't go. Don't leave me. I'm sorry." He held the key up in front of her face. Brigid grabbed for it, but he pulled it away, giggling.

"Please," she said through the pain that reverberated from her right side all the way through her skeleton into her guts and her brain. "Just—" Let Dylan go, she wanted to say, but at least in this moment he wasn't *looking* at Dylan. Maybe he'd forgotten the girl was in the room. Maybe if Brigid didn't remind him, Dylan would be safe.

Angus held the key out before him, pinched between two fingers. "May God rebuke him, we humbly pray," he said, and then plunged the key into his own left eyeball.

The swollen eye popped like a blister, and that same blackish-red fluid gouted from it, spilling in a viscous sheet down the side of his face. Brigid screamed. Angus didn't.

"I'm sorry," he said. "I've failed you. I've let you fall into sin and degradation." He knelt over her, and she could smell the shame that flowed down his cheek, rancid and dank like stagnant water. "I've driven you into the arms of the devil, but it's not too late. You can still be saved."

His eye socket was a cavern of gore. Brigid forced herself to stare up into it, searching for the key, but couldn't see so much as a glint of silver amidst the viscid depths. If she wanted the key, she'd have to reach in and feel for it.

Despite the throbbing in her ribs, she stretched her hand toward his face. Angus swung the drawer again, hard. A bolt of pain shot up Brigid's arm from the elbow. She wailed and rolled to the side, clutching her arm. It hurt too much to move. She couldn't tell whether it was broken.

"I'm sorry, Brigid," said Angus again. This time the drawer hit her in the back. Air exploded out of her lungs, and she writhed and wished she could scream. "We're both sinners. But God is merciful. He forgives our trespasses, as we forgive those who trespass against us."

"Stop," Brigid tried to say, but she still couldn't breathe, and all that came out was a croak. She felt the shadow of the drawer rising over her again.

With a desperate flail that amplified the pain in her elbow and ribs to unthinkable levels, Brigid managed to roll mostly out of the path of Angus's next swing. The corner of the drawer hit her shoulder, breaking the skin, a sharp pain but a superficial one.

Angus grabbed her by her bleeding shoulder and rolled her

onto her back. He looked down at her with pursed lips, his one remaining eye squinting down thoughtfully as he hoisted the sock drawer high. His knees pressed into her from either side, grinding the ragged edges of her broken rib together. Brigid would not be able to roll out of the way this time.

Dylan, she thought. She did not want Dylan to see what came next. If she got the key and threw it onto the bed, maybe Dylan could escape while Angus was occupied with beating Brigid to death.

With one last, wretched burst of strength—with a scream that rattled her teeth on the way out, as she pushed her body into a realm of pain she'd never imagined before—Brigid lunged upward, curling her fingers toward Angus's black, oozing eye socket.

She clawed at empty air, missing by at least six inches.

As her arm fell, as the drawer came down, Brigid forgot about the pain. She was beyond pain. She was even beyond fear. All she knew was a sorrow that stretched to the edge of the universe and beyond. She had not saved her daughter. She would not even live long enough to breathe a useless apology. But, oh, if there was a God, it had to know that she was so fucking sorry.

There was a horrible cracking sound, but it didn't hurt, and Brigid was grateful. It was a small mercy, here at the end, that she wouldn't have to feel her body's final destruction. Then the drawer crashed into her head, just above her left temple. Stars flared in her vision, then collapsed into black holes. The pain was next, arriving late just so it could make a dramatic entrance, a flourish of suffering, a crash cymbal between her teeth. Brigid's head rocked to the side, and she screamed yet again.

But she didn't die.

Her hand found its way up to her head to double check, and yes, there was the wound, a point of reverberating pain—but only a little blood. No hole in her skull; no brain leaking out among fragments of bone. Angus had hit her, but not as hard as he'd meant to. Had he changed his mind at the last moment? Was he losing his strength, belatedly passing out from the trauma to his eye?

No, she realized. Angus was looking back, over his shoulder. Something had caught his attention, distracted him at the final moment, and that was what had taken the strength out of his blow.

"Not again," Angus said in a tone of pure exhaustion.

Brigid pushed herself up onto her elbows, ignoring the various tremors of pain that rushed through her body, to see what he was seeing.

Dylan hovered above the bed. She was splayed out on her back, red hair sweeping down from her head, but not touching the mattress—her body floated in midair at least three feet above it. Her arms were spread to both sides in the same attitude of crucifixion Angus had adopted a few minutes ago. From each of her wrists dangled a few inches of steel chain.

Brigid's brain—aching, probably concussed—finally worked out that the cracking sound had been Dylan breaking her handcuffs.

Or was she still Dylan? Defying the laws of physics was more of an Adelaide specialty; maybe Brigid's mother had surfaced again in a belated rush of maternal protectiveness.

But as the girl swung her legs around and sat up—still hovering in midair, perched on an invisible mattress high above the actual bed—her face was unmistakably Dylan's. So was her voice as she said, with an anger clear and sharp as a diamond, "Get the *fuck* away from my mother."

Angus glanced back at Brigid, so he wasn't looking at Dylan as she pushed off nothing and launched herself across the room. It might not have mattered if he was. Dylan moved fast, *so* fast it shouldn't have been physically possible, and Brigid wondered at her own ability to feel surprised by that, after everything. She swooped on Angus like a bat, and he didn't even raise a hand to stop her before she sank her teeth deep into the junction of his neck and shoulder.

Brigid wasn't watching Angus's face as his body went rigid, as he let go of the sock drawer and let it thud to the carpet, as he reached frantically behind him, too late, trying to pry Dylan loose. All she saw was her daughter's face, her eyes wide and bright and *hers*, delight unmistakable despite her grimace as she wrenched her head back and took a ragged mouthful of flesh with her. Dylan moaned with pleasure as she chewed, swallowed, then frowned and hooked a finger into her mouth to pull out a scrap of flannel collar.

Blood sluiced from Angus's neck. Instead of clapping a hand over the wound, he flailed behind him, swinging his now-empty hands and hitting nothing. Belatedly, Brigid recognized her opportunity. She shoved her knee up between Angus's legs, pushing him back and sideways. He toppled off her without resistance. Dylan, still clutching his shoulders, fell too.

They landed on the carpet in a bizarre embrace, Dylan's legs wrapped around Angus's waist, holding him close. He thrashed and tried to escape, but fruitlessly. Dylan bit into his shoulder again. His blood drenched her face.

It took Brigid a long time to climb to her feet, anguish singing from her ribs, her elbow, her head. By the time she was standing, Angus had fallen silent. He still appeared conscious, though, his good eye open, his face a rictus of pain as Dylan burrowed deeper into his shoulder with her teeth.

"Dylan, stop," said Brigid weakly.

Her daughter met her eyes and let go of Angus's shoulder, holding up a finger as if to say *just a second* while she finished chewing what was in her mouth. After she swallowed, she said, "He was going to kill you."

"I know," said Brigid. "He still wants to. And I don't care that much if you kill him, but I don't want you to go to prison for it. I don't know anything about how to dispose of a body."

Dylan bared her bloody teeth. It took a moment for Brigid to recognize the gesture as a smile. "I have some ideas."

"Dylan," Brigid said. "You can't. You don't know what you're saying. This is something you'd have to live with forever." She thought of Serafina, placid and empty in a hospital room, sunlight falling on a white paper dress and no one inside whatsoever. "This could break you."

"No," said Dylan. "There are some things you don't have to protect me from. Sometimes you can let me protect you instead." She dipped a finger into the gash on Angus's shoulder and licked it clean. "Besides, I've been starving for literally days."

"Someone will find his body," Brigid said helplessly. "The cops, or Zandy—"

"The cops aren't coming, Grandma already told you that," said Dylan impatiently. "You never called them. And anyway, even if someone comes, they won't find him. This room is just a copy, one of the ones it made for people to get lost in. You have to take the long way to get here. No one's going to bother."

Trying to comprehend that statement made Brigid's head hurt more, so she returned to her initial point. "You don't know what it means, taking someone's life. You have no idea how it's going to affect you. I don't want you to have to carry that."

Dylan met her eyes. There was blood drying in her eyelashes, and it only made her more beautiful. "Mom," Dylan said with infinite tenderness. "He's already gone."

Brigid glanced at Angus's face, at the single red eye that was still darting back and forth, the chest that still rose and fell with every panicked gasp, though both were slowing now. Her thoughts were murky and slow, but they eventually caught up with Dylan's meaning.

Angus, as he had been, was no more—just as the Serafina Brigid had met as a child, furious and defiant, no longer existed. Serafina had died by inches; Angus's extinction was faster but no less absolute. The thing inside had devoured a vital part of him. And it had happened because of Brigid. Because she had purged her monsters into him.

Sometimes you can let me protect you, Dylan had said, and now Brigid understood. Brigid had already killed Angus's mind. Dylan wanted to take some of that burden by killing his body.

Brigid wanted to cry, then realized she was already crying. None of this was fair. Dylan shouldn't have to share this weight. Dylan shouldn't even have to be here. Dylan shouldn't have to know that Angus Byrne existed.

But he did—and there was no unweaving that thread from the tapestry of Dylan's life. Angus had shaped Brigid, and Brigid had shaped Dylan, and it was too late to change any of it, and pretending otherwise wouldn't help.

"Are you sure, baby?" Brigid asked.

Dylan smiled again. It looked like a real smile this time, even under the gore. "*Please*, Mom," she said.

Angus's lips moved like they were trying to form words. Brigid didn't care to hear them.

"Okay," she said. "Do you want me to stay?" The thought nauseated her—though there was nothing left in her stomach to expel—but she would do what Dylan wanted. She would, after all this time, let Dylan decide.

Dylan shook her head. "The door's open," she said, and Brigid looked over her shoulder and realized it was true.

"I'll be right outside," Brigid said.

She closed the door on the way out, then sat down on the floor in the hall to wait. She heard everything.

Epilogue

Dylan sat cross-legged in the middle of the circle. "Should I be lying down for this?" she asked.

"Nope," said Cypress, popping the *p*. "You're not just the object of the ceremony, you're participating in it. You should be upright and active."

Dylan gave them a small smile, and Cypress grinned broadly back. Brigid was glad to see it. Cypress seemed to be taking a big-sibling role in Dylan's life these days. Dylan went to them with questions she didn't want to ask her mother, and Brigid tried to be happy about the development and not worry about whether Cypress was giving advice that Brigid would agree with.

It was Cypress who had suggested to Dylan that if she genuinely believed Kai Shriver's apologies, she could give him another chance. "People make mistakes. Sometimes they make really bad mistakes," they'd told her. "You get to decide whether you still want them in your life. It doesn't mean that what they did to you doesn't matter. You can give them a chance to do better. Only if it feels worth it to you."

Brigid would never have told Dylan any such thing, and she still cringed when she noticed Dylan texting with Kai, but she couldn't deny that their renascent friendship seemed to be making Dylan happier and more confident.

Brigid envied that. She wished she had Dylan's ability to put the past behind her, to risk trusting and caring even after all she'd been through. She wished she could talk to Zandy without feeling like she was scaling a barbed wire fence, already bleeding in a dozen places.

Zandy *wanted* to understand. She wanted to know what had happened to them inside that house, and why her mother never seemed to run into Angus around the neighborhood anymore. She looked at Brigid with a kind of frustrated curiosity, like a knot she was trying to untangle. Brigid could see that the things Zandy didn't know were gnawing at her, and she yearned to tell Zandy everything. She was trying, damn it—trying to unlearn her lifetime of keeping secrets, to throw open all the doors in her mind.

But every time she opened her mouth to begin the story, she felt herself cringing, anticipating Zandy's skepticism like a slap. She saw the same thwarted urge in Zandy's face, wanting to ask a question but swallowing it unsaid. They both wanted so badly to bridge the silence between them, but neither could quite bring themselves to do it. They hadn't touched each other romantically since Brigid and Dylan had stumbled out of Angus's house for the last time.

Brigid had more than half expected Zandy to disappear from her life. She would have been heartsick, but not angry. But despite the tension between them, Zandy didn't go anywhere. She still texted Brigid about cute dogs she saw and funny things her students said. She invited Brigid and Dylan to Eileen's annual post-Thanksgiving Leftoverfest. She came to Dylan's school choir concert and out to dinner with them afterward. For now, they stayed in that precarious balance, tacitly agreeing that Zandy wouldn't ask questions Brigid couldn't answer. When Cypress told Brigid they needed one more person for the cleansing ritual, she'd known Zandy was the only one she could call.

Cypress bustled back and forth, setting up the spell circle in the back room of the magic shop. It was still dark outside— Cypress said the best time to do a cleansing was before sunrise, with the new moon still in the sky. Nadine was carefully laying out the objects they needed. She and Cypress had already had one argument over which incense was the best for casting out an unwanted influence—or, more accurately, Cypress had argued, and Nadine had said "No" so firmly Brigid had found herself wanting to apologize.

Dylan was tense, drumming her knees with her knuckles. Brigid bit back the impulse to snap at her, tell her to cut it out. Instead, she said, "Almost done."

"Can't wait," said Dylan with a tight smile. "Finally be able to eat real food again." Brigid tried to smile back.

Quietly, in the space between the two of them, Dylan added, "Is there anything you want to say to her before she goes?"

Brigid thought about it. In a movie, this would be the moment for a cathartic reconciliation with her mother's spirit. Brigid would say "I forgive you" and Adelaide would use Dylan's mouth to say "I love you" and a crescendo of violins would lift them up into the sunrise, a new day, the past washed clean.

But she wasn't sure she could say "I forgive you" and mean it. She was still angry at Adelaide—for taking over Dylan's body, for bringing her monstrous stowaway along, for sacrificing Brigid's childhood on Angus's insane altar. She was angry, too, when she thought about what she'd read in that notebook: Adelaide's spite and ugliness, the violence she'd planned. Though she knew that wasn't entirely Adelaide's fault—she'd felt that awful buzzing in her own head, she knew how it could twist what was true—she didn't know where to draw the line between her mother and the parasite with her. Having been host to the thing herself, she knew, too, that it didn't bring in desires of its own, only found the bitter and ugly things that were already hidden away in the corners and under the carpets and brought them out into the light. What she had seen in the light of Adelaide's possession would never leave her.

Dylan was still looking earnestly into Brigid's face, waiting for a response. Brigid wondered whether Dylan found it as difficult to forgive Brigid as Brigid did to forgive Adelaide. After all, Brigid had brought her daughter to Angus's house, just like her own mother had. She had endangered and threatened her daughter and imagined hurting her. Did it count for anything that her fantasies of violence hadn't gone as far as Adelaide's, that she hadn't come as close to realizing them? Brigid thought it might, but she also knew it wasn't up to her. The only person who could decide she deserved Dylan's forgiveness was Dylan.

Maybe she could set a good example, she thought. If she could make a convincing gesture of reconciliation toward Adelaide, it might nudge Dylan to be a bit more lenient with her own mistakes.

And then what? Brigid chastised herself. If she pretended

to forgive Adelaide, Dylan might pretend to forgive her? What would be the benefit of that? She didn't want forced affection or dutiful charades from her daughter. She wanted Dylan's genuine love and trust.

"Mom," said Brigid, and Dylan's eyes widened. She straightened her shoulders, preparing to receive and pass along the message—though Brigid was fairly sure Adelaide heard whatever Dylan heard, no matter whether Dylan was consciously sharing her ears. Brigid took a deep breath.

"I'm still really angry at you," she said. "I don't know if I'll ever stop being angry. You let some really bad things happen to me, and you caused my daughter to get hurt. I know you didn't mean to, and that doesn't make it okay." She realized she was shaking, her voice creeping into a higher octave, and took a moment to consciously relax her shoulders. "And I love you, Mom. No matter what." It was the kindest true thing she could say.

After a quiet moment, Dylan nodded. "She loves you too."

If she was going to set any kind of example for Dylan, Brigid thought, she wanted it to be that her daughter could speak up when she was angry; that she didn't have to protect anyone from the pain of knowing they'd hurt her, not even Brigid herself. She squeezed her daughter's hand and hoped Dylan understood.

"All right, Grandma Ghostie, time to go into the light," Cypress announced.

"Please have a modicum of respect for the deceased," Nadine said in a voice that reminded Brigid her employee had spent thirty years teaching elementary school.

Cypress ignored her. "Is everyone ready?"

"Yes," said Brigid.

"Yes," said Zandy, the last and quietest member of their circle.

"Let's get a move on," said Nadine.

Cypress traced their circle with a stick of incense. They all sat where Nadine pointed them, one at each compass point with Dylan in the middle. Brigid was north; Zandy sat to her right, at west. They were too far apart to touch, and that was probably for the best. Brigid hoped one day she'd be able to hold Zandy's hand without either of them flinching.

Nadine had reassured Brigid, when they were planning the ritual, that it didn't matter whether the other participants believed Adelaide was inhabiting Dylan's body. All that mattered was their focus, and Dylan's will.

"It's not about the deceased finishing their business with the living," Nadine had explained. "Everyone dies with unfinished business. That doesn't usually mean they stick around this plane. It's a question of what the living need from the dead, and whether they're ready to let go."

Dylan was ready to let go of Adelaide. She didn't want or need her protection anymore. The ritual would work: Adelaide would be released into whatever came next, and Dylan's body would be her own again.

And the thing Adelaide brought with her would be gone, too. Brigid was almost certain of it. She hadn't mentioned the stowaway to Cypress and Nadine; she doubted even their flexible belief systems could accommodate a ghost possessed by a demon. But it didn't matter. This was a cleansing, and a cleansing removed all impurities.

Nadine lit a white candle and placed it on the floor in front of Dylan. Cypress began the invocation.

Brigid breathed deeply. The air smelled like lavender and rosemary. There was no buzzing in her head, just the tidal rise and fall of her own blood.

She watched Dylan watch the candle, the gold reflection in her daughter's blue eyes. The light was so beautiful. Dylan was so beautiful. They would get through this. Surely, the hard part was almost over.

Acknowledgments

T hank you to my agent, Kate McKean, for sticking with
all these years and always being my sounding board and
champion.

Thank you to Jess Zimmerman, a brilliant editor and a true
joy to work with (except for all the times you make me do actual work). You helped me find the heart of this story and I could
not be more grateful.

Thank you to the entire team at Quirk Books. Every author
should be lucky enough to have such a supportive, knowledge-
able, and enthusiastic crew in their corner.

To Sumiko Saulson, my HWA novel mentor while I was
writing the first draft of this book, thank you for the direction
and motivation.

Thank you to all the friends who gave me suggestions for a
clarity spell, especially Faylita Hicks, whose insight about the
danger of seeing oneself clearly helped the whole story come
into focus.

I am ...teful to my community of horror writers for all the in... n, support, and occasional bitching, especially Matt Lyon... hia Gómez, M. Lopes da Silva, Millie Price, Angela Sylv... ailey Piper, Paula D. Ashe, and Ashley Santana.

...T you to Dane Kuttler, for braving this book and more (I p... e you don't have to read it again), and to all the friends, too... y to list, who have one way or another kept me sane.

...nk you, always, to Jana Clark, my first writing teacher and th...e who left the deepest mark. This book (and all the others, ...nd future) exists because of the things you taught me.

...hank you to my father, Ranger Miller; my mother, Michelle ...ler; my siblings, Kara, Kevin, and Sam; and my stepmother, ...ot. Your support means the world to me.

Thanks and apologies to my grandmother, Catherine Duffy Miller, who was, for the record, not the kind of Catholic depicted in this book.

Thank you to my daughters, who inspire my deepest fears and greatest hopes. I love you so much.

And to Charlie, the love of my life, for all the support, all the encouragement, all the nights and weekends you gave up so I could finish writing this book, and so much more—I couldn't do any of this without you. "Thank you" is not enough, but thank you, nonetheless.

LINDSAY KING-MILLER is the author of *The Z Word* (Quirk Books, 2024) and *Ask a Queer Chick: A Guide to Sex, Love, and Life for Girls who Dig Girls*. Her fiction has appeared in *The Fiends in the Furrows*, *Tiny Nightmares*, *The Jewish Book of Horror*, *Fireside Fiction*, *Baffling* magazine, and numerous other publications. She lives in Denver with her partner and their two children.

QUIRK  BOOKS